Intersection
of Lies

Tonya Sharp Hyche

Novels by
Tonya Sharp Hyche

Swept Away
Just For You
Breathless
Fearless
Intersection of Lies
Glass Shadow (Early 2013)

"Just as with Swept Away I could not put Just For You down. Another unpredictable, fast-paced, page-turner leaving me gasping for breath. Interesting characters both good and evil. This book will meet all your expectations of a suspenseful crime thriller. Tonya Sharp Hyche has become my new favorite author."

MARION H.
(AMAZON.COM REVIEW)

Breathless

"I took Breathless to read on my summer vacation and could not have been more entertained. The characters were well developed and the suspense kept me engaged…I can't wait for the next one!"

KATHLEEN
TEXAS

Fearless

"I have read all of this new author's books and what keeps me coming back for more is her fast and suspenseful plots that keep twisting and turning which will keep you guessing to the very end. I was very intrigued to see where the Fearless storyline would take the reader (given it is the sequel to Just for You) and I wasn't disappointed. Once I started reading it, I could not put it down and was completely drawn into the characters and plot. If you love a "who dunnit" where you won't be able to predict who dunnit, then Fearless is for you - buy it, put your feet up and settle in for a great read, you won't be disappointed! My only warning is you may not want to put it down!"

KAREN
(AMAZON.COM REVIEW)

To Christa Hyche,
My beautiful, loving, giving and caring mother-in-law,
you are one special lady!

Intersection of Lies

Chapter 1

Friday, October 12
Atlanta, Georgia

"Your Honor, in light of the newest evidence presented, we ask that all charges against my client, Ronny Jordan, be dismissed."

Lilee Parker jumped up. "Objection, Your Honor. The defendant…"

The Honorable Emma Carr raised her hand for silence. "Counselors, approach the bench."

Lilee sharply eyed Andy Kane, the public defender, who was grinning from ear to ear. She walked briskly around her small table and met him in front of the judge.

"Mr. Kane," the judge began, "you have made a strong argument with evidence backing your claim." She turned her attention toward Lilee. "Unless the state has something to disprove the evidence presented, I have no choice but to drop all charges against the accused, Mr. Jordan."

Lilee felt heat rising on her face and turned to face Ronny Jordan, sitting behind the defendant's table with a smirk on his face. The twenty-one-year-old was guilty of the assault and burglary of her client, Kelley

Wells. The sixty-three-year-old small business owner had been badly beaten and left for dead as the young man grabbed a mere fifty-eight dollars from the cash register. Now, because of some technicality, he was sure to walk. Lilee turned back toward the judge, unable to face Mrs. Wells as she sat among her family and friends.

Standing five foot six with the help of her two-inch heels, she raised her head to meet Andy Kane, the good-looking blond attorney towering over her at six foot two.

"Counselor," the judge said, "I need something."

Lilee pleaded with the judge with her eyes before finally speaking. "Your Honor, the man was identified by the victim. That alone should be enough to finish this case and send it to the jury."

The judge frowned. "That might be true, Ms. Parker, but your department has mishandled the evidence, and I have no choice but to side with the defendant."

Not giving up hope, Lilee asked for what seemed like the impossible. "Your Honor, may I have twenty-four hours to look into this matter before a decision is made?"

Andy Kane muffled his laugh. "Your Honor, I would like to remind Ms. Parker that the state has had three months to plan for this trial, while my client, who couldn't afford bail, sat in a city prison."

"Only because he had a prior conviction and the court deemed it necessary," retorted Lilee.

Andy placed a hand on his hip and shook his head. "Your Honor, the prosecution is trying to muddle the situation. The fact remains that the evidence has been tainted; therefore, it is inadmissible in court."

Judge Carr looked at the victim seated behind the state's table. Mrs. Wells' husband held her hand as her daughter kept a protective arm around her shoulder. All were looking her way. Next she glanced over toward the defendant, Mr. Jordan, a large man at around six foot three, weighing two hundred fifty pounds. She imagined the fear the woman must have felt that day, despite his appearance today in his new suit and short crew cut. He too had lots of family seated behind him showing their support.

Slowly she turned to face the counselors at the bench. "With the new evidence, I regrettably dismiss all charges against the accused, Ronny Jordan."

Lilee opened her mouth to protest but stopped when the judge added, "You need to have a long discussion with your team, Ms. Parker."

Lilee watched as Andy smiled toward his defendant and made his way over to his table. She walked back to her own table slowly, trying not to hang her head in shame, but at the same time, she couldn't face the Wells family.

"Would the defendant, Ronny Jordan, please stand?"

Ronny eagerly stood by his attorney who was almost his same height.

With all eyes on the judge, she continued. "In light of the new evidence presented, the state's case against Ronny Jordan is dismissed. I thank the jury for their time and patience during the last week; you are now released of all your duties. This court is adjourned."

Cheers went up across the room as Ronny's family hugged him and congratulated Andy Kane. Lilee heard sobs behind her and turned, finally facing the victim and her family. Immediately Mr. Wells was in her face. "What the hell just happened? Just because a piece of evidence was thrown out doesn't mean he didn't beat my wife and leave her for dead!"

An officer of the court stepped in. "Please take a step back, Mr. Wells."

Lilee tried to console him by reaching out for his arm, but he recoiled at her touch. "We aren't finished here. Your office will be hearing from us."

Lilee's assistant, Charli Pepper, guided her backward. "Come on," she said. "Let's use the side door and avoid the press."

"No, it's fine. I will talk to them."

Charli frowned. "Sorry, Lilee. Someone higher up has already made that decision."

She didn't have to ask whom. Her boss, Daniel Maggs, the district attorney, had shown up in the courtroom five minutes before Andy Kane tore her case apart. Apparently someone had tipped him off. If she had to guess who, that would be her fierce competitor within the department, Wes Schultz. Frustrated, Lilee threw her notes into her briefcase and closed it as Charli gracefully guided her out the side door.

Charli Pepper was twenty-six, three years younger than Lilee. They were as close as sisters but looked nothing alike. A brunette, Charli stood two inches taller, while Lilee was a fair-skinned blond. What they had in common, though, were their green eyes, beauty, and brains to go with it. Two highly motivated professionals, they made one hell of a team. This was a sad day for both of them; neither was accustomed to losing.

Charli opened the back exit door leading to the secure parking lot but stopped as a voice called from behind.

"Hey, Lilee! Wait up!"

Charli mumbled at the sound of Andy Kane's voice as Lilee turned to face him.

"Look, no hard feelings," he said. "That was a tough break."

Lilee looked at him with detest. "Why are you standing here talking to me? Don't you have an audience waiting for you out front? Or, wait; is your guilty conscience taking over now?"

Andy spread his hands out as if shrugging. "It's my job, Lilee, to give the best defense possible. Nothing less."

Lilee turned her back to him and started to leave.

"Wait! Charli, can you give us a minute?"

Charli hesitated and slowly walked away after Lilee nodded.

"What?" Lilee asked impatiently.

"Can we get together this weekend?"

Lilee's eyes widened, and Andy continued timidly. "Just for coffee. I would like to talk; that's all."

Finding her voice, she coldly replied, "I don't think so, Mr. Kane. Now if you will excuse me, I've still got work to do."

Andy reached for her arm and smiled, "I'm not going to give up, counselor. Another time."

Before she could respond to his boldness, he released her arm, turned, and went whistling down the hall.

Chapter 2

5:35 p.m.
305 Maple Leaf St.
Atlanta, Georgia

Christa Hart hit the control mounted on her Jaguar's visor and waited impatiently for the iron gate to open on her property. Her day at the office had dragged on longer than expected as she'd hashed out the newest designs with her business partner of fifteen years, Andrea Raines. The two co-owned Elegant Grace Designs, an idea that had started out as a hobby for two wealthy women and somehow turned into a very profitable business. When her twins left for college, Christa began spending more time at the office, trying to fill the void they left in her life. Her husband, William, had always put in long hours as a doctor, and now, more than ever, she needed her business to help fill her days and long nights until the boys arrived back home each weekend for Sunday lunch.

Glancing at her watch, she decided to leave the gate open and park in the circular drive. No sense in fooling with the garage door or gate since she and William would be leaving at six for a dinner party at the club. As she parked her car, she hoped Nina, her housekeeper, had picked up her blue dress from the dry cleaner as she'd instructed that morning. Lately she'd noticed Nina becoming more absentminded as she quickly approached sixty. William had made some remarks as well, and they had talked about hiring another lady to help her. They couldn't bear to just let her go after eighteen years with the family.

Getting out of the car, Christa grabbed her purse and briefcase and hurried up the six stone steps to the glass double doors. As she neared, she noticed that one of the doors stood cracked open a few inches. Not seeing anyone through the glass, she turned to look for Nina's car along the side of the home but couldn't see anything through the thick shrubbery. Setting her belongings down outside the door, she walked back down the steps and around the house to find Nina's blue car, parked in its usual spot, and a closed garage. Not seeing anyone outside, she walked back around the front, climbed the stairs, picked up her purse and briefcase, and pushed the door open.

In the foyer, a vase of fresh flowers sitting on the large, round table greeted her. Flowers were delivered every Friday, a tradition she had started more than twenty years ago. Her husband found it silly, but she smiled at the beautiful aroma filling her home.

"Nina! I'm home."

Not hearing a reply, she shut the door behind her, took a few steps toward her right, and entered her large study, covered from floor to ceiling in dark wood. Walking around the antique desk, she set her briefcase down on the floor and then thumbed through the day's messages that Nina left each day. Not seeing anything too important, she left the study with her purse.

"Will! I'm home," she announced as she climbed the winding staircase overlooking the foyer. Hearing a noise, she stopped and looked at the foyer below. Nothing. Assuming it had been Nina in the kitchen, she continued forward another step. She heard water running and assumed Will must be in the shower. She stopped. *My dress,* she thought. *Probably still hanging in the laundry room near the garage.*

Turning around, she walked back down the stairs and under the staircase toward the back of the large house. Passing the formal living room, she saw no one and continued on. Just as she turned a corner, she saw movement in the backyard. Startled, she walked into the living room and peered out the large glass window. The large palm trees surrounding their resort-style pool blew in the wind. She studied the cabana house. The door was closed and the blinds pulled. All looked normal.

Turning back around, she asked, "Nina? Are you in the kitchen?"

Her phone vibrated in her pocket, and she jumped. "Oh my God! I'm going to give myself a heart attack."

Christa set her purse down on the coffee table, pulled the phone out of her designer jacket, and read the display. Andrea Raines. She ran her free hand through her platinum blond hair as she answered. "Hello."

"Christa, glad I caught you. I forgot to get the Hickam file from you."

Knowing Andrea didn't live too far away, she replied, "No problem. I can drop it off on our way out tonight."

"Are you sure? I don't mind coming to get it."

"No, dear. We're going to be leaving in the next ten minutes to go to the club, so you're on the way."

"Thanks. Derrick is working tonight, on call again, so I told the Hickams I would meet them at their estate later tonight," Andrea said.

"Great! I will see you soon, Andrea."

"OK. Bye."

Pocketing the phone, Christa forgot all about the noise. She hurried into the kitchen and, seeing no one, continued on down the small hallway toward the oversized laundry room and opened the door. Immediately she saw her blue dress hanging up on the long rod beside William's dress shirts, just as she suspected. Grabbing her dress, she quickly turned around and froze. A large man wearing a ski mask stood before her holding a knife.

She finally found her voice and screamed as the knife came down. Christa met the man's cold, dark eyes as she fell to the floor still clutching her dress.

***

At City Hall, Lilee and Charli sat at a large oval table on the fourth floor of the district attorney's office at his request. Their boss of four years had been ranting and raving for the last twenty minutes about the police department's screwup and their inability to find their mistake.

Daniel Maggs, a well-liked district attorney, took great pride in his long-standing record of achievement within the Atlanta community. Maggs was pushing sixty amid lots of talk around town of his impending retirement. He was angry. No way did he want to end his career on the Wells case.

Lilee watched as sweat beads formed along the edges of his white hair and the short, stocky man wiped his glasses with his handkerchief. Seeing an opening to end his rampage, she quietly asked, "Mr. Maggs, what do you want me to do now?"

Holding his glasses out and seeing them clean, he placed them on his face and stared back at her. "Nothing. I want both of you to leave and report back here at seven a.m. on Monday."

Charli replied, "Yes, sir; we will."

Lilee stood and met his gaze, and he caved. "Ladies, I'm sorry. This isn't entirely your fault. But I do need the weekend to sort it all out so we can figure out where to go next."

Lilee fumed inside at his words. *Not entirely our fault?* she thought. *Hell, it wasn't our office that handled the evidence.* But before she came back swinging, Charli grabbed her arm and pulled her away.

When they were down the hallway, safely out of earshot, Charli said, "Shake it off, Lilee. Things will look better tomorrow."

Lilee stopped walking and looked at her assistant. "You don't actually believe that, do you?"

"Yes. Now, it's almost six, and we have been instructed to leave, so let's leave and start our well-earned weekend."

Lilee let out the deep breath she didn't realize she'd been holding. "You're right. Let's get out of here. I could use a drink."

"Now you're talking. Let me call Mark."

As Charli dialed, Lilee thought about how happy Charli was with Mark. They still acted like newlyweds even though their marriage was going on eighteen months. She smiled as her friend's face brightened with the sound of his voice, instantly reminding her that she was all alone with no one special in her life. Her fiancé of ten months, Landon Baynes, had decided to break off their wedding three months earlier. Something about him needing more time. She frowned. More time had turned into one visit and three phone calls—nothing more.

Charli put her phone in her purse and saw the frown. "Heard from Landon this week?"

"No. We're through."

"What? No!"

"Yes, we are. In fact, why don't you and Mark go on. I'll catch you another time."

Charli looked concerned.

"I'm fine. Tonight is a good night to rearrange my closet. I've been waiting long…" her voice broke, "…enough."

Charli shook her head. "I'm not leaving you alone tonight. Sorry. You're either coming out with us, or I'm coming home with you."

Lilee reached out and touched her friend's arm. "You are too good to me. But really, I want to be alone tonight. This is something I really need to do for myself. Please understand, and enjoy your evening with Mark."

Her friend didn't look convinced, so she added, "How about we go for a run tomorrow morning at the park?"

Charli searched her eyes and then reluctantly agreed. "OK. Eight o'clock?"

"Let's make it nine."

"OK, see you then. But call if you need anything."

Lilee smiled and walked away. As she opened the door, the cool October air greeted her. Early fall was beginning to settle in. Reaching into her briefcase, she found her keys without slowing her steps. Two rows over, her silver Mercedes stood alone in the parking lot. She hit the button on her remote, the vehicle chirped, and she quickly entered. Setting her briefcase on the passenger's seat, she tried sticking the key in the ignition and realized she was shaking. She dropped the keys to the floorboard and bent over to pick them up.

Bang! Bang!

Lilee jumped, hitting her head on the steering wheel. Looking toward the window, she was relieved to see that it was only one of her colleagues, Wes Schultz, knocking.

Placing the key in the ignition, she lowered the window. "Wes! Did you have to scare me like that?"

"Sorry. Um, I just wanted to say that I'm really sorry about what happened today."

She shot him a look that could kill. "Really? If you cared so much, you would've told me earlier so I could have prepared instead of being ambushed like that in front of everyone!"

"Hey now, Lilee, I had no clue."

A look of doubt crossed her face, so Wes continued. "You think I was the one who told Maggs?"

"Well, did you?"

"No, Lilee! Look, I know it's been game on for the last two years, but I would never allow a colleague to be dragged through the mud like that in a court of law."

Her expression didn't change.

"Gosh, Lilee, what's wrong with you? We're on the same team, you know."

She held up her hand to stop him. "Look, Wes, I'm tired, real tired, and I just want to get home, OK?"

Wes backed away. "Sure thing, Lilee, but we're gonna talk about this again on Monday."

Lilee broke eye contact and raised her window. Slowly she raked both hands through her long blond hair and took a deep breath. Finally she placed her car in gear and left the parking lot. As she pulled into heavy traffic, she didn't notice the other car pulling out behind her.

Chapter 3

Andrea Raines paced back and forth in her living room. Once again she picked her phone up off the coffee table to check her messages. Nothing. She looked at her watch: seven o'clock. She was scheduled to meet with the Hickams in thirty minutes to discuss their renovations for a guesthouse, and she still hadn't received the file from Christa. She tried calling again. No answer. Frustrated, she picked up her purse and keys and left for the country club, five minutes away from her estate.

Andrea pulled out of the empty garage and pressed the button to drop the door. Outside her gated driveway, she turned right on her street and was immediately consumed with guilt. *She was probably in a hurry and just forgot,* she thought. *If I wouldn't have forgotten the file to begin with, this wouldn't be happening!*

Soon, Andrea pulled under the covered entrance to the Park Square Country Club, where the regular valet attendant greeted her.

Opening her door, she said, "I'm just going in to grab a file from a colleague. Five minutes max."

The young man nodded. "I'm going to move it over a little, but that should be fine."

Andrea climbed the stone stairs and turned to see her black BMW being moved to the left. Hearing the automatic glass doors open, she turned and walked through. Immediately she saw Marty standing behind the dark mahogany counter smiling at her. She returned the smile just as he recorded her name on a log sheet.

"Hi, Marty. I won't be long. I just need to grab a file from Christa Hart."

Marty creased his brows. "I'm sorry, but the Harts haven't arrived yet."

Andrea stopped walking toward the main hallway leading toward the dining area and turned to face him. "Oh, I thought their dinner party was around six thirty, or possibly seven?"

"Yes. Six thirty."

Andrea nodded, pulled her phone out of her purse, and checked her messages. Nothing. Again she tried Christa's number. Voice mail again. *This is not like them,* she thought. *They wouldn't be this late for a dinner party without calling.*

"Thanks, Marty. I'm going to head over to their house now. But if I happen to miss her, please tell her I stopped by and to give me a call."

"Yes, Mrs. Raines."

Andrea hastily descended the stairs in her high heels, grabbed the keys from the attendant, and pulled away. She tried in vain to identify the driver of each passing car on the two-lane highway. None were either of the Harts' vehicles. Anxiety began to build over the next twenty minutes as Andrea studied the traffic and began to think the worse. *What if they were in a car crash, and all I've thought about was losing that stupid Hickam project?* She covered the last two miles without coming across any accidents or ambulances. Seeing the Harts' iron gate open, Andrea let out a sigh of relief as she pulled her dark vehicle into the driveway behind Christa's gold Jaguar.

Andrea quickly climbed the few stairs and rang the doorbell. As she waited, she looked through the double glass doors and saw the house fully lit, but no movement. After ringing the doorbell again, she twisted the knob and found it unlocked. Hesitating briefly, she pushed away any ridiculous thoughts and opened the door. *After all, Christa and I are best friends.*

She stepped in and called out "Christa! William! It's me, Andrea."

Patiently she waited for any response. Looking behind her she saw only darkness, as the sun had set on her drive over. Timidly, she walked forward and turned to find a semidark study. Flipping the switch, she found it empty and saw Christa's briefcase lying on the floor. The Hickam file was now within her grasp. *Should I just take it and leave?* She glanced at her watch. If she left now, she would only be about twenty minutes late. She hesitated before leaving the study empty handed, calling out more loudly, "Christa? William!"

Andrea looked up the spiral staircase. Seeing no one, she walked on and found the empty formal living room with Christa's handbag on the coffee table. Determining that Christa must be upstairs getting ready, she walked back to the large foyer and began climbing the spiral staircase. When she was halfway up, she heard water running. Relief washed over her face and a smile appeared. *Well, looks like they decided to stay home for a little alone time. I'll just grab the file and leave a note.*

Just as she turned, she saw what appeared to be water flowing across the wood floor at the top of the stairs. Taking more steps forward, she saw that water had run down the hallway from Christa's master suite. Panic rose inside her as the second carpet-covered step turned a darker blue as the water spread. Soon the next step began to slowly darken as well.

"Oh my God! Christa!" she yelled, quickly climbing the remaining steps and stepping into a hallway one inch deep in water. To her right, the master bedroom door stood open. She ran down the hallway yelling, "Christa! William!"

She ran in and found an empty master bedroom, the carpet soggy and the bed made. Turning left she found the double doors to the bathroom closed and water pouring out from beneath them. Andrea ran forward and opened the doors, fearing the worst for her friend.

Praying Christa hadn't died from her apparent fall in the shower or bath, she swung open the double doors and let out a piercing scream as her eyes found William—bloody, naked, and slumped over in the shower with multiple cuts all over his body.

Knowing instantly he wasn't alive, Andrea turned and fled. Reaching the hall, her feet lost traction when they left the carpet and met the wet wooden floor. She fell hard but found the strength to scramble back up, soaking wet, and run. She held the banister tightly as she moved down the stairs screaming, "Help! Someone help!"

Too scared to check the rest of the house for fear that she would be the next victim, she opened the glass door and ran down the remaining steps to her car, her screams never stopping. Deciding she was in no shape to drive, she continued running down the driveway screaming for help. When she reached the street, a neighbor exited his vehicle and ran to her.

"Call 911!" Andrea cried. "Something terrible has happened at the Harts'!"

Scott Engleton looked at Andrea and nodded. "OK. Calm down. What happened?"

Andrea just shook her head and fell to the ground, wrapping her arms around her chest in heartache.

***

Detective Forest Styles sat at a bar drinking a cold draft beer and watching a news report from the small television hanging in the far right corner.

"Buddy, can you turn that up, please?"

Buddy, the cranky old bar owner, wiped his hands on a towel and grabbed the remote. "Don't know why. The news is depressing as hell!"

Forest smirked. "Yeah, don't I know it."

As the reporter continued to recap the latest development of the trial of Ronny Jordan, Forest felt his heart rate increase. "Damn! What the hell happened now?"

Buddy hit the mute button when it went to commercial and remarked, "Told you!"

Forest got up from the bar stool and laid a ten down. Turning his beer up, he drank the remaining cold brew and set the empty mug on the counter.

"Leaving so soon?"

"Yeah. Got somewhere to be."

"You take care of yourself. Don't take chances."

Forest looked at the retired cop, now approaching sixty. When Buddy retired from the force at fifty-five, he leased a spot across from the Atlanta Police Department and opened a bar. It was his way of staying connected and supplementing his retirement at the same time. It served everyone well.

"Will do. See you next week."

Forest left the bar at eight p.m. and looked both ways before crossing the street. Pulling his keys free from his jeans, he unlocked his black Mustang. Just as he opened the door, he heard his partner, Trevor Watts, yell, "Hey, Forest! Wait up!"

Damn, what now? he thought as he slammed his car door and turned to see Trevor Watts' large black body, weighing two hundred and fifty pounds, running toward him.

At five eleven, Forest had to look up when Trevor's six-foot-six-inch frame hovered over him.

"We got a mess in Park Square," Trevor said.

Forest thought of the well-polished area, oozing with money and large estates. "What happened? A cat get stuck up a tree and someone fall trying to get it?"

"You wish. That would be too easy."

Forest leaned back against his Mustang and closed his eyes. Since leaving work twenty minutes earlier, he had only allowed himself one beer before his hot date tonight at eight thirty.

"Aw, shit! You had that date tonight, didn't you?"

Forest opened his green eyes. "I did, but not anymore. Am I right?"

Trevor nodded his head. "Yeah, I already called the missus. She was smokin' mad! The grandkids are over tonight, and she wanted me to help."

A smile broke across Forest's face at the thought of Louise Watts running around after three kids, all under the age of five. He had been to Trevor's house plenty of times over the last six years they'd been working together and had met his entire family. His two daughters were great, as were the grandkids, and Louise cooked the best fried anything this side of Alabama. "So what's for dinner?"

"Fried green tomatoes, pork chops, and mashed potatoes." Trevor shook his head and added, "Oh, and she made pecan pie since the grandkids were coming."

Forest cringed. "Well, let's hear what you got and get it over with and maybe I'll join you, because I'm sure my date isn't gonna wait around."

Trevor took a more serious stance and tone. "You won't make your date, and my food will have to be warmed up. It's ugly."

Forest met Trevor's hard stare. "Spill."

"At 7:55 p.m., two DOAs, and one stabbing victim was taken to the hospital in critical condition."

Forest groaned as he hit the lock button on his remote and shoved his keys back into his pocket. "Let's take the sedan. You drive."

Chapter 4

Lilee Parker had her CD player cranked up as she pulled Landon's clothing out of her closet piece by piece. Holding a glass of red wine, she twirled to the beat of the music as she threw his winter clothing across the room, ringing a cardboard box. "Piece of shit! Might as well taken all of it the day you left!"

Grabbing a leather jacket off the hanger, she held it a little too long before tossing it. It smelled of him, even after several months without wear. She remembered the day she bought it for him, an early Christmas present last year. He was so proud of the jacket and wore it often. A tear rolled slowly down her cheek. She wiped it with her free hand; turned the music off; sat down on her large, empty bed; and took another sip. She was already on her third glass, and it was only eight fifteen. Taking the last sip, she set the glass on her nightstand and thought, *What the hell went wrong*?

But she already knew the answer. He'd moved on with someone else. She knew it in her heart, even though he continued to deny it. He had blamed it on her job, saying she worked too hard and too many long hours to have a fulfilling marriage. Looking at the full box, she wondered, *Was he right?*

A noise from the hallway jolted her back to reality. "Bimbee, is that you?"

Lilee stood, left her bedroom, and turned on the hall light. Paper crinkled as she heard the cat meow. Rounding her living room, she saw the feline furball sitting on top of the kitchen table tearing a plastic cereal bag.

"Bimbee! Get down, you bad cat!"

Startled, the cat jumped down from the table and fled out the back door through the small pet window.

"Stupid cat! I should put you in the damn box as well!"

She grabbed the plastic bag with a few crumbs left inside and tossed it into the waste can. She thought, *Why is Bimbee still here? It's Landon's cat. I don't even like cats!*

She walked over toward the refrigerator, opened it, and scanned the shelves for something edible. Seeing yogurt in the back, she pulled it out and looked at the date. "One more day. Good enough."

She grabbed a spoon and sat on the cushioned bar stool at the counter. As she ate she thought about how she had lost seven pounds since her breakup with Landon. Since she was small to begin with, the weight loss was obvious to everyone around her. Politely, no one had said anything, but she knew what they were thinking. When she saw her mother the previous Sunday, she had screamed at her, "Are you sick? A strong wind could blow you over!" She had lied and told her mom she'd had food poisoning from a garden salad and that it had taken nearly two weeks to get over it. She had promised to come over again on another Sunday when her mom suggested she cook a feast along with dessert to put some more meat on her bones.

She finished her yogurt and looked at the nutrient label: one hundred and sixty calories. Adding that to her cereal bar for lunch, it totaled three hundred and fifty for the day. Leaving the kitchen, she walked back to her bedroom, grabbed her cell phone, and dialed up for pizza delivery. She gave her order and then shouted, "Ninety minutes? You have got to be kidding!"

A young voice answered, "Sorry, ma'am. It's Friday night, and football season. It might be only one hour, though."

"Fine. Go ahead and place the order." She gave her address and credit card number and ended the call.

Walking back over to her closet, she looked once more for anything else that belonged to her ex-finance. Nothing. She folded and taped the box and wrote "Landon's clothing" in big letters across the top. She thought about adding a word between those two but decided to act her age of twenty- nine, not sixteen.

She walked back over to her closet and began rearranging her clothing to cover the emptiness left behind. It took her only twenty minutes to color code and arrange by items. Pants led to shirts then to skirts then to lounge. Still it wasn't enough to fill the large walk-in closet. The master bedroom, bath, and closet were just too big for one person. The one-story, twenty-eight-hundred-square-foot house sat on one acre. They had picked it out together a year ago. *Now what am I gonna do with a four-bedroom house with a large enough master bath to sleep in?*

The new home had all the bells and whistles: granite counter tops, stone fireplace, large back porch, and three-car garage. The only thing missing was a swimming pool with hot tub, and she had planned on starting that project in the fall when the prices of pools dropped. Now, that idea didn't seem so great. Thankfully, she hadn't made the mistake of adding Landon's name to the title. She had wisely listened to her grandfather and paid a large down payment with money she received from a trust. Landon had split the monthly payments with her and paid all utilities.

Her eyes drifted toward her computer to the stack of mail. *No time like the present.*

Glancing at the clock, she read the time: nine o'clock. Her stomach growled, *Damn. Forty-five more minutes!*

Lilee logged into her bank account and began setting up bill payments for four new bills. She completed the task in under fifteen minutes and logged out. Standing, she stretched and suddenly felt extremely tired. She yawned as she slid the large cardboard box to the corner and looked at the clock once more: 9:20. Just as she took a step toward her bathroom, she heard a noise. Thinking it was the pizza delivery knocking on the front door, she left her bedroom and walked down the hallway toward the foyer. Just as she hit the foyer light switch, she heard a loud thud up against her wooden door and immediately panicked when she noticed she'd left the front door unlocked.

She quickly ran to the door, turned the dead bolt, and let out a deep breath as her heart continued to pound. She looked out the peephole timidly but only saw darkness. No pizza delivery boy. Looking right, she flipped a light switch and then peered out the clear side-glass window. Nothing. No car in the driveway, and definitely no pizza.

Instead of opening the door, she ran toward the garage door and opened it, revealing her silver Mercedes, the garage door securely closed behind it. Relieved again, she twisted the dead bolt and went to the back door. She knew it was locked because the only door she'd opened when returning home was the front door when she'd retrieved her mail, but she had to check, just to make sure.

Seeing the lock twisted, she instantly thought of Bimbee locked outside. She looked at the pet door but had no way of knowing if she'd come back inside or not. "Bimbee! Come here girl. Are you in here?"

Nothing.

She walked over to the pantry and pulled out a can of cat food. Tapping a spoon to the lid, she yelled, "Bimbee! Come eat, girl!"

Again, nothing.

Lilee thought of the noise at the front door. Was it Bimbee? Her mind raced to wild animals roaming around at night, from foxes to wild dogs. *Could something have gotten her?*

She glanced at the clock in the kitchen: nine thirty. It had been an hour since she had called for pizza, and he did suggest it could arrive earlier. Lilee looked around. The house felt cold and spooky. Walking through the house, she began closing doors to all the guest rooms and baths. Next, she turned on the lights in the living room. Still she felt spooked. Living alone in such a large home was not what she had expected a year ago. Now she started thinking about selling and getting something smaller, like a townhouse.

"Oh, stop it!" she said, breaking the silence. "You're fine all by yourself!" And as if she needed to prove it, she marched toward the front door, unlocked it, and swung it open.

She screamed. Bimbee lay on the front porch, sliced opened with a knife protruding from her belly, in a pool of blood. Glancing around, she saw no one. She slammed the door and bolted it, shaking hysterically. Running back toward her bedroom, she picked up her cell phone and began dialing 911 just as she heard another noise up against the front door. *Oh my God! Who is doing this?*

"911. What is your emergency?"

Instantly she saw Ronny Jordan's large body in her mind. He wore that smirk she saw on his face in the courtroom. Pictures of Kelley Wells' bloody, beaten body flooded her mind, and she dropped the phone.

She quickly flipped the light switch off by her bed and knelt to the floor. Grabbing her phone, she leaned up against her nightstand, out of sight from anyone who might be peering in her many windows. She whispered, "Someone is outside my home! They killed my cat with a knife!"

"Ma'am, give me your address and name."

"34 North Spring Lake. Lilee, Lilee Parker"

"OK, Ms. Parker. I want you to stay on the line. Help is on the way."

"Um, I'm a city prosecutor," Lilee explained. "There's a lot of people that I've…" Her voice broke.

"Ms. Parker, a unit has responded, and he's in the area. Should be less than seven minutes."

Lilee grabbed her watch off the nightstand and began to follow the slowly moving black line over each number.

"You still there, Ms. Parker?"

"Yes."

"Did you see anyone outside your house?"

"No. I just heard a loud noise. And…and then I checked all my locks before I opened my front door and found my cat, dead."

"How long has it been since you heard a noise outside?"

"When I called you."

"OK, Ms. Parker. Try to relax. Help should be there in less than five minutes. You will not hear a siren. The officer will check the area first, and then I will let you know when to open your front door. Do you understand, Ms. Parker?"

Lilee closed her eyes and tried to steady her breathing. "Yes."

"Do you live alone, Ms. Parker?"

"No. I mean, yes. Yes, I live alone."

"Do you have a dog or any other animals?"

"Just my cat."

The operator asked more questions and remained calm and in control as Lilee tried her best to answer. Soon, Lilee saw headlights flash across the walls of her bedroom and then the sound of a car pulling into her driveway.

"An officer has arrived at your property, Ms. Parker. Stay inside with the doors locked until I give you instructions."

What seemed like ten minutes passed as the lady asked more questions about her home and the neighborhood. Finally the operator said, "Ms. Parker, please go to the front door to let the police officer in your home. He is standing on your porch."

Lilee slowly got up off the floor and then ran down the hallway to the foyer. Rounding the corner, she froze when she saw the message written on the glass window in blood: *DIE BITCH!*

"Ms. Parker, are you still there? The officer is outside. You can let him in."

Lilee nodded instead of speaking. She moved forward slowly, looked through the peephole, and saw a man in a police uniform.

"Yes. I'm opening the door now."

Lilee unlocked the door, and the officer quickly stepped inside and locked the door behind him.

He calmly said, "I will talk to the operator now."

Lilee handed him the phone but tuned him out as she stared at the message written in what could only be Bimbee's blood.

Chapter 5

Five policemen were standing in Lilee's doorway taking photos and dusting for prints when the pizza delivery guy showed up. One of the officers on the porch shouted, "Pizza! I'll get it." She watched as the tall officer jogged down her steps and greeted the deliveryman. They exchanged words for a good three minutes before the officer finally took the pizza, and the young man got back into his small car and drove away. Lilee looked at her watch. It was now ten o'clock: exactly ninety minutes, as promised.

Officer Norman, who had arrived first and secured her home, took the pizza from the officer and turned to face Lilee. "Let's go into the kitchen," he suggested.

Slowly Lilee obeyed, leaving the others at the front door. Choosing the same bar stool as before, she plopped down with a look of defeat as the officer set the pizza box down and opened the lid.

"Smells good! You're probably starved. It's ten o'clock."

"Not anymore."

Officer Norman took a seat beside her and prodded. "Just one piece. It will help you sleep better tonight."

Lilee looked at the pepperoni pizza and then picked up the smallest piece.

"Now if you choose that one, you're gonna have to eat two." He smiled.

For the first time, she took a good look at him. He was handsome and probably around her age. Nice with a caring personality that came across as genuine, not forced.

"Do you have a first name, Officer Norman?" she asked, taking a bite of pizza as he nodded with a smile.

"John."

"Do you know me? I mean, have we met before?"

"Yes," he said. "But I was with a larger group. We were all working together on a case a few years back."

She nodded. "Sorry. I don't remember."

He smiled again, and this time she noticed a dimple on his left cheek.

"Oh, I'm sorry," she said. "Would you like some pizza?"

"Well, I've already eaten, but it does look good."

She smiled as he picked up a slice. As he ate, he opened his note-pad and read over the notes that he had taken over the last twenty minutes since arriving. A couple of minutes passed as neither spoke. Finishing her slice, Lilee moved off the bar stool, grabbed two glasses from the cabinet, and filled them with tap water. She handed him a glass.

"Thanks. So, we know about Ronny Jordan, but we'll need to put together a list of other cases, and we'll have to check them all out."

"It's gonna be long," Lilee warned.

He laughed. "How long have you worked for the city?"

"Four years. Four very long years."

He nodded and then looked around her kitchen. "Nice home you have."

"Thanks."

An older officer walked in and interrupted. "Excuse me, Ms. Parker, but we're all done now."

Lilee slid off the bar stool and walked back into the foyer. The evil message had been wiped clean, and they had bagged and removed Bimbee. She looked down at the bloodstain. The older officer noticed and tried to reassure her. "Whoever was here is long gone, but we'll keep an officer outside tonight. And, sorry about your cat."

She nodded and watched as the officer exchanged a few words with John and then left, leaving her and John alone in the foyer. Lilee stepped forward, locked the door, and returned to the kitchen as John followed.

"Do you have someone you can call to stay with you tonight, or perhaps go to a friend's house?"

Immediately Landon Baynes' image popped in her mind. She wanted him. He made her feel safe. Maybe, just maybe, she should call him. They were once engaged. She did mean something to him. "Yes. Just give me a minute."

She grabbed her phone off the kitchen counter and walked over toward the living room. Landon was still listed as her favorite, so she quickly pressed his name before she lost her nerve. A female voice answered after the third ring. Stunned, Lilee pressed the red button, ending the call. *Damn it! My number will show up on his caller ID,* she thought.

Wait. That is why she answered, not him. Fuming she turned around and faced John again. "I…I don't know who to call. It's so late."

"I learned a long time ago that it's never too late to call your best friend," John said.

She saw his dimple appear again as he smiled, and her heart melted. She answered, "You're right. I'll call Charli."

Charli answered on the fourth ring, sounding a little breathless. "Lilee, what's up?"

Lilee closed her eyes. "Nothing."

John walked over and placed a hand on her shoulder and whispered, "I can sleep on the couch."

"I…I just wanted to call and tell you that running is not going to happen tomorrow."

"Oh? Why not?"

"Too much wine. I'm going to bed and have no plans to set my alarm."

"Well, OK. Call around lunch though, or when you get up."

"I will. Bye, Charli."

Ending her call, she smirked. "I'm a sad case tonight."

"No, you're not. Just a bad day; that's all."

"There are two guest rooms. You don't have to sleep on the couch."

Lilee watched as he looked from the couch to the master bedroom. "I think Officer Phillips was right. Whoever was here is long gone tonight. But, I'll take the couch. It's in a better location."

"I'll go grab a pillow and a blanket then," Lilee said.

"Thanks."

A few minutes later, Lilee came back into the living room and placed the blanket and pillow on her long leather couch. She then put the pizza in the refrigerator and said, "Good night. I'll scream loud if I need anything."

He nodded. "We still have a patrol car outside, remember."

Lilee looked toward her front door. She could still see the message, even though it had been wiped clean. "I appreciate that."

In her bedroom, she immediately brushed her teeth and then climbed into her king-size bed—alone. With the lights off and her covers pulled up to her chin, she closed her eyes but sleep wouldn't come. Ronny Jordan filled her mind. He was so big and had the strength to crush her instantly. Shivering, she turned over on her side and hugged a pillow, remembering the officer outside and the one asleep on her couch. It took another fifteen minutes of tossing and turning before sleep finally tugged her under.

***

Detectives Forest Styles and Trevor Watts watched as the body of William Hart was carefully placed on a stretcher and then covered with a white sheet. Blood soaked the white cotton fabric as he was pushed out through the bathroom door. With gloves on, Forest opened a few drawers in the bathroom inspecting their contents. He found nothing unusual and no recreational drugs.

Forest scanned the bedroom and began looking behind art pieces for a safe.

Trevor spoke. "The closet is massive, but no safe in here either."

Forest opened a dresser drawer and found several pieces of jewelry. "Doesn't look like robbery. Nothing seems touched or missing."

"No, and too many stab wounds."

Forest raked a hand through his short brown hair. "Shit, it looks like a hit. Someone clearly had it in for the doctor and his wife."

They examined a few more rooms and then made their way downstairs and entered the study. Two officers stopped and looked up. Jason, the younger one, spoke. "Found a safe. It's behind the top cabinet. Still locked, and nothing looks disturbed in here."

The sound of another stretcher rolling across the floor caught their attention, and all stopped to watch as the elderly housekeeper rolled by. Blood also spotted her sheet as it covered the full length of her body. Forest stepped forward and asked the EMT, "Any word on the condition of Mrs. Hart?"

"She was still alive the last I heard."

Forest nodded as he watched them continue out the front door and then turned to Trevor and spoke. "OK, we have Christa Hart arriving home sometime around five thirty to five forty-five. We know she took a call from her partner, Andrea Raines, but we don't know if Mrs. Hart was in the home or en route at the time."

Looking around he pointed at her briefcase and continued. "She's in a hurry because she needs to get to a dinner. So, she lays her briefcase down and then walks straight to the back of the house to get her dress."

Together they entered the living room and saw Mrs. Hart's purse on the coffee table. "Why wouldn't she leave the purse in the study with her briefcase?" Forest asked aloud, but he was really just talking out the sequence of events. He then added, "Maybe she was planning on taking her purse upstairs with her and changing it out with another purse for dinner. Lord knows she had plenty to choose from."

"So as she walks through to get her dress, she hears her phone ringing, so she removes it from her purse and leaves it on the coffee table," commented Trevor.

Forest nodded. "That makes sense. She probably was in the home when she got the call."

The two men walked past the living room and through the kitchen. Trevor offered, "If she's in a hurry, she wouldn't walk around the large island."

"Yeah. Therefore never seeing her housekeeper lying dead on the floor," agreed Forest.

Continuing on, they stopped at the entrance to the large laundry room and saw all the blood along with a blue dress in a transparent plastic dry cleaning bag lying crumbled on the floor and spotted with blood. "She was clutching the dress," Forest said, "so she must have taken it down and then turned around and met her attacker."

Trevor replied, "So she never makes it upstairs to find her husband."

"She was clueless as she walked through her own home," Forest agreed. "Damn."

Trevor looked at his notes and then read aloud. "Hospital said Dr. Hart left around four forty-five, so if he didn't make any stops, he should have arrived by five fifteen at the latest."

"OK. We have the doctor entering the home," Forest said. "I would assume he spoke with the housekeeper first, then made his way upstairs for his shower. The perp was probably already in the home and killed the doctor first and then the housekeeper."

"No way of knowing who was attacked first," Trevor replied. "But one thing is for sure: the perp waited on Mrs. Hart. This wasn't robbery. This was a well-plotted hit to take both of them out. Poor housekeeper. She was just in the wrong place at the wrong time."

"Detective Styles?"

Forest turned around and saw Jason. "Yeah?"

"The sons have arrived at the hospital, and it looks like Mrs. Hart's gonna make it."

Forest nodded. "Thanks. Come on, Trevor. We might've just caught our first break."

They turned to go but stopped when Jason continued. "Oh, also, some-one pulled a nasty prank on a city prosecutor tonight. Killed her cat and left a threatening message."

Trevor asked, "Which one?"

"Lilee Parker. You know, the one that let Ronny Jordan get away today."

Forest remembered the news story from the bar and asked, "What time was this?"

Jason shrugged. "Not sure. But we have men watching her tonight and patrolling her neighborhood."

Forest looked at his watch. It was now eleven o'clock. He looked up at Trevor. "Got to love Friday nights!"

Trevor laughed. "Yeah. And you were stupid enough to plan a date."

Forest punched his partner in the shoulder, "Oh yeah, big guy? You told your wife you would help babysit!"

Trevor rubbed his shoulder. "Yeah. Let's get to the hospital. Maybe we can still make it home before sunrise."

Chapter 6

Ronny Jordan lay kicked back in a recliner working on his sixth beer when his little brother waltzed through the front door at eleven fifteen. "Johnny Rae, wherz you been?" Ronny asked.

At eighteen, Johnny Rae stood a little over six foot. He was skin and bones compared to his brother's thick physique of over two hundred and fifty pounds of pure muscle. Their momma entered the room holding a baby on her hip. "Child, where you been? It's after eleven?"

"Nowhere."

Ronny slammed down the recliner footrest. "What da hell you mean, nowhere? You been somewhere. Now answer Momma!"

Carly looked at both her boys. She had raised them herself after walking out of an abusive marriage fifteen years earlier. To this day, no one knew if their father was dead or alive. The only thing they knew for sure was that a child support check had never come in the mail. Carly worked two jobs and had refused any services from the government. She was a proud single black mom and didn't care to add to the statistics of the great state of Georgia.

As a result, she worked twelve-hour shifts a day and relied on family and friends for help with raising her boys. Now, whenever she needed help with Johnny Rae, Ronny would step up to the plate. It had been great, until he got himself arrested and landed in jail for three months awaiting trial. The last couple of months had been near unbearable as she cared for Ronny's child and fought with a moody teenager.

"Just driving, driving around. Why's everyone on my case?"

"We haven't seen you since the courthouse," Carly said. "That was hours ago."

Ronny got up and walked toward his little brother. When he was within inches of his scrawny body, he turned to his momma. "Go on back to bed with Ronny Junior. I handle this."

Carly looked at the time. "I do have to get up at five." When no one responded, she slowly turned around and walked back to the small bedroom down the hall.

In a soft, chilling voice, Ronny spoke. "Now, I's only gonna ask this one more time. Wherz you been? And don't you lie to me."

Johnny Rae nodded. "I swear, I didn't do nothing. I just followed her, followed her home. I wanted to know where she lived."

Ronny's eyes widened. "Whoda hell you talkin' about? The Wells lady?"

Johnny Rae looked down and shook his head.

Ronny, quickly running out of patience, grabbed his brother by the shoulders and whispered, "Who?"

Johnny Rae swallowed then softly murmured, "The blond chick; that lawyer that was mean to you."

Ronny covered his face and took a deep breath. "Did you touch Miz Parker?"

"No. I…I promise. I just followed her home and…and watched her."

"Shit, boy! You trying to land my ass back in the slammer? Whose car do ya think you were drivin'?"

"Sorry! I was angry. Just mad and angry, that's all. I didn't think."

"You damn right, you didn't think!" Slowly Ronny walked back over and sat in his recliner, picked up his beer, and took another long swig as he thought. Finally he continued. "Don't talk of thiz again. You weren't there. You were with some whore somewhere, but not at Miz Parker's house. Understand?"

Johnny Rae slowly nodded his head. "Aren't you mad? You've been wastin' away in a cell for three months with no pay. You didn't beat that old woman up!"

Ronny avoided eye contact. He *had* beaten and robbed the Wells lady, but he would never let his family know the truth. So he lied. "Yeah, but nowz I out. All over. No mores thinkin' about it." Ronny picked up his beer and took the last swig. "Get me another beer."

Johnny Rae walked toward the small kitchen, grabbed one from the fridge, and soon returned.

"Don't ya got work tomorrow?" Ronny asked.

Johnny Rae nodded.

"Go to bed. The last thing we needz is your sorry ass fired because you tired."

Ronny reclined back again and watched as his brother left the room. When he was all alone, he picked up the phone and dialed a friend.

41

"Yo, Ronny, my man. Whatz up?"

Ronny got straight to the point. "We needz to talk."

***

Hospitals in downtown Atlanta were not usually a quiet place to be on a weekend once darkness fell on the city. Security was tight, and guards ran all visitors through a metal detector. So far the nurses had processed four gunshot wounds, two rape victims, four battery and abuse victims, three stabbing victims and two cases of drug or alcohol abuse. No, it wasn't a slow night when Christa Hart arrived at the hospital late Friday evening. Once the staff was alerted that she was the wife of one of their own doctors, most cases were set aside as the best were summoned to the operating room to try to save her life.

It had been a tough save. They were lucky that Christa Hart was a fit, healthy, forty-five-year-old fighter with a strong will to live. Unfortunately, her husband, Dr. William Hart, also fit for forty-five, had no fighting chance. He had apparently been stabbed until his pulse no longer beat. The wife had been spared. None of the twelve stab wounds had hit a major artery or organ. How? This was the question on the minds of the entire medical staff. She was clearly one lucky lady who was going to live, but with a tough emotional road ahead of her.

Nurse Marla Kay Abbott made more notes on Mrs. Hart's chart as Dr. Griffin spoke. "Do not leave her side. If any of her numbers elevate or drop, page me immediately."

Marla Kay nodded. Her eyes were moist. She loved William Hart, and they had worked closely on several cases together over the last eight years since she'd joined the hospital at the young age of twenty- two. Now that she was nearing thirty, one would think she had seen enough to become immune, but this was different.

"Are you OK, Ms. Abbott?"

She nodded slowly and wiped her eyes. "Yes, I am."

Dr. Jeff Griffin placed a hand on her shoulder. "We are all going to miss William, but we need to concentrate on saving his wife with no mistakes. William would want us to do everything we can for his boys to have a mother."

She nodded again. "I will stay right here and won't take my eyes off the machines."

"Good. I have to go out and talk to the twins now. They are going to want to see her. Try to cover up as much of her wounds as possible."

Marla Kay stared at Christa. *How?* she thought. Her neck, face, and arms were badly bruised and stitched up. But she responded, "Yes, of course, Dr. Griffin."

As the doctor left the room, Marla Kay stepped forward and ran her hand through Christa's beautiful blond hair, smoothing it down. Next she pulled the light blanket up to her chest and eased one arm underneath. There wasn't much she could do with the right arm since it was hooked up to an IV. She did try to pull the top cover of the blanket over that shoulder, though, leaving only her elbow to her hand exposed. *There,* she thought. *That is the best I can do.*

Marla Kay only had to wait another five minutes before a door eased opened and Christa's twin sons, Timothy and Todd Hart, age nineteen, entered the room with red eyes and grim expressions. They had already been told about their father and housekeeper. Now they were panicked that they were about to lose their mother as well. Marla Kay stepped aside and gave them some room as Dr. Griffin entered behind them and closed the door.

"Why don't you use the next five minutes for a break," he said. "I will stay with them."

She nodded and slowly peeled her eyes off the twins. Her heart was breaking for them, and she wanted to say something, anything to comfort them, but just couldn't find the right words. She eased away and then quietly left the room.

Timothy was the spitting image of Christa. He had her blond hair, blue eyes, and fair skin. He was the quieter one, less adventurous compared to his brother, Todd. His twin looked more like their father, olive skin and dark hair, but with blue eyes like his mother instead of their father's green eyes. Both were fit and athletic with bright futures ahead of them as they both studied medicine at Auburn University. They had been called immediately by a close family friend, Scott Engleton, who lived next door. Their kids had all grown up together, and they all had each other's contact numbers for emergencies.

Once the boys heard the news, they dropped everything and a friend had driven Tim's car and broken every speed limit from Alabama to Georgia to get them there in time to see their mother once more. Now it appeared she was going to make it, but neither believed it as they looked at her frail body, swollen and bruised.

"She looks bad, but she is healing, and it is important for us to keep her medicated where she can sleep. The body heals faster when she sleeps."

Timothy looked at Dr. Griffin. "When will she be awake?"

"Probably around lunch tomorrow. It will be safer then to ease her off the medication and allow her to wake up."

Todd touched her face and then his hand rested on her shoulder, he was about to lift the blanket but was stopped by his brother's stern voice. "Don't. She wouldn't want you to see her injuries."

Todd picked his hand back up and turned to the doctor. "How did she survive? They said she had multiple stab wounds, just like…like father?"

Dr. Griffin simply answered, "It's a miracle. She lost over 60 percent of her blood supply."

"It wasn't her time," Tim said.

Todd stared at his brother, who had always viewed the world differently from him. Unlike Tim, he viewed everything in black and white, just like their father. He wanted the medical explanation for how all her major organs had remained intact with so many punctures to her small body. He wasn't insensitive; he just always wanted all the details that explained the situation, whether it was good or bad.

"The hospital has set aside a room for you two. Please use it to try to get some sleep. Tomorrow is going to be tough. A lot of decisions will have to be made. I promise that someone will come and get you if there is a change in her condition."

Tim nodded. "Thank you. That is very kind."

"What about the police? Where are they? I want to speak with them," inquired Todd.

"I don't know who's in charge, but they were informed she wouldn't be able to answer any of their questions till late tomorrow."

"Thank you again for everything, Dr. Griffin," Tim said. "I'm sure Todd and I will find them."

"Boys, your father was one of the most gifted surgeons I knew. He was truly a remarkable man, and this hospital will miss him dearly."

Tears formed in Tim's eyes as he softly said, "Thank you." Then he slowly opened the door and eased out with Todd following behind.

Marla Kay saw the boys and broke away from the chatter at the nurses' station. "Excuse me."

The twins turned around and saw the nurse from earlier approaching.

"I'm Marla Kay Abbott, and I will be taking great care of your mom. Please just ask if you have any questions."

Todd took a step toward her. "I know who you are."

Marla Kay's face turned white. "What do you mean?"

Todd stepped within an inch of her pretty face and whispered softly, "You are my father's slut, and I would appreciate not seeing you around my mother."

Tim watched the exchange and quickly took action. "Come on, Todd. This isn't the time or place."

Todd grabbed Marla Kay's arm tightly. "Do you understand me? Stay the hell away from my mother!"

He slowly let go of her arm, shrugged away from his brother, and took off down the hall. Tim met her eyes and shook his head. "I'm...I'm sorry," he said and then took off after his brother.

Marla Kay's face flooded with tears and she buried her face in her hands. Dorothy, her good friend, quickly rushed to her side. "I will speak to Dr. Griffin. Go home. I will call you tomorrow."

Marla Kay nodded, quickly turned in the direction opposite where the boys had gone, and fled down the hallway as other nurses raised their eyebrows and shook their heads. "See?" one of them said. "Another reason why you don't get involved with married doctors!"

Dorothy, who was the head nurse on the floor, turned around and gave them an ugly look. "Keep your comments to yourself, Misty!"

Misty frowned; tossed her long, dark hair over her shoulder; and left.

Dorothy watched the other nurses slowly get back to work and then took a deep breath before heading to Christa Hart's room.

Chapter 7

Forest Styles had decided to call it a night after hearing that no new information could be learned from the hospital. His partner had dropped him back off at the station, and he had driven home after they had decided to meet at the hospital the next morning around eleven, when Mrs. Hart was expected to be awake. It was after midnight when he pulled his Mustang into his garage.

Forest lived alone. He had tried marriage once, but it didn't last. She said she understood his job and unpredictable hours, but, three months after exchanging "I dos," she quickly changed her mind. Forest unlocked both locks to his door and entered his kitchen, closing and locking the door behind him.

Flipping the light switch, he scanned his small home and quickly entered a code in his alarm system. Turning back around, he immediately noticed the answering machine flashing. Walking over, he placed his keys on the counter, hit the button, and then turned to grab a cold beer from the refrigerator.

"I got your message. Look, I understand, but I'm just not willing to try a third time. Sorry. Have a nice life, Forest."

He wasn't surprised. He had stood Diane up three straight weekends now. He closed the door, twisted the cap, and took a long sip as the machine went through three hang-up calls.

"Forest, it's Daniel Maggs. You have probably heard by now about one of my team members, Lilee Parker, being threatened tonight. As a favor, would you personally check into this matter? I would appreciate it. You can reach me on Saturday anytime."

Forest waited for more, but that was it. Stepping forward, he hit delete. Daniel Maggs didn't have to leave his number, because Forest had it memorized. Daniel was his uncle. An image of Lilee Parker filled his mind. She was a spitfire in the courtroom and had rarely lost a case. *I wonder what happened with Ronny Jordan?* he thought. *How the hell did that get screwed up?*

Taking his phone out of his clip holder, he walked through the small living room and into the only bedroom in his townhouse. The other bed-room had been made into a study. Plugging his phone into his charger, he set his alarm for six and then removed his piece and laid it on the small dresser. Next, he stripped down, got into bed, and immediately fell asleep—with no more thoughts of Lilee or the Harts.

***

Lilee awoke with a fright at 3 a.m. She must have had a nightmare, because Officer John Norman was standing at her door with the light on holstering his pistol as he saw her sitting up in bed, obviously OK.

"Oh, God! I'm sorry. Did I wake you?"

"Yeah, but that's OK. Nightmare?"

She blushed. "Yeah. Ronny Jordan had me trapped in a corner and nowhere to run."

John shook his head. "I'm sorry. You gonna be able to go back to sleep?"

"I should." She looked up at him. "Are you?"

"Sure."

She crossed her arms over her thin T-shirt and coyly replied, "Liar."

He smirked. "Yeah, you're right. You got my adrenaline pumping. But nah, seriously, I can go back to sleep. Just holler if you need something."

When he turned around she softly whispered, "John?"

He turned to face her as she said, "Stay, please."

John walked three wide steps, took her in his arms, and began kissing and holding her tight. Soon he was on top of her, raising her t-shirt as his hands caressed her body. Her body jolted at his touch and she opened her eyes.

Suddenly Lilee rose up in bed and looked around. No one was there. *Oh, thank God,* she thought. *It was all just a dream. Am I losing my mind?*

Pulling the covers back, she got out of bed, walked into her master bath, and closed the double doors behind her. Finding the light, she filled a glass with water and drank. As she set the cup down, she noticed she was shaking. Squeezing her hands together, she tried to push all the anxiety she was feeling away. She looked at herself in the mirror and thought, *Damn, am I that lonely?* Suddenly she heard a tap on the door and jumped.

"Ms. Parker? It's Officer Norman. Are you OK?"

Lilee looked at the door and then back at her reflection in the mirror and watched as her face turned pink blushing at the sound of his voice. "Yes. I'm fine. Just needed some water."

Slowly she turned away and opened the double doors and saw him.

He glanced over her and very professionally stated, "Let me know if you need anything."

She nodded and he turned and left. It was at that moment she realized she was only wearing a long T-shirt that barely covered her underwear.

She had removed her sweats before jumping into bed. Mortified, she flipped the switch off and ran and jumped back in bed.

The sun was shining when Lilee awoke again. She looked over to her clock and read the time: nine thirty five. Startled, she jumped up. She couldn't remember the last time she'd slept so late. Noticing her door was open but seeing no one, she quickly grabbed her sweats off the floor and pulled them on. Still feeling a chill, she opened her bottom drawer and removed a long cotton housecoat. The temperature had dropped during the night, and her wooden floors felt cold. Opening another drawer, she grabbed some socks as well.

Now that she was decent, she entered her bathroom, used the facilities, and brushed her teeth. She brushed her hair, pulled it up into a ponytail, and left in search of Officer John Norman. She had no choice. It was time to face him after greeting him half naked in the middle of the night. *Oh, what he must have thought!* Making her way down the hallway, she heard a noise coming from her kitchen. Rounding the corner, she said, "Good Morn…" and stopped when she saw a strange man sitting at her bar.

"Where is Officer Norman?"

"Good morning, Ms. Parker. I'm Detective Forest Styles. Officer Norman has already left."

Lilee eyed the good-looking man sitting there drinking coffee from one of her coffee cups. He had also been reading the paper—her paper, no doubt.

"Oh, I see."

"I made coffee. I hope you don't mind."

She walked toward a cabinet, removed a cup, and began pouring as she responded, "No, of course not."

Turning around, she took a sip of her black coffee and noticed he hadn't taken his eyes off of her. Feeling a little awkward, she turned away, opened the refrigerator, and grabbed the box of leftover pizza.

As she set it on the island in front of him, he smiled. "Now you are a lady after my own heart. Cold pizza for breakfast. Nothing like it!"

She cracked a smile, but it faded quickly when she caught a glimpse of her picture in the paper and read the headline. She closed her eyes and asked softly, "How bad is it?"

"Bad. But you're lucky!"

She opened her eyes and stared intently into his green eyes. "I'm sorry, but lucky how?"

He closed the paper and turned it around for her to read the giant headline on the front page. "See? No one will think twice about you or the screwup after they read about the murder of Dr. Hart in Park Square."

Her eyes widened as she began to read. "How horrible."

"Yeah, it was. I was there last night for several hours."

Lilee looked back up at him. "Who exactly are you again?"

"Detective Forest Styles. Been with the Atlanta Police Department now for six years."

"Why haven't we met before now?"

"We have once before, but it was brief. We just haven't worked on any cases together. But I've seen you in action. You're a good lawyer."

She studied him as he took another sip of coffee. He did seem sincere with his comment. "Thanks. Um, if you were at the Hart house last night, why are you here with me now? I mean, are you not in charge of the Hart case?"

"I am. But I'm running a favor for my uncle."

Confusion was clearly written all over her face. Before she could ask for clarification, he added, "Daniel Maggs is my uncle."

She dropped her pizza back in the box and asked, "You're related to Maggs?"

"Well, he's my aunt's husband. So not a blood relative, no."

"So I guess Maggs has already heard about last night."

"Yeah. I had a message on my machine last night when I got home. I haven't returned his call yet."

"Well, John and I...I mean, Officer Norman and I started a list last night of my cases. He said it would take a while to sort through them."

"It will. A list of names will be produced, and then each will be questioned on their whereabouts last night."

"I think it was Ronny Jordan."

Forest surprised her when he said, "Nah, he can't be that stupid. Got to be someone else."

She narrowed her eyes and then looked at her cup of coffee, slowly tracing a finger around the edge.

"Ms. Parker, why isn't your alarm monitored?"

She opened her mouth to respond but struggled at finding the right words. "Um, well, it wasn't necessary."

"You live alone don't you?"

Softly she replied, "Not always; just recently."

"Well, I called a security company. I've used them for years. They're coming by. Please consider purchasing the package. They're a good company."

She turned and refilled her cup. "Do you want another cup?"

"No, thanks. I got to get going. Lots of ground to cover with the Hart case today."

Taking her full cup, she turned back toward him and commented, "Yeah, I imagine."

Forest folded the paper, took his last sip of coffee, and stood. "Look, there's a patrol car still stationed outside. Just let them know if you need anything."

She glanced at his gun as he turned and grabbed his jacket off the other bar stool. He noticed and asked, "Do you own a gun?"

She shook her head.

"Get one, and I'll show you myself how to use it."

She watched as he lifted another slice of pizza.

"Thanks for the pizza."

"Sure. No problem."

She walked him to the front door, where she looked outside and found the patrol car sitting in the same spot as the night before. The officer in the car waved, and Lilee returned the gesture.

"Lock the door back," Forest said. "Security company should be here within the next thirty minutes."

Lilee watched his backside as he walked out the front door and felt her heart miss a beat. Suddenly, as if he felt her stare, he turned around. "Lilee. You don't mind me calling you Lilee, do you?"

She shook her head.

"Well, Lilee, I will see you later." He turned back around and then stopped and faced her once again. "You know, Lilee, Landon Baynes is a fool."

She watched as a smile formed on his face and then he turned once more, walked over to a black Mustang, and climbed inside. Firing up the engine, he waved as he sped away. It took a moment for her to realize she had stopped breathing. Catching her breath, she quickly turned away and went back inside, locking the door behind her.

Chapter 8

At ten o'clock Officer John Norman pulled out of the grocery store parking lot in his patrol car. Now officially off duty, he was looking forward to the next two days off work. He had planned on going fishing, but an all-nighter had left him too tired. All he could think to do now was to go home, stretch out on his recliner, and watch the Georgia Bulldogs play some football. Easing out into traffic, he pulled ahead into the fast lane, one of the greatest perks to being a cop. He smiled. Like always, everyone got out of his way.

A mile later, John took the entrance ramp to the interstate. Setting his patrol car on cruise control at seventy-one, he relaxed behind the wheel and turned up the volume to his favorite country CD. Images of Lilee Parker soon filled his mind. *Damn, she was a beauty!* He still wasn't sure she realized how she'd been dressed in the wee hours of the morning. But still, she had opened the door.

Should I have stayed? The question lingered in his brain with no clear answer. He would see her again next week when he came back on duty, and the thought made him very happy. Just then, all thoughts of Lilee disappeared as a black SUV came flying by in the slow lane, passing him. *What the hell?*

Turning off his CD, he turned on his police scanner and looked at the radar mounted on his windshield: 87 mph. *What the hell is this idiot doing?*

John was officially off duty, but this excessive speed was dangerous. Even more worrisome was the fact that they had knowingly sped past a cop car in broad daylight. He pressed the gas pedal and sped up to eighty as he pushed a button mounted on his dash and spoke.

"Officer John Norman, number 9453. Over."

"Go ahead 9453."

"I got a black SUV, recorded speed 87 mph, traveling southbound on I-75. Is there an alert out?"

"Negative on a black SUV."

Silence followed, and then the operator added, "Go ahead and proceed with caution. I register your location, and I'm calling for backup."

John flipped his siren and pressed down on the gas pedal, raising his speed to ninety. The black SUV was now swerving and traveling up to 96 mph. Finally John got close enough to read his plate to the operator.

"Do you copy the plate number?"

"Affirmative. Running it now."

Suddenly the black SUV entered the right lane and slowed down, turning on his right turn signal.

"Black SUV pulling over on the side of the highway."

"Affirmative. The plate is registered to a Dr. Henry Boggs, south Atlanta."

John took a deep breath and remarked, "Just another doctor in a hurry."

"Maybe, Officer Norman, but proceed with caution."

John looked out his side mirror for oncoming traffic. All clear. He quickly got out of his car, placed a hand on his weapon, and flipped the safety switch. He walked up to the driver's side window cautiously just as the driver lowered it. "Could you step out of the"

Baaang!

Officer John Norman never saw the gun. He fell to the ground with a bullet hole to his forehead. The black SUV shifted into gear and sped off back onto the interstate, spraying gravel and dust all over the fallen officer's body, leaving no witnesses.

Forest Styles pulled into Atlanta General Hospital at ten fifty-five, five minutes before the planned meeting with his partner, Trevor Watts. He immediately saw the excessive amount of law enforcement walking around their parked patrol cars. Forest quickly parked, exited his vehicle, and had begun jogging toward the entrance when he spotted Trevor talking to an officer.

"Hey, what's up?"

"An officer got gunned downed along the interstate less than an hour ago."

Forest assumed he was now in surgery with the large presence of officers. "How's he doing?"

"Dead. No chance. Gunshot to the forehead. The vehicle he called in was registered to a Dr. Henry Boggs."

"Aw, shit!"

"Gets worse. Dr. Boggs has been in surgery for the last three hours, and his black SUV is missing from the parking lot."

Forest frowned and shook his head. "Who was the officer?"

The young officer standing by Trevor answered in a cracked voice. "John, John Norman."

Forest felt the blood drain from his face. "No. I just saw him this morning. That can't be."

Trevor asked, "Where?"

"At Lilee Parker's house. He had stayed over last night on patrol after she received a death threat."

The young officer put his hands on his forehead and spoke again. "He was off duty. Going home. Shit!"

Forest placed a hand on his shoulder. "I'm sorry. You knew him well."

"Yeah. We went through the academy together."

An awkward moment came and went as no one spoke. Finally the men said good-bye, and Forest and Trevor entered the hospital in search of Christa Hart's doctor.

"Mrs. Hart is still in ICU located on the second floor," said the elderly lady volunteering at the help desk. "Once you get off the floor, follow the signs to ICU. There will be a call button for you to press, and someone will be out to assist you."

Forest thanked her, and they stepped toward the elevators. He pressed the up button, and, as they waited, he couldn't push Lilee and Officer Norman out of his mind. *Someone needs to tell her, in person*, he thought.

Trevor looked his way. "You OK?"

"Yeah. Just…life can change in a flash, can't it?"

"It can, especially in our line of work." The elevator doors opened, and they stepped on. Trevor pressed the number two and asked, "So tell me about Lilee Parker."

"Daniel had left me a message to look into it. So I went over there this morning and chatted with her. She seemed fine, and the guys are on it, already talking to some of the people, getting their alibis."

"Rumor is our department messed up on the Ronny Jordan case. Is he the number one suspect?"

Forest thought about his comment. He hadn't heard the rumor, and Lilee hadn't badmouthed the department that morning. *Interesting*, he thought.

The elevator door opened, and all conversation on Lilee Parker ended as they came face-to-face with Dr. Griffin and the two sons of Christa and William Hart.

"I'm Dr. Jeff Griffin."

Both detectives shook his hand and introduced themselves. Timothy Hart spoke next. "I'm Tim, and this is my brother, Todd."

"Is she awake?" Forest asked.

Dr. Griffin shook his head. "Not yet, but it shouldn't be too much longer. A nurse will come get us."

"Do you have any leads as to who did this?" Todd asked.

Forest looked at him and said, "Let's all take a seat."

Todd and Tim both had red, tired eyes due to lack of sleep. Both wore wrinkled, button-down polos, and their hair looked a mess. Forest had read about the boys that morning. Both were high achievers academically and both had lettered in double sports in high school. They now attended Auburn University with a full ride scholarship to study medicine. Forest had been impressed. No run-ins with the law over drugs, alcohol, or speeding tickets. The boys were squeaky clean—at least on paper.

Trevor opened his notepad. "When was the last time either of you saw your parents?"

Todd answered. "Sunday. We always come home Sunday morning and leave Sunday night."

"Did either of you speak to your parents this week?"

Tim looked down and mumbled. "No. We had midterms this week. We were too…"

Todd finished in a somber voice, "Busy studying."

"On Sunday, was there any hint of a problem or possible tension between your parents?" Forest asked.

Todd got defensive. "Are you asking if our parents were fighting?"

Forest replied calmly, "I'm looking for anything out of the ordinary that just maybe seemed off or odd."

Tim shook his head. "It was a normal Sunday. We ate lunch, watched some football, discussed our classes; nothing stands out that would lead to…well, this."

"Todd?"

"Yeah. Just a normal Sunday."

Trevor turned to Dr. Griffin. "Did you work with Dr. Hart this week?"

"Yes."

"How did he seem this past week?"

"I've asked myself that question over and over, and nothing. I mean, nothing explains why or how this could happen."

"Did he lose a patient recently under his care?" asked Forest.

"I thought about that too. William was a gifted surgeon. It was rare for him to lose anyone under the knife."

"But it happens, right?" Forest asked gently.

Dr. Griffin nodded his head. "I can only think of two cases over the last year that ended badly."

Looking at the boys, he explained. "Neither was your dad's fault. Both cases were lost causes by the time your dad agreed to help."

"We will need those names," Trevor said.

Dr. Griffin nodded.

"Excuse me, Dr. Griffin."

All turned to face a nurse who had spoken behind them.

"Mrs. Hart is awake now."

Chapter 9

As a car rode past Lilee Parker's home, its driver noticed a patrol car parked out front. Never slowing down, the car continued on unnoticed. *Damn! Another time, Ms. Parker.*

Two minutes later, Charli Pepper pulled up in Lilee's front yard and was instantly greeted by Officer Bishop.

"Hi, Mrs. Pepper. How are you today?"

"I'll be fine once I see for myself that Lilee's OK."

"Shaken up," he said, "but she's tough."

Thinking of all the cases and battles they'd faced together over the last few years, she quickly agreed. "Yeah, she is. Excuse me now."

"Yes, ma'am."

Before Charli could knock on the door, Lilee opened it. She watched as Charli's eyes found the blood stain on her porch. "Oh my God! Lilee!" she cried and then opened her arms and embraced her dear friend. "Why didn't you tell me this last night when you called?"

"Sorry. Come on in. I just made another pot of coffee."

Closing the door, they made their way into the kitchen, where Charli took a seat on the bar stool and watched as Lilee poured two cups.

"So do the police have any ideas or leads?"

"If they have, they haven't told me yet."

Charli reached for her cup. "I bet it was Ronny Jordan. He's been sitting in prison now for three months, probably planning this all along."

"He's number one on the list, but…I don't know."

"You don't think it's him?"

"Well, I did at first, but I don't know. Maybe the police are right. He'd be really stupid to commit a crime on the day he was released."

"Stupid is as stupid does." Charli laughed. "We see it all the time!"

Charli took a sip of her coffee and watched as Lilee smiled briefly and then her expression changed as the seriousness of the matter set back in. "Why don't you pack a bag and stay with us tonight?"

"I don't know," Lilee said, shrugging. "We'll see. The day is still young."

"Have you talked to Maggs yet?" asked Charli.

"Yes. He was really upset."

"So was I! You should have told me last night!"

"Sorry," Lilee said again. "Look, hey, do you know a Detective Forest Styles? He's Maggs' nephew."

Charli smiled. "Oh, yeah. He's hot. Why? Did you meet him?"

"Yeah, this morning. How is it you know him, but I don't?"

"Because you never come up for air. It's work, work, work with you!"

Charli was right. Lilee really never bothered to get to know people within the police department. Maybe if she had, slipups like the one with Ronny Jordan might not have happened. She took another sip of her coffee and then walked around the bar and sat beside her friend.

"Is he gonna help with the investigation?" Charli asked.

"No, I don't think so. Apparently he stopped by as a favor to Maggs."

Charli saw the spark in her eyes. "Oh? Tell me about it."

"Well there's not a whole lot to say. We chatted; he's nice."

Charli smiled. "Pretty easy on the eyes too."

Lilee smirked. "Well, yes, I would have to agree with that."

"Who knows? He might end up helping."

Lilee shook her head. "He's got the Hart case."

Charli saw the paper folded on the island. "I can't believe what happened last night at Park Square. What is this city becoming?"

"Detective Styles was there. He said it was bad, real bad."

Charli frowned and then turned the paper over to hide the headlines. "I've got an idea. Since my hubby had to go in for work, why don't you go and get dressed and let's go out for lunch?"

Lilee picked up her coffee cup and nodded. "I think that's a great idea. I need some new clothes too. Give me ten minutes."

As Lilee walked away, Charli couldn't help herself. She turned the newspaper back over and stared at the picture of the Harts and then scanned the article. Next, she turned the page and saw a picture of Ronny Jordan beside his attorney, Andy Kane. "Piece of shit. Both of you."

She quickly stood up, walked back toward the foyer, and scanned the front yard. The patrol car still sat there. Her eyes found the dark bloodstain again, and suddenly a cold chill ran down her spine. She looked back up to verify the policeman was actually sitting in the car and then took another sip of her coffee to fight the coldness.

***

Christa Hart slowly opened her eyes, and her sons surrounded her. She tried to smile but felt the pain and grimaced.

"Mrs. Hart, I'm Dr. Griffin. Do you remember me?"

She nodded.

"I know you're in a lot of pain now and have many questions. But you are one lucky lady. Your body just needs time to heal. You're gonna make it."

Tim held her hand. "Mom, do you remember what happened?"

Christa slowly closed her eyes, and visions soon filled her mind. She remembered walking into her home, seeing flowers, and smelling their beautiful aroma. *What must have gone wrong?* Opening her eyes once again, she tried to look over her body but stopped at the pain.

"It's OK, Mom," said Todd.

Dr. Griffin saw the look of horror spread across her face. She remembered. Suddenly screams filled the room and she tried to grab hold of her boys. Dr. Griffin stepped forward and gently held her down. "You are safe now, Mrs. Hart. No one is going to hurt you anymore."

All watched as her body went limp. Her cries turned into tears as she pushed words through her trembling mouth. "Will. Where is William?"

She knew the answer. She could see it in her boys' faces. She shook her head and muttered, "No. No, he can't be."

Tim leaned forward and hugged his mom gently. "We…we will get through this, Mom. We love you very much. Todd and I, we'll be here every step of the way."

Todd placed his hand on her head as Tim stood back up and gave him some room.

"Mom, there are some detectives here. It's important that you talk to them. They have no leads. Anything you can give them would help."

She nodded slowly and then watched as her boys stepped away, and she saw the two strange men in her room for the first time.

"I'm Detective Forest Styles, and this is my partner, Trevor Watts."

She didn't speak.

"Mrs. Hart, did you see your attacker?"

She nodded slowly.

"How many?"

"One," she said softly.

Forest was careful to only ask questions with one-word answers but at the same time did not want to influence her thoughts in any way. That could be used later to confuse the case.

"Do you know who it was?"

She shook her head no and closed her eyes.

Todd walked around to the other side and placed a hand on hers.

She opened her eyes, and their eyes met.

Forest continued. "Was it a male or female?"

She turned to face him. "Male."

"What race?"

She shook her head and then closed her eyes. She began moaning, and it turned ugly quickly as more pain ripped through her body. Dr. Griffin stepped forward and quickly readjusted her pain meds. Soon, she began to relax. Next, he turned to the detectives. "I'm sorry, but I think that's enough for now. We can try again tomorrow."

Forest nodded. "Thanks, Doctor. Tim, Todd, I'm sorry. If either of you can think of anything, please call."

Todd took the card Forest extended but quickly turned back toward his mother and placed a comforting hand on her exposed, frail hand. Slowly her light moans faded to a whisper, and then she was out.

Forest and Trevor left the same way they had entered and once again found the waiting area outside ICU. A nurse gestured toward them, and then Forest saw Andrea Raines stand and rush toward them.

"Detectives! Any word? No one is telling me anything."

Forest reached for her hand and squeezed it. "Todd and Tim will be out shortly. I know this is a rough time, but do you think you can answer some questions for us?"

Andrea's eyes left his face and looked behind him as Forest felt the presence of someone else.

"Gentlemen."

Forest turned to find a tall man, around six one, with dark grayish hair standing in a white coat. He read his nametag: Dr. Derrick Raines.

"Dr. Raines. Detective Forest Styles."

Trevor extended his hand next. "Detective Trevor Watts."

"Gentlemen, my wife has been through enough. I think tomorrow will be better suited for questions. You may come out to our home, say around early afternoon."

Forest didn't push. He looked at Andrea's red eyes and sad face. "Around two o'clock?"

She nodded.

"We have your address," Forest agreed. "We'll see you tomorrow."

"Thank you for your understanding, detectives. We'll see you tomorrow," said Dr. Raines in a dry voice.

Forest stepped away as Dr. Raines embraced his wife and held her tenderly. Carefully he watched the exchange as they waited for the elevator to open. Soon the two men stepped inside the elevator, and Forest remarked, "Something tells me this case is going to unlock a lot of skeletons in a lot of closets."

Trevor smirked. "Yeah. No robbery. Must be love, money, or revenge. Now, we just got to figure out which one."

***

Ronny Jordan paced back and forth on the small porch, irate. "I wuz home last night wif witnesses. I ain't got nothin' to do with no big city prosecutor!"

Officer Lewis continued to push his buttons. "What about your friends, Ronny? Did you make a special request perhaps? Maybe a little favor was asked?"

Ronny's face turned mean, and he was at the point of boiling over. "I told ya no. Now if you don't have a warrant for my arrest, get da hell off my porch!"

"We'd like to talk to those witnesses, Ronny, and then we'll be leaving."

"Ain't gonna happen. Just me and Ronnie Junior here, and he don't talk."

Officer Lewis persisted. "Where's your mother, boy? We'll go to her?"

"Damn you fools! You don't need to go trampsing into Momma's work. Leave her be."

"How sweet. Don't want your momma further embarrassed by her son's actions."

Officer Coolridge placed a hand over his heart and added, "Yeah, my heart is just melting for his love and compassion over his momma."

That did it. Ronny exploded. "Get da hell off of my porch or I's call Mister Kane. Now!"

Officer Lewis stepped forward and placed a hand on Ronny's chest. "You want to hit me, big guy? Cause I would love to take your sorry black ass in and lock your ass up once more."

Ronny held his breath at the officer's touch. Sweat began to form on his forehead, even though it was a mild seventy degrees outside. The last thing he needed to do was have CPS come in and take Ronny Junior away and have his ass thrown back in jail. His momma wouldn't be able to take that. She would snap this time around. He was sure.

"No, sir. Come back at five thirty. Momma's shift ends at five."

Officer Lewis continued glaring into his eyes, mere inches away, before finally removing his hand and then stepping away. "See you then Ronny. And you better hope she's here, cause if not, we're dragging your ass back in. And that's a promise, not a threat."

Ronny never moved from his spot as the two officers got into their patrol car and left. When they finally backed out of the driveway, he let out a long breath. *Damn you, Johnny Rae,* he thought. *What da hell did you get me into?*

Chapter 10

Tom Franklin ran his own auto body shop on the corner of Tenth Street in downtown Atlanta. He had built a solid reputation of fairness and good work over the last twelve years—something hard to do in his line of work. Last year he'd been able to move his wife and two small boys into a nicer house just three blocks from his business. It had worked well, and he often came home for lunch each day.

With today being a Saturday, he was especially busy but had promised to close up come four o'clock. His wife had planned a date night with just the two of them. He smiled. It sure was nice for Sheila to get out of her sweats, put on a little makeup, and get dolled up. He couldn't blame her, though. Her days were just as long as his. She ran a successful alteration business out of their home, allowing her to stay home and care for their youngest son, who, at only three, was not yet old enough to attend school like his six-year-old brother.

Scanning the parking lot for any new customers, he saw none and stepped back inside and locked the door. Next he turned off all the lights and then walked back into the large shop located behind his office. The large overhang door still stood open to let the nice breeze in. He looked at the time again: three fifty. Looking at his latest project, a nice F350 up on the lift, he decided he had enough time to finish. All he had to do was get a shower, and this should take no longer than fifteen minutes. *One less thing to do on Monday*, he thought.

Tom had two other mechanics, but both took off at noon on Saturdays, and no one worked on Sundays. Sheila had put her foot down many years ago that Sunday was for church and family, and that was not going to ever change. He smiled again. She was right. The extra money couldn't compete with being a good father, something he'd never had. So they spent Sundays going to church and then to the park after lunch. He loved baseball, and both his boys had gloves and were working on their throws. He smiled again at the memory of Jacob and Patrick running around with their little gloves that fell off their little hands so easily as they ran around.

As he stepped under the large truck, he looked up at it and began putting parts back on, tightening each bolt. Engaged in his work, with only five more bolts to go, he never noticed a presence entering the shop from the open garage door. Carefully the person walked along the concrete floor without a sound toward the lift's control panel. A hand covered in a leather glove pressed a button.

Cries echoed through the garage as Tom cussed and vainly tried to move as the F350 came crushing down with a thud. Somehow Tom had been able to move, but it had only been a foot—not enough. He lay motionless, pinned beneath a tire of the blue truck. The figure wearing the gloves walked over and looked down at the crumbled body. "See you in hell, Tom!" And with that, the dark, twisted soul pressed the garage door button and left.

***

When Charli pulled into Lilee's driveway at 4:45 p.m., both women immediately spotted a black Mustang parked behind the patrol car.

Lilee spoke first. "Looks like Detective Styles is back. I wonder if this is good news or bad?"

Charli put her car in park and shut off the motor. "I can stay a little longer. We'll find out together."

Lilee nodded and then opened her car door as Officer Bishop and Detective Styles walked over. "Ladies, enjoy the day?"

Lilee held up two large shopping bags. "I did. Amazing how shopping can change one's mood. So, how are things going here? Any updates?" Immediately Lilee saw something in both of their eyes. "What? What happened?"

"Why don't we go on inside, and we'll talk there?" Detective Styles suggested.

Lilee looked over at Charli and then back to the Detective. "OK."

Once in her home, Officer Bishop and the Detective checked the house as Charli and Lilee sat in the living room waiting.

Soon Officer Bishop reported, "All clear. I'm going back out. Call if you need anything."

Forest Styles walked over and took a seat across from the women.

Lilee, who had been patiently waiting now for a good five minutes, said in a tense voice, "Now, can you tell us what's going on? Because I know it's something."

"You read people well, Ms. Parker."

Lilee sat back and tilted her head to the side. "Well, it's my job, remember? And please, call me Lilee."

He nodded. "Lilee, I'm sorry to tell you this, but Officer John Norman was killed today in the line of duty. I'm so sorry."

Forest watched as the color drained from her face and she opened her mouth to speak but found no words. Suddenly she placed both hands over her face and mumbled, "No. No; not John."

Charli knew John Norman and asked in a pleading voice, "When did this happen?"

"It was this morning. He was technically off duty, and he stopped a vehicle on the interstate that was driving at dangerous speeds. The vehicle had been stolen, but no one knew it at the time. He was shot at close range."

"Oh my God!" Charli cried. "We heard it on the news, but…we didn't know who it was. This is awful!" Charli closed her eyes as tears began to roll down her cheek.

Lilee looked back up and removed her hands. "We…we just talked last night. He was such a good person, so kind, caring. I…I this is hard."

Forest nodded.

Charli asked, "Is there any way this could be related to Lilee and what happened here last night?"

"Everything's being looked at closely, but it looks more like wrong place at the wrong time, and Officer Norman just happened to be the one to pull over the perp."

Lilee stood up, walked into her kitchen, and pulled out a bottle of wine from her wine rack. Seeing her struggle with the opener, Forest stood up, walked over, and immediately placed a hand on top of hers. "I'll do this."

Lilee looked up with her wet green eyes and slightly nodded. Next she walked over and grabbed a wine glass. Turning around, she asked Charli, "Do you want some?"

Charli stood up and walked over. "No, and I'm afraid I have to leave. We've got that dinner meeting at six. Do you want us to swing by and get you afterward?"

Lilee shook her head. "No, I will be fine. There will be an officer outside, right Detective Styles?"

"Yes, and please call me Forest."

Charli watched the exchange between the two and then offered. "OK, well, please call me if you need anything. We can always cancel our plans."

"You are sweet, but that won't be necessary," Lilee said. "Besides, this dinner is important for your husband, so you need to get going and quit worrying about me."

Charli stepped forward and gave her a tender hug. "Easier said than done. I had fun today. Look, call me tomorrow or if you need me, promise?"

Lilee released her friend and nodded. "I had fun today too. Thanks."

Charli said, "Good-bye, Forest."

Forest replied and then turned to look at Lilee. She was a mess. Her mascara had smudged and the hand holding the empty wineglass trembled. He carefully reached out and took it from her and poured the red wine to half full. Slowly Lilee walked around, sat on the bar stool, and then picked up the glass and began to drink.

He watched her movements carefully. She was clearly shaken by news of Officer Norman. *How well did she know him?* he wondered. Soon, she placed her glass down and stood. "Will you join me? It's nice on the back porch this time of day. Oh, and I have water or juice to offer."

He surprised her by saying, "Actually wine sounds good."

"Oh, I'm sorry. I just assumed you were still on duty."

"No. I wanted to be the one to tell you the news in person. Didn't want you to hear it from someone else."

Lilee watched as he took another glass down and poured more wine. When he was done, she said, "Thank you for that."

Forest followed her through the living room and watched as she unlocked her French doors and then stepped out onto the large covered patio.

"This is nice," he said.

She took a seat on a cushioned couch and gestured for him to sit beside her. "Thanks."

Moments passed with neither speaking another word as they drank from their wine and looked out onto the well-manicured backyard. It was quiet and nice, and neither seemed to want to break the silence as they continued to sip their wine.

Lilee dabbed at her eyes and finally broke the silence. "So, any leads on last night?"

"No, to both cases."

Instantly Lilee thought of the Hart case. "Is Mrs. Hart still gonna make it?"

"Yeah, looks like. She spoke some today, but not a lot. She's in a lot of pain."

Lilee turned and faced Forest. "No more. No more talk of death and murder. Tell me about you. I want to know Forest Styles."

He looked into her green eyes. "I enjoy fishing and watching football."

She smiled. "I've never been fishing, but I love football!"

Forest looked genuinely shocked. "Never been fishing?"

"Not even with a snoopy rod when I was little."

"Well, that's just wrong. I'll take you."

Lilee took a sip from her wine and stared out across the yard. "I would like that very much."

Forest smiled. "Yeah. Me too."

"Ever been married?"

He lost his smile. "Once. It didn't work out. How about yourself?"

"Almost. It didn't work out. But you already knew that."

He remembered his comment from that morning about Landon Baynes being a fool. "Yeah, but are you dating someone now?"

She turned back toward him. "Why do you ask?"

He set his wineglass down on the coffee table in front of him, turned toward her, and gently placed a hand on her cheek. In a soft, sexy voice, he lowered his mouth close to hers and said, "Because when I kiss you, I want to know if someone's gonna be hunting me down?"

She slightly shook her head and then his lips found hers and he kissed her tenderly. Sparks flew as she felt warmth spread over her body. He smelled and felt good, and her body was immediately awakened by his touch. Soon he pulled away, leaned forward, and picked up his wineglass again. As he leaned back, he placed his free arm around her and pulled her close without saying a word.

Time seemed to stand still for the next five minutes as each relaxed and continued to sip from their wine. It had been a long day, following a long week for her. She was tired, too tired from it all. Her long hours, her breakup, her lost case, last night, and now the death of John Norman. It was overwhelming. Now, for the first time in several months, she felt at peace within his warm embrace. She had no idea where this was going, but, at the same time, she didn't want this feeling to end.

More minutes passed, and then Forest slowly removed his arm. "How about another glass?"

She nodded.

He smiled and then leaned in and kissed her on the forehead as he stood up. She watched as he walked back through her house. He looked so fit in his button-down shirt and blue jeans. She could hear the soles of his boots as he walked across the tile. She smiled as she turned back around and continued to look out. Just as she set her empty glass down, she saw movement out of the corner of her eye. She looked quickly to her right but only saw the tall shrubs bordering her fence line. She continued to stare but saw no further movement of any kind.

Forest walked out with the bottle of wine and looked over to where she was staring. "What is it?"

"Nothing. Just a squirrel or a bird."

Forest moved directly in front of her and then turned around to take a closer look. Seeing nothing, he eased his stance and took his seat again. "Do you always keep your gate locked?"

"Sorry. There're no locks on the side gate."

Forest looked at her and shook his head. "I can swing by tomorrow morning and fix that."

She watched as he poured more wine. "That's kind but I…"

"I have the tools," he interrupted. "I don't mind."

"OK."

He took a sip from his glass and said, "I'm starved. How about you?"

She thought about how she had picked at her salad at lunch. Charli had fussed at her for not eating. To pacify her friend, she had eaten a large stick of bread with butter but hadn't felt hungry. Now, for the first time in a long time, she felt hunger and a real need to eat. "Food sounds like a really good idea. Shall I order some Mexican or Chinese? I know of some good restaurants that deliver."

He smiled. "I'm one step ahead of you."

"Oh?"

"Yep. I ordered Mexican, to be delivered at six."

She looked down at her watch and noticed that is was now five forty-five. "How did you know?"

"I looked in your refrigerator this morning. It's empty."

He smiled and she returned the gesture. "Well, I could make some margaritas to go with dinner."

"Why Lilee Parker, are you trying to get me intoxicated where I'll spend the night?"

"Actually, I would feel safer if you stayed the night." She blushed and then added, "With or without the alcohol."

He narrowed his eyes and looked intently at her. She blushed again and then explained, "I have a couple of guest rooms."

He smiled and touched her hand. "OK. The guest room it is."

Dinner was delivered at six as planned, and the two ate chicken fajitas and chips and drank two glasses each of margaritas. After a good SEC football game between Florida and Alabama, both decided it was time to turn in.

"Thank you, Forest, for everything. Tonight I will get much-needed rest."

"You're welcome. I enjoyed your company." He stepped in close to her and lowered his mouth to hers for a tender kiss. She felt the spark once more between them and instinctively wrapped her arms around him and kissed him back. Forest held her tight, but, knowing she'd had a bad day and too much alcohol, he forced himself to pull away. "I'll see you in the morning," he said softly.

Slowly she nodded, took a step back, and then turned and left him standing alone in the living room. He watched as she left and then suddenly peeked her head back around the corner and said, "Tomorrow, Forest." She smiled and left once more.

Forest held his breath, hoping she would return once more, but she didn't. He opened his mouth and took a deep breath as he walked toward the front door and checked the lock. Next he looked at the alarm and noticed it was still armed. She had given him the code earlier as a precaution when they'd both set it. Satisfied, he turned to walk away but found it quiet difficult, knowing her bedroom was right around the corner. Walking toward it, he saw her door closed and then turned and began walking in the opposite direction, choosing to follow his mind rather than the growing ache he felt in his lower body. He continued on down the narrow hallway, checking all the rooms, and then chose the bedroom closest to both the living room and her.

Forest pulled the covers down on the guest bed and set his gun on the nightstand. Climbing into bed, he thought about how he had promised to take care of Lilee at his uncle's request. Now, he began questioning why he'd jumped so quickly at the idea. Sure, he'd wanted to tell her in person about Officer Norman, but he couldn't deny the fact that he wanted to see her again as well. As more minutes passed, he determined that he liked her a lot, and yes, he definitely wanted to get to know her some more. Lying down, he closed his eyes and, with the help of the alcohol, soon drifted away.

Chapter 11

A group of teenagers gathered around a park bench smoking and drinking, well hidden by the darkness and away from street traffic. All were over sixteen and came from broken homes, and most had dropped out of school. Marilynn was the only one in the group on a timely track toward graduation, with dreams of going on to college. Most laughed at her, but she didn't care. "One can dream, can't they?" she would always say. She was currently dating Johnny Rae Jordan. Her parents were not pleased because of the trouble his brother had gotten into. Despite their protests, she continued to see him. She liked him and saw potential and a caring heart underneath all that persona of bad boy attitude.

"Girl, what you going on about now?" Johnny Rae asked Molly, who like Marilynn, was seventeen. Molly and Marilynn had been friends for years, even though Molly had fallen a year behind in her studies.

"Seriously. I saw him do it."

Johnny Rae turned mean. "Shut up! You didn't hear anything or see anything. Do you hear me!"

Marilynn stepped between them and pushed Molly away. "Go. I will talk to you tomorrow."

"No," Johnny Rae said. "I ain't finished with her."

Marilynn narrowed her eyes at Johnny Rae and got in his face. "Yes, you are."

Johnny Rae held her stare without blinking. She didn't back down. Finally he looked away, threw his cigarette to the ground, and grabbed her arm. "Let's get out of here."

Finally, she thought. She couldn't stand his loser friends. They were all a bad influence on him, and the less he hung out with them and the more with her the better. As they walked off, she heard the group heckle from behind.

"Fool is one love sick puppy."

"Yeah. I wonder who does the slapping around? Probably her."

More laugher rang out, but she grabbed his hand, continued walking, and calmly asked him, "What time do you get off work tomorrow?"

She knew he wanted to turn around and end the jokes. She watched and waited patiently for him to make a decision as they continued moving forward slowly. Finally he answered, and she knew she had won the battle—this time.

"Four o'clock. Shift starts early, at six."

"Well, why don't we head on back? It's almost ten. I got some studying to do anyway."

"Don't know why. You have A's in everything."

She smiled. "That's because I study."

He stopped walking and looked into her brown eyes. She waited patiently once again for him to say something. She knew she was pretty, but she wanted an education to go along with it, and she wanted to be a veterinarian. She swore nothing was going to stop her, not Johnny Rae, not Molly, and not her messed-up parents who fought all the time. She tilted her head and finally asked in her sweet voice, "What, Johnny Rae?"

"Remember what we talked about the other day?"

She did. She tried to hide the excitement in her eyes as she thought about what to say. "Um, well, Johnny Rae, we talked about a lot of things. Can you be a little more specific?"

He coughed and cleared his throat, "The, um…the GED."

She stepped closer and prodded, "What about the GED?"

"Um, I was thinking…thinking your were right."

This was news to Marilynn. Good news. Since turning eighteen that summer, Johnny Rae had dropped out of school and gone to work six days a week. She had been so upset that he wasn't going to stick out his senior year. When they locked up his brother for three months, he had lost his job, obviously, and with it came no pay. His momma was already working extra shifts to make ends meet. She admired Ms. Carly, because she was strong and had a hard work ethic. It had been a sad day indeed when Ronny got locked up and Johnny Rae quit school to help make ends meet.

She wrapped her arms around him. "You want to take it?"

He nodded.

"I think that's a great idea, Johnny Rae! I'll get the paperwork from the school counselor on Monday."

"Well, it's just an idea. Probably flunk it anyway."

"No. Don't say that. I will help you study for it. You will pass. I promise!"

He shook his head. "I don't know about you, Marilynn. You crazy!"

She pulled away from the embrace and started walking again holding his hand. "Nope, Johnny Rae. Just crazy in love!"

***

Dr. Derrick Raines and his wife of sixteen years, Andrea, lay side by side sleeping in their king-size bed. Derrick had one arm wrapped around his wife as she jerked slightly. She was having a nightmare.

She was running through the woods. Someone was chasing her. She screamed, but no one came to rescue her as she continued to run from some strange form chasing her with a knife. Suddenly she saw the Hart estate up ahead. It gave her hope, so she picked up her speed. Running up the stairs, she quickly looked behind her but saw no one. She was now all alone.

Andrea pulled on the glass double door, but it was locked. "No!" She screamed as she banged on the glass. She turned around once more and saw the man again. She turned back around and continued banging on the door, but no one came. She pushed away, fled down the steps, and forced herself to run harder around back toward the guesthouse, the cabana by the pool. Maybe it was unlocked. *Oh, God! Please let it be unlocked.* She rounded the last corner but tripped over a small net the boys had left out in the yard. She looked behind and found the strange man with no face raise the knife. Struggling she crawled forward and finally got back on her feet. She was now within a few feet of the cabana. She was going to make it.

She twisted the doorknob, and it opened. Thank God! She quickly entered and locked the door back. The small guesthouse had only one door but several floor-length windows. She raced toward them and pulled all the blinds shut.

"Andrea, what in heavens are you doing?"

Andrea turned and found William Hart naked in bed. He pulled the cover off his body and patted the empty mattress beside him. She screamed.

Andrea's body lurched forward in her bed. Derrick quickly rose and comforted her. "Shhh now. Just a bad dream. You're safe."

She felt his warm body wrap around her. She was so cold, and she was shaking. He spoke gently as he pulled her red hair away from her face. "Let me get some pills for you."

"No. Really. I don't want to take anything."

"Dear, they aren't going to hurt you. They will help give you some much needed rest."

"I know. I just always feel so groggy the next day."

He glanced at the clock. "It's ten forty-five. If you take them now, you will be fine in the morning. Now if you don't and you have another nightmare at two and then take them…"

"OK. Fine. You're right."

He got up. "I know I'm right. I'm the doctor."

Andrea flipped on the lamp beside their large wooden bed and debated getting up and changing shirts. Her back felt damp, and it was making her cold. She was just about to get up when Derrick returned with a pill and a glass of water. "Here you go. This will help you."

She nodded and quickly swallowed the pill. When he turned to leave with the glass, she asked, "Can you grab me another T-shirt from my drawer?"

Their closet was inside the large master bath, and this would save her a trip. Soon he returned, but empty handed.

"Where's my shirt?"

He gave her a naughty look as he climbed into bed and quickly removed her damp shirt. Suddenly it dawned on her what he had given her. "You didn't!"

He smiled a wicked smile and then climbed on top of her. "I did. Now, be the good wife, Andrea, that I deserve."

She slowly closed her eyes, and her mind began to pull away as the drug began to take over. Her vision blurred, her heart began pounding rapidly, and soon she was hoisted up into the air as Derrick had his way with her. She moaned as the pain turned to pleasure and she let go. She spent the next fifteen minutes rocking back and forth on top of Derrick as her body continued to spasm with each release. She cried out and gave more and more of herself till she was spent. Finally she collapsed on top of him and felt herself being instantly rolled off. He quickly straddled her and pressed her face into the pillow, holding her down till the brink of suffocation. As she jerked, he rode her harder and then finally released his tight hold and moved as she flipped over, gasping for breath. Sitting up, she slapped him hard across the face. "Too far! Too far, Derrick!"

With his face burning from her touch, he quickly threw her back down and rolled back on top of her. "Derrick! Off! Enough!"

He continued.

Breaking her arm free, she punched him this time, making contact with his nose. Instantly he stopped, flipped her over, and began spanking her madly with his bare hand. Soon blood hit her back from his nose and he suddenly stopped. He quickly rolled off and left for a shower, leaving her shaken and curled up into a ball. Soon the drug completely took over, and she was lost as it pulled her under to darkness.

Chapter 12

Lilee awoke the next morning to tapping outside her bedroom window. At first she was alarmed by the noise but soon realized it was nine o'clock and the noise was Forest installing a lock on her gate. She smiled, sat up in bed, and stretched upward. Looking around her room, she stopped smiling when she spotted the box of clothing that belonged to Landon. *Damn. Just when I think I've moved on, something always takes me back.*

Getting out of bed, she walked over and bent over to pick up the box. No luck. It was too heavy. Hearing a noise in her kitchen, she stopped and then pulled a housecoat on over her T-shirt. Making her way down the hallway, she soon spotted an officer she hadn't met.

"Good morning, ma'am. I'm Officer Steel. I hope we didn't wake you?"

Lilee smiled. "Good morning. It's no problem. I needed to get up. Oh, and you made coffee. Great!"

"No ma'am. Detective Styles did the honors."

She smiled. "Um, Officer Steel, do you mind moving a box for me? I…I need to get it out of my bedroom and into my garage."

"Sure. I didn't get a chance to work out this morning."

89

She laughed and gestured for him to follow. She watched as he set his coffee cup down and then she turned and he followed her to her bedroom. "That's the box. It's heavy, so be careful."

With ease, the officer picked up the box and then turned back down the hallway. Lilee quickly ran around him and then opened the garage door. "Just put it in that corner; that will be fine."

The officer did as he was told and then came back in and shut the door behind him. "Okay, ma'am. I'm gonna head back outside and check in. Is there anything else?"

"Oh, no. But thank you. I really appreciate that."

He nodded and soon left out the front door.

Seeing him leave, she went back into the kitchen and poured a cup of coffee. Deciding it was nice outside, she took her coffee to the back porch door, opened it, and felt the warm rays of the morning sun as she stepped onto the porch. Hearing the sound of a hammer once more, she left the porch in search of Forest. When she rounded the corner, her heart missed a beat as she spotted him carefully examining his work as he closed the gate to make sure it locked properly.

"Good morning."

He turned and smiled as their eyes met. "Good morning. Sorry if I woke you."

"Nah. Besides, it's after nine now."

He walked toward her. "Yeah, I couldn't wait much longer. I have a busy day today."

Thinking of the Hart case, she nodded. "Would you like some breakfast before you leave?"

"Sorry, I can't. Rain check?" He grinned and she blushed and looked down for a moment. He placed his tool in a small box and then closed it. "I got to be at the hospital at eleven. Hope to be able to question Mrs. Hart again."

Lilee tried not to frown. "I understand. Thanks for dinner last night, and the lock."

"Anytime. Look, I would feel better if you stayed inside, though, and skipped the back porch excursion alone. You know, just until we have a better handle on who did this."

She tilted her head and teased, "Don't trust your locks?"

He smiled. "I do. I just don't want to take any chances with you."

His serious tone made her instantly feel chilled. Lilee looked around. Her once peaceful backyard now looked eerie as large shrubs and tree limbs cast shadows along the fences.

"Hey, I didn't mean to frighten you. I'm just being cautious."

She nodded and then began moving toward her back porch as he picked up his small toolbox and followed her. Once they were inside, she locked the door back and then turned to face him. "I know you are busy with the Hart case, but if you hear anything, please let me know."

He reached out and traced her face with his finger gently. "I will. Promise."

She nodded and he pulled her close, giving her a sweet kiss on the forehead.

"I'll be back later, if that's OK?"

She nodded as their eyes met. "Be careful."

He released her and walked toward the front door. Opening it, he turned. "You be careful too. Bye now."

She waved and he left.

***

Andrea awoke alone in bed. She blinked slowly and looked around for Derrick. He wasn't there. She slowly sat up and collected her bearings. She pulled the sheet off of her, climbed out of bed, and walked into the bathroom. Seeing her image, she froze. Stepping forward, she ran a hand over her face and continued staring. Large circles and puffiness had formed under her eyes. She looked horrible. She had cried so much the day before, and now her face was paying the price.

Turning away, she turned on the shower lever and began removing her clothes. Bending over to pick them up, she felt soreness in her back. When she turned to toss her clothing in the hamper, she noticed a dark black bruise on her right cheek. *What the hell?* she thought. She searched her memories from the night of the Hart attack. *Did I fall? Did I hit something?* She continued to search her memory, but nothing. Slowly she turned away and walked under the hot spray of water, pushing the thoughts out of her mind.

An hour later, Andrea arrived downstairs dressed in a soft pink velour lounge suit, her makeup done and her shoulder-length red hair cuffed neatly around her face. Seeing her husband seated at the table drinking coffee and reading the paper, she quickly walked over and gave him an affectionate touch and a kiss on his cheek.

"Good morning, dear," he greeted her. "I just made a fresh pot of coffee. How did you sleep?"

She walked toward the coffee pot and responded over her shoulder as she poured a cup. "Very well. I do feel a little sore this morning, and I have a large bruise. I must have fallen sometime Friday night, and I just can't remember it."

As she turned around with her coffee, she saw Derrick's face as he looked up. "Derrick! What happened to your face?"

"You don't remember?"

She shook her head, walked toward him, and placed her fingers against his upper lip gently.

"You had a nightmare last night. You were screaming, and you elbowed me."

She removed her hand and covered her mouth. "Oh God, Derrick. I'm so sorry. I…I don't…"

"Don't worry about it," he interrupted. "I'm fine. Should be gone by tomorrow."

She looked down at the article he was reading. The Harts had made the front page news again. She took a seat and read the headline. "Service is Tuesday. What about Christa? Is that too early? I mean, will she be able to attend?"

Derrick folded the paper. "Probably not tomorrow night's visitation, but she should be released in time for the funeral service; it's at two."

"I want to see her."

"Yes. We have the detectives coming today, remember?"

"Oh, yes. Um, what time again?"

"Two. If you like we can go in around three. I have some patients I need to check on as well."

Andrea took a sip from her coffee. "It's so quiet. I miss the girls."

"Donny and Michelle will bring them home later tonight. Already spoke to them."

The Raines had known Donny and Michelle Hughes for over ten years now. They lived at the end of the street and had immediately offered to help after hearing the news of William and Christa Hart.

"Are they OK?"

"They sounded fine. Michelle was taking all four girls shopping. Brave woman, if you ask me."

She smiled as images of Kimmy and Mekenzie grabbing everything they saw and wanting to try it on filled her mind. Their girls were twelve and fourteen, the same age as Michelle's girls. They often hung out together, and wherever the four landed it was sure to be loud.

"I think I will call them," she said and left him sitting there as she went in search of her cell phone. She found it charging in their study. Seeing her briefcase, she instantly thought about work and quickly realized she hadn't made any phone calls to cancel their upcoming appointments. She sat in her leather chair and opened up her calendar. Sliding a finger over a name and number, she picked up the desk phone, completely forgetting all about the girls.

***

Lilee walked toward her front door and looked outside. Seeing Officer Steel sitting in his patrol car, she checked the lock and then turned toward her master bedroom to get a shower. Closing her bedroom door, she locked the knob. Then she closed the double doors to her bath and locked them too. She felt a little foolish but remembered the words spoken by Forest earlier.

Soon she was under the warm spray and washing her body and hair. When she finished shampooing her hair, she rinsed it, poured some conditioner into her hand, and began to slowly massage it through her long blond hair. Just as she returned under the spray, the water pressure dropped and then the water slowly stopped pouring. *What the hell?*

She squinted to see but instantly felt the burn of the conditioner. She stepped carefully out of the doorless shower, found a clean towel on the nearby hook, and wiped her eyes and face. She slowly opened her eyes and blinked till the pain was gone. Next she quickly dried off, wrapped her hair up in the towel, grabbed her housecoat, and went in search of Officer Steel.

Opening her bedroom door, she walked down the hallway and peered through the side glass window. The patrol car sat empty. *Where is he?* Panic seized her as she looked at the control pad and noticed her alarm was not armed. She walked back toward the living room and looked around. No one. She was alone. Timidly she walked over to the French doors and scanned the backyard. *Where is Officer Steel?*

The alarm suddenly sounded and the lights went out. No power. *Something is wrong!* Hurriedly she fled toward her master bedroom and quickly locked the door. Taking a deep breath, she ran to the window and lifted the blind. Sunlight through the windows made it easy to see inside since it was midday, but without the power, her house phone no longer worked. *My cell phone! Where is it?*

She tried to think through the blasting noise of the alarm. *In the kitchen.* She cautiously opened her bedroom door and peeked out. Seeing no one, she ran down the hallway back toward her kitchen and scanned the counters until she saw it. As she picked up her phone, it immediately started ringing and she jumped, dropping it to the floor. *Damn it!*

She grabbed the phone and the back piece that had fallen off and stood— bumping into someone behind her. She froze as her heart stopped beating and terror seized her body.

"It's me, Officer Steel."

She closed her eyes and tried to breathe, but she felt lightheaded and dizzy. Suddenly she was leaning too far to the side, and he grabbed her and pushed her back up toward a standing position. She slowly opened her eyes and met his brown eyes. He was worried. "We need to move. Too many windows."

She didn't respond as he led her down the hallway back toward her bedroom. Once they were inside, he locked the door and then quickly checked the bathroom and closet. "I've called for backup. Should be here soon."

Finally she found her voice. "Wh…what happened?"

He shook his head. "I don't know. I heard the alarm and then I immediately called backup and found you."

She was confused. "How did you get in?"

"The back door was unlocked."

"No. It was locked."

He looked at her and asked, "Are you sure?"

She thought back to when she had used the door last. It had been that morning when she and Forest walked back inside. *I did lock it, right?* Doubt filled her mind as she tried to visualize entering the house and telling Forest good-bye. *Wasn't it locked earlier when I looked for Officer Steel?* Her head was starting to hurt, and it didn't help any that her hair was wet, making her cold.

Finally she said, "I can't be sure, no."

He nodded. A radio chirped and he picked it up. Lilee turned around and walked toward the window. She saw two patrol cars speeding into her driveway with their lights flashing. "Stay here," Officer Steel said.

She nodded and watched as he slowly unlocked her door and carefully looked around. He twisted her lock back, stepped into the hall, and then closed the door, leaving her all alone once more.

The noise of the alarm was deafening. *Why is it going off?* she wondered. *I never set it.* Suddenly, as if her thoughts were heard, the alarm stopped. Her ears were ringing still, and she could still feel a vibration going through her head.

Tap, Tap. "Ms. Parker, it's Officer Steel. Please open the door now."

Lilee heard the words but felt frozen in place.

"Ms. Parker?"

Finally she forced her body to move and shouted, "I'm coming!"

She opened the door and she was faced with three officers staring at her. Feeling a little uncomfortable, she crossed her arms over her thin cotton housecoat. She suddenly realized that she had lost her towel at some point and her shoulders were wet from her hair.

"What happened?" she asked. "I was in the shower, and the water stopped. I came into the kitchen and then the power went out. What is going on?"

Officer Steel answered in a very calm voice, "Someone turned off the water, and then they cut the power line."

"What? Why would someone cut off the water?"

"Someone is taunting you," said an officer she didn't know.

"In broad daylight, with an officer outside?"

Officer Steel responded, "I'm sorry, Ms. Parker. The gate was opened in the back, but the lock wasn't broken. Whoever it was must have scaled the fence and then turned off both utilities in the backyard."

She turned around, walked back into her bathroom, and stopped at the window with the blinds slightly opened. When Officer Steel followed her, she spoke. "He was watching me. Knew I was in the shower."

Instantly she felt sick.

"Ms. Parker, I need you to pack a bag. The area is too large to keep you safe without a dozen men. A hotel will be safer."

She nodded slowly and then walked into her closet. She could barely see with the outside light filtering in.

"Here, take my flashlight," Officer Steel offered.

"Thank you."

She threw some clothing in her black suitcase and then, noticing they had left her alone, she removed her housecoat and pulled on a pair of jeans and a sweatshirt. Last, she pulled her wet hair up into a clip and packed up her makeup and toiletries. *Guess my hair is going to get deep conditioned today,* she thought.

Chapter 13

Carly Jordan climbed the few stairs leading to her small porch. She had decided to come home for lunch and enjoy the ten minutes of sunshine along the way. Opening the door, she found Ronny and Ronny Jr. sitting on the floor building a tower out of blocks. "Well, don't you two look cute?"

Ronny Jr. saw her and immediately held out his small hands. She smiled.

"I's make you a sandwich, Momma," Ronny said. "Sit."

She set her small handbag on the worn sofa and then knelt down by the baby and began to stack a few blocks.

"What time Johnny Rae come home?" Ronny asked.

She had to think. Keeping up with everyone's schedule was tiresome. "I think he said four. Why?"

"I's hadn't seen him since Friday night."

"Well, work and his girl keep him busy."

"What girl?" Ronny asked.

"Her name is Marilynn, Marilynn…hmm, well, I forgot her last name. Sweet girl."

He turned to face her with a sour expression on his face.

"She is, Ronny! Wait till you meet her. She's different."

"How's she different?" Ronny asked. "Thiz I got to hear."

"For one, she's still in school and will graduate top of her class next May, maybe even valedictorian. She's already on the A honor roll, and there's talk of a scholarship for university."

Ronny started laughing. "If all thaz true, why da hell she with Johnny Rae?"

Carly placed a hand on her hip. "Now stop that talk. Your brother's a good boy, stays out of trouble too."

Ronny slowly turned back around to finish making her sandwich. "I gonna find a job, Momma. Tonight."

"Tonight? Ronny, what kind of job you hoping to find on a Sunday night?"

"Good kind of paying job, thatz what."

She frowned. The last job she wanted her son to take was as a bouncer at some Atlanta strip club. Before she could say anything, he continued. "Pay iz fifteen dollars an hour with bonuses."

She watched as he picked up her sandwich and glass of sweet tea and brought it over to her. "I knowz ya don't like it, Momma, but pay iz good. Can't turn it down."

She grabbed her lunch and replied, "But Ronny, the work is…"

He stared hard at his momma as he interrupted. "I's be home with Ronny Junior days and work at night."

The baby heard his name and began clapping and smiling. She looked down and saw the cute little thing. He was such a good, happy baby. "When do you plan on sleeping if you work till three a.m.?"

"Three thirty tilz you leave. I can nap when Junior naps."

She was skeptical. "I don't know."

"It'll work, Momma. Besides, I probably only get five days a week."

She didn't say anymore as she ate her sandwich and continued to play with the blocks. Suddenly they heard a knock at the door. "I's get it, Momma."

She watched as he walked over and looked out the window. "I's be back. Eat da sandwich."

She narrowed her eyes. "You can invite them in, you know."

"Nah, itz all good."

He opened the door quickly and stepped outside, closing the door behind him. When her curiosity got the best of her, she set her tea on the coffee table, pushed off of the floor, and stood. She walked over to the window and pulled the curtain aside.

Ronny was talking to someone by a dark automobile with his back turned to her. She couldn't see the other person because he had climbed back into the car, and Ronny was blocking her view. *What are you up to now, Ronny?*

As if hearing her thoughts, he quickly turned around. She let go of the curtain and stepped back.

***

Trevor Watts greeted his partner at the elevator on the second floor.

"She's awake."

"Good," said Forest.

"I instructed her sons to wait in the waiting room."

Forest glanced over and found Todd and Tim Hart sitting on a couch with somber expressions. "How did that go over?"

"Not good, but they complied. I did tell 'em the doctor would be in there with us the whole time, in case she became upset again."

Forest stepped forward and nodded at the boys but didn't stop as he moved on down the hall toward the ICU wing. He pressed a button, and a nurse soon appeared and opened the door. Dr. Griffin, standing at the large, circular counter, turned and gestured them in.

"Detectives."

"Doctor. How's Mrs. Hart doing today?"

"Better. Less pain, and she's sleeping less. Come on; she's expecting you."

"Thanks. We'll do our best to keep the questions to a minimum," offered Trevor.

The doctor nodded and then led them down the hallway and opened Mrs. Hart's door. He stepped inside and spoke softly. "Mrs. Hart, the detectives are here now."

Hearing his voice, she turned her head and scanned them with her eyes. The detective stepped in, and then Forest shut the door back. "Ma'am, I'm Trevor Watts, and this is my partner, Forest Styles. We were here yesterday."

She nodded.

Forest stepped forward and placed a gentle hand on top of her exposed hand. "Dr. Griffin tells us you're doing much better today. I'm glad. We'll be quick. Anything you can tell us will be much appreciated."

Trevor continued. "Yesterday you told us you saw one male. Do you know the race?"

She nodded. Time seemed to still as she opened her mouth and said, "White."

"Were you able to get a good look at his face?" Trevor asked.

She shook her head and forced a sound. "Mask."

Forest looked at his notes and saw Christa's height of five six and her husband's of five eleven. He asked, "Mrs. Hart, was the man taller than your husband?"

She nodded.

"OK. Now I want you to answer in numbers. One if he was just a little taller, two if he was a lot taller."

"Two."

"Good. OK, Mrs. Hart. I'm five eleven, the same size as your husband, and Detective Watts is six six."

Forest moved and stood directly beside Trevor. "Now Dr. Griffin is…"

He waited for the doctor to step beside him and answer, "I'm six two."

"Which do you think was closest to the man's height?"

She closed her eyes and shook her head. No one said a word as she remained quiet with her eyes closed. Moments passed, and then she opened them and stared hard at Forest. "Doctor."

Trevor nodded. "You're doing great, Mrs. Hart. Now, you said he was white. Do you remember if you saw any tattoos, birthmarks, burns, or injuries, like a bruise?"

She shook her head.

"Hair color?"

She shook her head.

"Long sleeves?"

She nodded.

"Gloves?"

She nodded.

Forest touched her hand again. "Last question, Mrs. Hart, and I want you to take your time. Do you know of any reason why someone would come into your home to harm you and your husband?"

All three men watched as tears formed in her eyes as she remained silent. Patiently everyone waited as she closed her eyes and blinked away the tears. She shook her head slowly.

Forest nodded. "Alright, Mrs. Hart. We'll let you rest now, but if you can think of anything that would help, please tell Dr. Griffin, and he will call us. OK?"

She nodded.

Trevor walked closer and squeezed her hand. "Thank you, Mrs. Hart. We'll keep you posted."

Forest turned as Dr. Griffin opened the door behind him. The three men stepped out into the hall and he closed the door behind them. "She didn't give you much."

"No," Forest said. "Thanks for putting together that list of patients. Someone's looking into that now."

Trevor asked, "On a personal note, are you aware of any problems they might have had in their marriage?"

"Why do you ask?" the doctor asked. "Has someone said something?"

Forest replied, "We're just trying to cover all the angles."

Dr. Griffin frowned, and they waited a few moments before he finally spoke. "There's a chance that he might have had an affair. But I'm really not comfortable saying because it's only speculation." He stopped and looked behind him toward the nurses' station and then continued. "Hospitals are the worst when it comes to rumors."

Forest opened his notepad. "Got a name?"

He hesitated. "Look, I could be wrong about all of this."

Forest tried to speak in simple terms. "Dr. Griffin, a doctor and housekeeper are dead, and one lady inside that room has a long road ahead of her. So please, just give us a name and leave the rest up to us."

"We'll be discreet," offered Trevor.

"Dr. Hart was a brilliant surgeon, and I would hate to see something like this come to light and cast a shadow on his outstanding reputation within the medical field and the community."

Neither detective spoke, instead letting the silence fall between them. Finally he gave in. "Marla Kay Abbott, a nurse. Now if you'll excuse me, I have some rounds to make."

"Call us if you can think of anything else," Forest said.

Dr. Griffin never stopped. He simply waved his hand in the air to acknowledge.

Forest turned to Trevor. "Let's go see the boys now."

Trevor smiled. "Now this is going to be fun."

They found the boys still sitting on the couch when they left the ICU. Tim saw them first and nudged his brother.

"Anything new?" asked Todd.

Forest took a seat directly in front of them and said, "Yes. But I have some questions for both of you. Do you mind answering them now?"

"Sure. Anything that will help," offered Tim.

Trevor took a seat in the small leather chair between the two couches and then caught the boys off guard by asking, "Are you aware of the amount of life insurance your parents owned?"

Tim spoke first. "No."

"Wait a minute. Do we need a lawyer present?" asked Todd in a stern voice.

"I hope not. Do you have something to hide?"

"No, nothing," Todd remarked hotly. "We loved our parents very much."

Tim looked at his brother and then to Watts. "He's right. We do love our parents. Our family is close. Yeah, we might've had disagreements now and then, but we always worked them out."

Forest opened his notepad and read. "Three million dollars to the two of you, and five million in the event of their deaths coinciding."

Neither boy spoke. They were genuinely speechless.

Soon Todd broke the silence. "I don't understand why he had so much. We both had scholarships, and the house is paid for."

This was news to Forest. He hadn't gotten all the information yet on their finances. "Yes, it's a lot of money. Did your parents gamble?"

Tim was furious as he sat back, crossed his arms, and shook his head. "You aren't gonna find anything like that with our parents. They were good people. My dad golfed, and mom had her work as a hobby. They didn't do anything illegal that would cause this to happen."

"Yeah? Well, there was something," Trevor replied, "because this was a deliberate hit. Nothing seems to be missing from the home."

Tim shot to his feet. "Don't you drag my father's good name in the mud. He was a great..." His voice cracked.

Todd stood and tried to console him. "They aren't, Tim. They're just trying to figure all of this out."

Tim shrugged Todd away. Todd studied his brother closely. Odd. It was always Tim who held his temper in check. Something was bothering him, and Todd had yet to figure it out.

"I need some coffee," Tim said, and all watched as he quickly walked away and stepped onto the elevator that had just opened.

Forest looked back at Todd and gestured for him to sit again. "Todd, there has to be some reason why someone entered your parents' house and killed your father so viciously. Help us."

Todd frowned.

Forest saw doubt in his eyes. There was something. "Go on."

"My dad had an affair. But it's over."

Seeing the shame in his face, he treaded carefully. "How long ago, and for how long?"

"I don't know how long it lasted, but it ended last year."

Trevor asked, "Do you know why it ended?"

"Yeah. My dad fell back in love with my mom. They renewed their vows and went on a second honeymoon to Europe."

"When was this?"

Todd twisted his mouth as he pondered the question. "After we graduated high school. Sometime in June."

"Did your mom know about the affair?"

"If she did, no one ever told me."

"So how did you find out?" inquired Trevor.

"I walked into dad's study one day and found him and Tim arguing. Later, on the ride back to campus, Tim finally calmed down enough to tell me about it."

Forest thought about what he'd said. Tim didn't find out until after they had started college last August. "When was this argument?"

"I don't know. Sometime earlier this year."

Trevor prodded, "Was it before spring break or afterward?"

"Oh, before, because Tim and I went to Cancun instead of going home."

Trevor picked up on his comment. "How long did this tension last between your father and you two?"

"A few weeks. A little longer for Tim."

Trevor closed his notepad. "I'm getting the impression your family isn't as close as you two presented earlier."

Todd narrowed his eyes. "Now that's where you're wrong, detective. Tim and I would die for our parents. Now if you will excuse me, I'm going to find my brother."

Forest watched him leave and then turned to his partner. "Looks like we need to find out who Marla Kay Abbott is and pay her a visit."

Trevor stood. "I think you're right."

Chapter 14

At twelve forty five, an officer left his watch at the hospital in search of the men's room. Seeing him leave and only a few nurses at the station, a decision was quickly made. Wearing soft-sole shoes, the figure didn't make a sound entering Christa Hart's room. It scanned the room quickly, and its eyes followed the small tube connecting the bag to her hand, where an IV line was taped. *That should do the trick.*

Light snoring sounds emerged from Christa's slightly parted lips as she slept. After glancing toward the door and finding them still alone, the figure turned a small dial to high, pressed a button, and carefully pulled a small device off of her sleeping body. She stirred but surprisingly didn't wake. Satisfied that Christa would no longer be a problem, the dark soul left without no one the wiser.

***

Forest and Trevor pulled into Marla Kay Abbott's driveway at one o'clock. The modest one-story stood in a nice neighborhood only a ten-minute drive from the Hart estate in Park Square. "This is awfully convenient," Trevor remarked. "The brilliant surgeon could have stopped by for a little fifteen-minute rumble, then been off home to the little unsuspecting missus."

Forest nodded. "Yeah. Convenient."

They got out of the sedan and glanced around. The street had some activity on the nice autumn Sunday afternoon. A few kids rode their bikes, and a family walked the narrow sidewalk pushing a small stroller.

As expected, the man looked their way with a hint of concern across his face. Forest waved and the man timidly waved back. The two men obviously didn't look like they belonged. It didn't take a genius to figure out they were cops, in a black sedan with a light mounted on top.

Forest looked back toward the stucco house. Nice landscaping hugged the home. The garage door was closed, leaving them no way to know if anyone was home. Following the sidewalk, they reached the entrance, pressed the doorbell, and waited. They were soon rewarded when the door opened, revealing a beautiful brunette wearing short shorts.

"Good afternoon. I'm Detective Styles, and this is my partner, Detective Watts. Is Marla Kay Abbott home?"

Her brown eyes followed as he raised his badge. She stepped forward timidly and looked closer. Satisfied he wasn't lying, she took another step back. "I'm sorry, but no, she isn't home."

"I see. The hospital said she called in sick."

She narrowed her eyes. "She isn't here. I'm sorry."

Forest eased up. "OK. Do you know when she's expected to return?"

He watched as she looked at her watch. "Around three; maybe a little later."

Trevor asked in a deep voice that startled her, "Where is Ms. Abbott?"

"I…I'm not sure."

"Do you live here with Ms. Abbott?" inquired Forest.

Instantly she tensed. "I'm sorry, but maybe you should come back around three. She should be home then."

Forest studied her. She could not have been more than twenty-one. Was this perhaps her sister? "We'll do that, Ms....?"

She swallowed. "Jenna."

"Thank you, Ms. Jenna. We'll return."

She stepped back slowly and closed the door. A lock sounded as she twisted the dead bolt.

"Well, that was interesting," Trevor said. "I think she was putting us off."

Forest started walking back to their sedan. "Yeah, but why?"

***

Officer Steel escorted Lilee down the carpeted hallway of the Grand Hotel, stopped at room number 330, and swiped the plastic hotel card along the magnetic bar. The light turned green, and he opened the door. Glancing around, he saw no one.

Next he checked the bathroom, made his way over to the balcony door, and pushed the curtains back to reveal a small, empty porch. He checked the glass sliding doors and found them locked. Pulling the curtains back, he turned around and smiled. "All clear, Ms. Parker. You'll be much safer here. We'll have a man at the end of the hallway and one downstairs."

She sat on the bed and frowned. "OK to call room service?"

"Of course. Sorry about lunch."

113

"No. Don't apologize."

"I put a call into Detective Styles."

"Oh?"

"He has a busy day, but he'll call."

"Any word yet about who was at my house?"

"No, ma'am, but we're still working on it. Don't worry. We'll catch him."

Her eyes dropped, and he could see her doubt. "We're doing everything we can, Ms. Parker. Please call this number if you need anything."

She looked back up to meet his stare and grabbed the card.

As he walked off toward the door, he turned back and warned, "Don't open the door unless the code name 'Snoopy' is given."

"Snoopy?"

He smiled. "Yeah. I'm partial to dogs."

She finally returned his smile. "Thanks, Officer Steel. I know you're trying."

He nodded and then walked out, closing the door behind him.

Lilee stood up, walked to the closed door, and pulled the silver latch over to activate the safety lock. Next she walked into the bathroom and noticed the garden tub. Deciding to soak in a hot bath rather than take another shower, she sat on the small edge, placed the plug in, and adjusted the water temperature. Looking up at the sink counter, she spotted a basket of soaps. She smiled when she saw a small bottle of bubble bath. Unscrewing the top, she poured it under the flow of the water, instantly filling the air with a vanilla scent.

Glancing at her watch, she saw that the time was now one thirty. She was starved. It only took a minute to decide what she wanted to eat. Picking up the phone, she ordered a cheeseburger with fries. "Umm, could you bring the food at two fifteen?"

Hanging up the phone, she walked back into the bathroom, removed her clothing, and lifted her leg to feel the water temperature with her toes. *Perfect.* She carefully held the side, stepped in, and lowered her body, submerging herself amidst the bubbles. The water soon reached the desired level, and she reached up and pressed the lever off. Immediately she heard her cell phone ringing in her purse, on the bed. *Great! Are you kidding me?*

Quickly she grabbed hold of the sides and stood up, carefully stepping out and grabbing a towel off the hook as she went. She made wet footprints as she walked across the carpet and grabbed her phone. *Unknown caller.* She turned around and looked at the lock. Still locked. Pushing all bad thoughts away, she pressed the small green button.

"Hello?"

"Hi, it's Forest. I got the message. How are you?"

She took a deep breath as she turned and walked back into the bathroom, dropping her towel. "I'm fine. At a hotel for the night."

She carefully eased back into the water, making a small splash. "What are you doing?"

"Just got back in the bathtub."

"Oh?"

She smiled as she leaned back, submerging her shoulders and chest. "So how is your day going? Learning anything on the Hart case?"

"Yeah, a little at a time."

"When do you finish up?"

"Not sure. Gonna meet with a team later tonight and comb through what we got. One thing is for sure, though: I won't be staying with you tonight."

Her eyebrows creased as she asked, "Oh?"

"Silly, you don't have a guest room at the hotel."

She blushed as she smiled. "Yeah, that would get some tongues wagging in the department."

"Too late. It's already started."

"What?"

"Yep. News travels fast. Everyone's envious that I stayed at the hot prosecutor's house."

She twirled the end of her wet hair. "I don't think they view me as the hot prosecutor."

"What world do you live in?"

"I…I don't…"

He interrupted, "Sorry, gotta let you go. We just pulled up at our address."

She shot up in the water and asked in a shrill voice. "Did you say we?"

He laughed. "Call you later, Ms. hot prosecutor."

116

The call ended and she grinned as she lowered back down into the water. Looking at the time, she saw that she had fifteen more minutes before her food arrived. Placing her phone on the ledge, she began to wash. When she was done, she pulled the plug to drop the water level and then began to turn on the water and adjust the temperature to warm. Satisfied, she leaned her head under the spray and finally rinsed out the conditioner from earlier in the day. Just as she was done, she turned off the water and heard her phone ringing once more. Picking it up, she again read, *Unknown caller*.

Thinking it was Forest again, she smiled as she spoke. "Hello? Forget something?"

"Yeah, you bitch!"

Lilee looked around frantically as she quickly braced against the side of the tub and stood. She heard laughter, and the male voice began singing, "Parker gonna die, Parker gonna die, Parker gonna die." Then he shouted, "I'm coming, bitch!" The line went dead.

She quickly tossed her phone on the mat, grabbed a towel, and dried off. When she wrapped up her hair, she grabbed another towel off the rack and noticed her hands were shaking. Pulling the towel around her, she heard a knock on the door and wobbled as her knees went limp and her stomach flipped. A wave of nausea consumed her. Fighting it, she took a deep breath and asked in a cracked voice, "Who…who is it?"

"Officer Butler, ma'am. I have room service."

"Just a minute."

She forced herself forward, grabbed the white housecoat hanging in the closet, and quickly pulled it over her slightly wet, naked body. Just as she was about to flip the silver lever, she stopped. He didn't give a code. *Why not?*

She felt her mouth shake as she asked, "What's the code?"

"Excuse me, ma'am?"

"The code that Officer Steel gave you?"

Silence.

"Officer Butler?"

"Oh, gosh. I'm sorry, Ms. Parker. I forgot. Can you give me a hint? By the way, this cheeseburger sure smells good. I would hate for it to get cold as Officer Steel chews my tail out for forgetting a simple password."

She eased forward and peered through the small peephole. All she could see was an arm holding a tray of food. *Forest told me not to take chances,* she thought. Biting her lip, she thought quickly and then answered, "It was one of the *Peanuts* characters."

"Oh, that's right. It was Lucy. No, wait…Charlie Brown."

Silence.

"Ms. Parker?"

Her heart had stopped. She had purposely used the word "characters" expecting that an intruder would pick a person and not the dog. He had failed. He wasn't an officer.

Chapter 15

Forest closed the car door and laughed. "She didn't think that comment was funny."

"Oh, really? I give her two days and she'll be done with you."

He looked at his partner and smirked. "Only two days. Gosh, do I have that bad of a track record?"

"Yep, and it doesn't help we just landed another big case."

Damn. He's right. Forest thought about Diane, a real class act he had met at a dinner party. For three weeks, he had tried to make their first date but failed. He frowned. Forest glanced around the well-kept yard of the Raines estate. A large fountain flowed in the center of their circular drive, giving the place a peaceful feel. "Nice place," he said as they waited for someone to answer their knock.

Soon Dr. Raines greeted them at the front door. "Gentlemen."

Forest noticed immediately that his upper lip was swollen. He shook his hand and replied, "Doctor. How is Mrs. Raines? Is she still up for a visit?"

"Yes. Thank you for asking first. Come on in?"

Forest nodded and entered the massive home. The large foyer had high ceilings, and an impressive chandelier hung directly above them. As he turned right, he saw that the staircase to the second floor was hidden down a hallway. This floor plan was opposite from the centered spiral staircase at the Hart estate.

As he followed the doctor, it became obvious his wife was a good decorator. The home felt warm and inviting—quite an accomplishment for such a large home that neared seven thousand square feet. He forgot all about the decor when he spotted Andrea Raines sitting on a dark brown leather couch in what appeared to be the family room. She stood.

"Detectives, please have a seat."

Forty-two years old, Andrea stood five eight and was very fit. Her husband, also forty-two, stood around six foot and was equally fit. Together they made a striking couple.

Forest nodded. "Good to see you, Mrs. Raines. We appreciate you taking the time to see us. I know this is a hard time for you."

She nodded and sat down again. Suddenly a small woman entered the room. "May I get you gentlemen something to eat or drink?"

"Water would be nice," Forest said.

Trevor added, "Yes, thank you."

Dr. Raines waited till she left and then spoke. "I have some patients to see later, around three, and I promised my wife she could visit Christa today."

"Of course," Forest said. "This shouldn't take long."

Trevor fired away. "Mrs. Raines, your phone record indicates you called Mrs. Hart several times on Friday evening. Can you tell us about those calls, starting with the one at five forty-seven p.m.?"

"Yes. Um, I forgot a file, the Hickam file, and I wanted to come over and get it. I had a meeting at their home. I needed the file, and it was in her briefcase. So, I called."

"Your call lasted a little over one minute. Do you know if she was in the home already or still in her car?"

Andrea shook her head. "I can't be for sure, but I knew she had to change, and I remember she told me she was leaving in the next ten minutes, so maybe she was already home."

The housekeeper arrived again and set down two waters on coasters.

"Thank you," said Forest before turning his attention back to Andrea. "How were you planning to get the file?"

"We live on the way to the club, and she had a dinner party there, so she offered to drop it by."

Forest read his notes. "The next four calls were each less than five seconds."

"Yes. Each time I called, it went straight to voice mail."

"I know this is hard, but try to break down for us what was going on each time you called."

She rubbed a hand through her red hair, looked away, and found Derrick's eyes. He smiled. Forest looked at the doctor and saw that his face was lined with worry even as he tried to comfort his wife with the gesture.

Slowly she faced Forrest again. "Do you like my husband's shiner?"

Both detectives turned to stare at Dr. Raines' swollen upper lip and noticed that his right nostril had a blue tint to it.

She continued. "I had a nightmare last night. I elbowed him."

"It was an accident, dear. It will just give everyone something else to talk about today."

She lost her smile. "Doubtful."

Noticing the men turned back toward her, she asked, "What time was the first call?"

"Six fifty."

"Yes. My meeting was at seven thirty. So, knowing she'd said she was leaving at six, and it only takes thirty minutes or less, I assumed she forgot. I know I tried a couple more times, and then I left to go to the club."

"It's only a five-minute drive from here," added Dr. Raines.

"I arrived and talked to Marty," Andrea continued, "a staff member, and he informed me that they hadn't arrived and were late."

Forest read his notes. The club had confirmed that the Harts had a six thirty dinner party and that Mrs. Raines had showed up inquiring about them. So far, all sounded right.

Trevor asked, "Did you call her from the club?"

"I did. That was the last time. On the drive over, I was concentrating on all the passing vehicles. At this point I thought they'd been in an accident, and I forgot all about trying to make my seven thirty meeting."

Forest looked at the time of 7:12, the last record of a phone call. He calculated in his head the twenty-five-minute drive, finding the bodies, and then the 911 call at 7:40. She wasn't lying. It would do no good to question the events at the house. They were already dead, except for Christa, who nearly bled to death waiting on someone to discover her. He flipped a page in his small notepad and read. "You've been in business with Mrs. Hart for fifteen years now," he said. "That's a long time."

She smiled. "It is. Elegant Grace Designs is our baby. Somehow we managed to turn it into a very profitable business."

Forest could clearly see the pride she felt as she spoke of her company. She had continued on about the start-up, the clients, and future work. It was her passion, and it would have required a lot of her time. He wondered about their marriage. Both had demanding jobs that required many hours. *What about their two children? Did they ever have family time all together?*

Forest looked at the doctor. "When did you get home that night?"

"I didn't. I was at the hospital. I'm the doctor on call this weekend and, well, one can plan on staying on Friday nights because they are so busy. But you already know that."

Forest grinned. "I do."

The doctor looked at his watch. "And speaking of work, I'm sorry, but duty calls."

Trevor said, "Just one more quick question."

The doctor nodded.

"Were either of you aware that William Hart was having an affair that ended last year?"

Forest watched Andrea's face as its color drained and her hand flew to her chest. He looked quickly at the doctor. He didn't share the same expression. He knew, but she didn't.

"No," she said. "That can't be. I don't believe it! That's just...just idle gossip that someone started at the hospital. Right, Derrick?"

She turned and faced him, and a frown immediately formed on her face. At that moment, she realized he knew. She suddenly stood. "Excuse me. Derrick can answer the rest of your questions."

Both detectives barely had time to stand before she bolted from the room. Dr. Raines stood as well. "Gentlemen, I really wish you wouldn't have asked that in front of my wife."

Trevor replied, "No disrespect, sir, but our goal is to find a killer."

He frowned.

Forest added, "You didn't answer the question. Did you know?"

He narrowed his eyes and stared hard at Forest. Finally he looked down at the floor and put his hands in the pockets of his dress pants. He mumbled, "I knew." He looked up at them and spoke clearly. "We didn't discuss it, though. It was one of those things where he knew I knew, but we elected to never bring it up."

"How did you find out?" inquired Trevor.

He looked around the room and gave the question some thought. "I don't remember. It was a long time ago."

"We were told it ended right before the Harts renewed their wedding vows and took a trip to Europe last summer. Is this accurate information?"

Dr. Raines grew uncomfortable. "Maybe. I'm not for sure."

Forest read his body language. "Dr. Raines, are you under the impression that the affair was still ongoing?"

"Look, I don't know. Lots of talk at the hospital. Generally nurses stop talking when a doctor approaches, but sometimes we still overhear things."

Trevor asked, "What's her name?"

Again more discomfort. "I really don't want to say, since I never saw any inappropriate behavior between the two."

"You're too kind, Dr. Raines. William Hart is dead. Give us the name, please."

The doctor glared at Trevor with a frown. Finally he gave in. "Marla Kay Abbott. She's a nurse."

Forest closed his notepad. "Thank you. We appreciate the help. Please give my apology to your wife. We didn't mean to upset her."

"You can see yourself out."

Forest glanced at Trevor and then turned around and walked back out the way they had entered. Outside, Trevor spoke. "We need to see Marla Kay Abbott."

Forest just nodded as he unlocked the sedan and climbed in behind the wheel. "Yes, we do."

Chapter 16

Lilee Parker ran toward the room phone and quickly dialed the number on the card. Nothing. She hadn't dialed a number to get out. *What the hell? What is the number?* Not taking the time to figure it out, she ran back into the bathroom and picked up her phone—just as she heard a loud clatter outside her door. *Just breathe, Lilee. Don't faint; don't faint!*

She pressed the last button, and Officer Steel answered immediately. "Don't open your door. Go into the bathroom and lock the door. I'll call you back when it's safe."

She quickly did as she was instructed and waited. And waited some more. She looked at her phone: 2:25. *What the hell is going on?* She paced back and forth. Soon she picked up a brush and began brushing out her hair. With each stroke of the brush, she tried to block it all out as if it were a dream. Next she grabbed the lotion and began applying it to her face. When she was done, she stared into the mirror and studied her reflection. She touched her cheeks. Turning her face side to side, she realized how thin she had become over the last few months since her breakup with Landon. *I need to eat more,* she thought. *Take better care of myself. I'm skin and bones. This can't be attractive.* Suddenly her phone rang, and terror reigned once more as she picked it up to answer.

"Yes?"

"Officer Steel. Ms. Parker, please go to the door now. The code word I gave you earlier was Snoopy."

She immediately opened her bathroom door, ran toward the bolted wooden door, and looked through the peephole. Seeing Officer Steel, she opened it. Three officers were present, and a large tray with a broken plate and a disassembled cheeseburger lay on the floor. Her stomach growled. She closed her eyes.

"Ms. Parker?"

She slowly opened her green eyes. "Gentlemen, if I don't get some food, I'm going to collapse."

For the first time since they'd met, Officer Steel cracked a smile. "Glad you still have a sense of humor, Ms. Parker."

***

At five minutes after three, Forest pulled back into the driveway of Marla Kay Abbott's home. This time, her two-car garage was open and a small yellow sports car was parked right in the middle. "Looks like we got lucky. I think she's home."

Trevor looked around the tidy yard as he got out of the passenger seat. "Yeah. Looks like it."

After ringing the doorbell and getting no response, Forest decided to try the side gate. "Beautiful day for outside." As they walked around, he heard voices.

He knocked loudly on the gate and then heard a female voice. "Just a minute."

They stood patiently for a few minutes waiting. Just when he was about to get concerned, he heard the same female voice from behind.

"Yes? May I help you?"

Forest turned to see a tall, slender woman in her early thirties. She wore shorts and a T-shirt and had her long black hair pulled into a ponytail. He studied her confused expression and wondered if Jenna had forgotten to tell her about them dropping by.

"I'm Detective Forest Styles, and this is my partner, Detective Watts. Are you Marla Kay Abbott?"

She took a step back and slowly nodded.

"We would like to talk to you about the Hart family. Is now a good time?"

She nodded.

Trevor stepped toward her and then looked around at some people walking around the neighborhood. "We might need to talk inside."

Marla Kay turned and saw the Elliott family kicking around a soccer ball in their front yard. She hesitated for a moment but waved after the family made eye contact with her. Turning back around, she said, "You're right. Let's go inside."

Forest was a little perplexed as to why they didn't go through the side gate and into the backyard. When they walked around, he saw that the front door had been left open and understood. As they entered the home, he suggested, "We can go in the backyard if you would like."

"No," she said. "Let's sit in the study."

Forest saw the study to his immediate right. The foyer was small, and one had to go through a hallway to see the rest of the home. Her suggestion didn't surprise him. Not many people willingly took them through their homes on unplanned visits. But still, the idea that someone else was home with her and she didn't want to introduce her visitors nagged at him.

"Please, have a seat."

They each sat on the leather sofa while she took the small leather chair. Forest scanned the large bookshelves hoping to get a better read for Ms. Abbott. Lots of books along the shelves—mostly medical books. He saw no framed pictures, which gave the impression she was indeed involved with a married man.

"How can I help you?"

Forest met her dark green eyes. "Let's start with your relationship with Dr. William Hart."

She narrowed her eyes and sat straighter. "He's one of the doctors I worked with."

Trevor flipped his notepad open and began writing. This irritated her because she couldn't see what he was writing. He finished and looked up. "How long did you work together?"

She crossed her arms and stated, "I met him my first year as a nurse. So that would be eight years ago."

"And when did the affair begin?"

Marla Kay looked as if she'd been slapped. Color appeared on her neck and face as she exclaimed. "How dare you? Come into my home and make such outrageous accusations!"

Calmly he replied, "So you deny there was an affair?"

Forest studied her as she blinked away tears. "The hospital can be so cruel. We were not having an affair."

"Who is Jenna?" asked Forest. "We met her earlier."

She wiped her eyes. "My younger sister."

"Does she live here?"

"Yes."

"Did she tell you we visited earlier?"

She began to get more rattled with the inquisition. "Yes. Look, I was close to Dr. Hart. We were good friends, but we were not having an affair. If this is why you're here then there's nothing more to add."

"If you two were close, did he ever confide in you about any trouble he was having with patients, friends, or his family?"

She relaxed a bit, crossed her legs, and met Forest's eyes. "Everyone has problems, but no, nothing that was so extreme that that…" Her voice broke and another tear fell. "His murder has been a shock for me."

Trevor asked, "How well do you know his sons, Todd and Tim?"

She wiped her face and then stood and walked over to her desk and grabbed a tissue. When she turned back around, she answered, "Not well. I've only seen them in passing at the hospital."

Forest saw it. She was lying. Something about the way she looked and her body language changed. "Were you ever introduced?"

"Yes, of course. All the staff had been introduced at one time or another over the years."

"Were they well liked among the staff?"

She moved forward and sat again, holding her tissue. "Yes. They were always polite and eager to learn medicine. So, yeah, they were well liked."

Trevor closed his notepad. "Ms. Abbott, Dr. Hart was savagely killed in his home by an intruder. Do you have any information that might help us find out the answer to why he was killed?"

She seemed rattled again. "No. He was a good man and a brilliant surgeon."

"One more question, Ms. Abbott, and we'll leave you."

The beautiful woman with red, puffy eyes nodded.

"What started the rumors about the affair?"

She looked down and folded and pressed her tissue into a small square. Quietly she spoke. "He was my mentor. I went back to school and became a nurse practitioner. He...he helped me."

Trevor opened his notepad back up and asked, "Financially?"

Slowly she raised her head and then timidly nodded. "I...I couldn't afford all of it. So, yes, he paid for some of my tuition."

"Who knew about this?"

She looked back at Forest. "No one. He told no one."

Forest stood. "If you can think of anything else that will help our investigation, please give me a call, day or night."

She took Forest's card and nodded. Slowly the tears began to fall again. "Please don't reveal that he helped me financially. It will only add to..." She looked down again. They waited. She closed her eyes before looking back up at them. "He was a good man; he didn't deserve this."

"We can't make any promises, Ms. Abbott, but we'll do our best," Trevor said.

She nodded and then escorted the men out the door. Outside, they noticed that the garage door was closed. Forest looked at Trevor and asked, "When did she close the door? And why?"

Trevor looked at the house and the closed door. "We would have heard it if it was lowered while we were in her study. She had to have closed it while we were near the backyard."

Forest studied the distance. "We were standing on the other side of the house for probably a good five minutes. It had to have been. Now, why did she close the door before greeting us?"

Trevor spoke as he lowered his large frame into the passenger's seat. "I don't know, but there's more. She's not telling us everything."

Forest shut the door and fired up the engine. "Yeah. I think you're right, partner."

***

Jenna held a three-year-old little girl on her hip as she peeped out the blinds. "They're gone now. How did it go?"

Marla Kay glanced her way and said in an irritated voice, "Get away from the window! They might see you."

Jenna rolled her eyes. "Relax. They didn't. Now tell me how it went."

The little girl with dark hair and big brown eyes held out her hands. Marla Kay stepped forward and took her into her arms. She smiled as she asked, "Did you enjoy your movie?"

"Um huh. I want drink. I'm firsty."

133

"You are? Well let's go into the kitchen and see what we can find."

As Marla Kay turned and left the study, Jenna folded her arms and said loudly, "We have to talk about this."

Marla Kay just lifted her hand to acknowledge but continued on past the foyer. Jenna frowned as she looked back out the wooden blinds to the empty driveway.

Chapter 17

Marilynn drove her 1998 Oldsmobile onto the dirt driveway of the small Jordan house. Turning the engine off, she took off her seatbelt and got out. She smoothed down her denim skirt and then closed the car door. Looking around, she found an empty yard so she walked forward, climbed a few steps, and knocked on the door. Soon she heard footsteps and then a chain being unhooked. The door opened to reveal Carly, with Ronny Jr. on her hip.

"Well hello, sweet child. Come in."

Marilynn smiled. "Thank you. Is Johnny Rae home?"

Carly looked at her watch. "Um, no. I think he got off at four. But I can't keep track of everyone's schedule."

"No, ma'am."

Carly gestured to the couch and took the recliner while still holding the baby.

Marilynn tried not to show her worry. Johnny Rae had failed to show at their planned destination at 4:05. She had waited until four fifteen and then drove in the direction of his workplace. But she'd found no sign of

Johnny Rae. She thought she was clever to enter the store and casually look around for him, but she never saw him. She didn't dare ask the boss man but did ask a clerk she saw stocking a shelf.

He had informed her that Johnny Rae had left a long time ago. She had acted like it was no big deal as she purchased a soft drink and then quickly fled the store before breaking down to cry. He had clearly stood her up and lied to her. Now she was sitting in front of Ms. Carly, and she didn't know what to do.

"Johnny Rae mentioned he was going to take his GED," she said.

A shocked expression formed across Carly's face. "Really? I don't believe it!"

"He is," Marilynn confirmed.

"Well, I'm so happy. You know, I think you had something to do with that. You're a good influence, Marilynn."

She returned her smile. "Well, I don't know about that, but I do try."

"Why don't you hold Ronny Junior, and I will fix us some sweet tea?"

Marilynn stood and held out her hands. "That sounds lovely."

The baby readily went to her, and Marilynn decided to sit on the floor to play with him. She saw a red ball and then rolled it over to him. He laughed, picked it up, and tossed it back toward her. Carly soon returned. "Isn't he a sweet baby?"

"He is." Marilynn thought about how he was going to grow up without a mother, and a small frown formed on her face.

Carly saw it. "Johnny Rae told you about his momma, didn't he?"

She slowly nodded.

"Fifteen years. But her lawyer says probably eight with parole, if there's no trouble inside."

It had taken Johnny Rae a long time to confide in Marilynn about the whereabouts of Ronny Jr.'s mother. A year earlier, she had gone out and never returned. She apparently got high and drunk and decided with a few others that robbing a store at gunpoint and then racing down Main Street at dangerously high speeds was a good way to spend a Friday night. She was wrong. The driver of the car hit and killed a homeless person, and the car was registered in her name. Everyone denied driving, and the finger-pointing game began. It ended badly with Marissa going away for fifteen years.

Suddenly the door opened and Johnny Rae stumbled in, ending all thoughts and talk of Marissa.

"Good Lord!" Carly said. "Are you drunk, Johnny Rae?"

He looked around the room and met his mom's stare. Marilynn had stopped rolling the ball and was waiting for him to look at her. He didn't. Ignoring her completely, he continued by into his room and slammed the door. Carly jumped up and ran after him.

For the next five minutes, all Marilynn heard was screaming. She was stuck. She couldn't leave because of Ronny Jr. He suddenly began crying, frightened by all the commotion. "Oh, sweetie," Marilynn pleaded. "Don't cry. Please!"

Too late. His sniffles gave way to wailing. She tried to pick him up and comfort him, but he hit her hands to push her away. She wanted to cry herself. Why had she fallen in love with Johnny Rae? It was such a chance meeting. She'd been carrying a large box, and he had offered to help. Afterward they had talked for an hour and then walked across the street for ice cream.

It was downhill after that. She had fallen—hard. That sweet boy with a gentle nature was now gone. Over the last year, he had changed. Now he seemed distant at times, and his temper was quick. She stared down the hallway at Carly's backside as she continued to question Johnny Rae.

Finally Carly threw her hands up and turned around. "I'm done, Johnny Rae. You got to learn from your mistakes now. I can't help you anymore."

She entered the small living room and bent over and picked up Ronny Jr. to console him. "I'm taking him for a walk."

Marilynn stood and helped her with the stroller. Once they were down the stairs, Carly buckled him in and then stood and faced her. "I'm sorry, child. I won't fault you for walking away. God knows I'm not going to stop you."

A tear rolled down her face as she reflexively reached out and hugged Carly briefly. Pulling away, she said, "I don't know how to walk away, Ms. Carly."

Carly smiled at her, but her eyes were sad. "I know child; I know."

Marilynn watched as she turned away with the stroller. She couldn't move. Her heart was breaking. She looked at her car and then back up at the house. Finally she made a decision. Walking toward the car, she quickly unlocked it and then opened the car door to leave.

That's when she heard him behind her. "Don't go, Marilynn! Please."

Her heart and mind were playing a tug of war. Her mind told her to run. She was going to college, to be something one day. Johnny Rae would only hold her back. *Run!* her brain willed her, but her heart won. She slowly closed the door, wiped her tears away, and turned to face him.

***

Forest was silent for the next ten minutes. He had listened to his messages and heard her voice. Now he was racing toward the Grand Hotel with his siren blaring. Trevor had offered to drive, but he had declined.

He couldn't be bothered with pulling over and trading spots. He had to get to her. As he drove cautiously through traffic, he wondered where these strong feeling were coming from. He had only spent a couple of hours with her. Now his chest felt like it was closing with the need to see her and hold her in his arms once more.

"Two blocks on the left," Trevor said.

Forest nodded his acknowledgment and then slowed as he turned into the hotel parking lot and silenced the siren. "I can get a ride back to the station."

Trevor smiled. "Are you sure? I think I want to meet her."

Forest stared at his partner with his attempt to calm his nerves. "No. Thank you, though. There's too much to do with the Hart case."

Trevor's deep laughter filled the black sedan. "I see how it is. I go back to work, and you go play with the beautiful little prosecutor."

Knowing he was only joking, Forest replied, "Sounds like a plan. See you in an hour." He opened the door and got out, and Trevor did the same.

Just as Forest turned to walk away, Trevor said in a serious tone, "Forest!"

He turned.

"Watch your back."

He nodded and then jogged toward the entrance. Trevor looked around the parking lot and then got behind the wheel and drove away, never seeing the person hiding behind the white van watching.

Officer Steel immediately greeted Forest in the hotel lobby. "We got a mess, Detective Styles."

"What happened?"

"A waiter was knocked out from behind and his uniform stripped. When he came to, he was tied up and gagged with his cart of food missing."

"And the officer on guard?"

"He was knocked out too. Also, the cameras on the stairwell were covered. He knew we were here, and he came anyway."

"Damn! How is she?"

"Shaken up pretty bad. We moved her to the second floor, room 212. There're two officers inside with her until a decision is made about where to take her. We got to get a handle on this!"

Forest raked a hand through his short brown hair. "Who knew her location?"

"Only a handful within the department. He had to have followed us."

There was no use stating the obvious. They screwed up. "I'm going up. We'll talk again when I return."

Forest quickly took the stairs. More officers on the second floor nodded as he walked by. He tapped on the door, and then a female officer greeted him. "Detective Styles."

"Officer Burrow."

Forest walked in and saw Lilee sitting on a chair in the far corner with her legs tucked beneath her. When their eyes met, he said, "Give us a minute, please."

The officers quietly left and shut the door, leaving them alone together.

Before he could get any words out, she jumped up and ran into his arms. Neither spoke as he held her tenderly. Moments passed before she pulled away. Her green eyes looked tired, and her blond hair was messy and damp as it fell across her shoulders over her tight gray T-shirt. She wore jeans and flip-flops and not an ounce of makeup, and she looked breath-takingly sexy. His heart tugged as she searched his eyes for answers.

"Forest, I'm really scared now. He's too bold to come here in broad daylight while I'm surrounded by officers."

He nodded. "You said you got a call. Tell me about it."

"It was after I talked to you." She smirked. "I thought you were calling me back."

He touched her hand and squeezed it. "It was a male voice, but, I don't know, he didn't sound young, but he came across as so immature."

"How so?"

"He was singing in a child's tone that I was gonna die."

"He might sound young and immature, but he's smart and strong to take out two people without a fight."

She shook her head. "I guess. I don't know; it's all so unnerving."

"I want you to come with me."

She ran a hand over her long blond tresses. "Where?"

"To the station, and then back to my place."

When she didn't answer, he continued. "You aren't leaving my side until we get a better handle on who's doing this."

Seeing fear in her eyes, he realized he was scaring her more. "I'm sorry. I don't mean…"

"No. I understand. Just give me a few minutes, and I'll change."

141

He watched as she turned and picked up a small bag and then headed to the bathroom. When she was about to shut the door, he moved toward her and said, "Wait."

She watched him as he neared. Then he took her into his arms and kissed her gently on the mouth. She didn't pull away, instead kissing him back. His hands caressed her back and then found her hair. He continued to kiss her until his mind took over once again, and he slowly pulled away. When he was within inches of her mouth, he spoke softly. "Nothing's going to happen to you. I promise."

She whispered, "OK. I'll hold you to that. Because, I would really be upset if I didn't have a chance to get to know you more."

He kissed her once more and then took a step back as she smiled and closed the door.

Chapter 18

The plan with Lilee Parker had gone all wrong. Officer Steel had proven to be too smart by giving Lilee a code. *Now what?* The figure studied the list once again and picked up a purple crayon from beside the little girl lying on the carpet by the couch. Slowly, the figure drew a line over William Hart's name in purple crayon. The second name, Christa Hart, couldn't be crossed off yet. No word yet on the news or from the hospital, so a question mark was drawn.

The third name was Officer John Norman, and another purple line was quickly drawn. A smile emerged at the memory of John walking toward the SUV to his unfortunate fate. Below John's name: Lilee Parker. The smile disappeared. *I'll just have to come up with a new plan; that's all.*

Below Lilee's name at number five: Tom Franklin, the stupid mechanic. He was crossed off, leaving five more on the list. So far, only three had been eliminated. The figure gave the purple crayon back to the little dark-haired girl, who smiled back. She had turned three the month before without any big birthday celebration. Last month was a bad month. But it was the three-year anniversary of that dark night that continued to be the source of hurt and depression.

The little girl got up and left the room, and the list was once again studied. Number six: Nick Woods. This one would be easy. They had recently met and started up a friendship. A smile emerged again. *Tonight, Nick Woods.*

***

Lilee Parker had changed into a black lightweight cashmere sweater, chose her black boots to wear with her designer jeans, and tossed the flip-flops. She had combed her hair and slicked it back into a low pony-tail, applied some light makeup, and painted her lips her signature pink shade. When she walked into the police headquarters, most people greeted her politely. If it weren't for the Hart case and the death of John Norman, she would have been less well received. Too much had happened since Friday's lost case against Ronny Jordan, pushing it far from everyone's minds.

"Go ahead and take a seat in here. No one will bother you. Is there anything I can get you?"

She looked around the small workroom that held a few couches and a large flat-screen TV. On the table she spied a couple of pizza boxes. "Yes. May I have some pizza?"

Forest walked over and raised the lid. Half a pepperoni pizza remained. "Go for it. There's soft drinks in the frig. Help yourself."

"Thanks." She reached out and grabbed his hand. He smiled as he looked into her beautiful green eyes and squeezed her hand back.

"I'll be two doors down. Come get me if there's a problem."

She nodded. "There won't be. Now go."

She watched him turn and leave and then found a drink and grabbed a slice of pizza. When she was done with her third slice, her phone rang. Immediately she tensed as she pulled it out of her pocket. She was relieved for only a second when she discovered it didn't say

"Unknown caller," but she tensed again when she saw the name: Landon Baynes.

She pressed the green button. "Hello?"

"Hi, Lilee. It's me."

She swallowed a lump in her throat. "Landon."

"Sorry I missed your call the other day. I'm on vacation in Miami."

"Oh. Well, it was nothing."

He smirked. "Lilee, I got a call from an Officer Steel about my where-abouts. Obviously there's something."

She didn't know how to respond. She didn't want him to know she'd called for help, and she sure didn't want to talk about how a female voice had answered the phone. "I…I have a large box of yours, winter clothing. It's in my garage."

"Oh, yeah. I'll come get that."

Silence.

"Lilee?"

"Yeah."

"I'm sorry about the trouble this weekend. I never want to see harm come your way. You need to be careful. You've always been too relaxed when it comes to your safety."

"You never told me that," she interrupted.

"Yes, I have. Many times. You just never listened."

"What's in Miami?" She couldn't help the words that tumbled out of her mouth. She regretted them immediately.

An awkward moment passed, and then he answered, "I've moved on, Lilee. She's from Miami Beach."

The lump formed in her throat again, and the pizza she had consumed began to flip around in her stomach. Quickly she reached for her drink and took a sip to make her swallow. Finally she was able to speak. "That was fast."

She heard a female voice in the background calling his name. "Um, I got to go now. I'll drop by next Saturday morning and pick up that box. Take care of yourself, Lilee. Bye."

She couldn't respond. She continued to listen, but the line was soon disconnected. She lowered her phone and pressed the red button. She was so angry at herself. *What possessed me to ask about Miami? Did I really have to know?*

Soon her phone rang again, and she felt a sense of relief as the name Charli Pepper appeared.

"Hi, Charli."

"Hey yourself. You never called me today when you promised you would."

"No. I'm sorry. A lot has gone on."

"Were you threatened again?"

Lilee stretched out on the couch and began to fill her in. A lot of fussing went on, and then Charli asked, "Where are you staying tonight?"

Twirling her ponytail, Lilee looked up at the ceiling and replied, "Detective Styles' home."

"What? Really? Whose idea was that?"

146

She smiled at the memory of him asking her. "His."

"Well, I'm not sure how I should feel about that. It either means you're in a shit load of trouble, or he's taking advantage of you."

She honestly replied, "Oh, God, I hope the good-looking detective takes advantage, because I desperately could use some…"

She stopped midsentence and jerked forward as Forest rounded the corner of the sofa. He was frowning. "Charli, I have to go. I'll be fine, and I'll see you at the office tomorrow. OK? Bye."

Timidly she asked, "What?"

"Christa Hart went into cardiac arrest today. Someone tried to kill her—again."

"Oh, no. Is she going to make it?"

"Yes. She's one tough lady; I give her that."

"How did it happen?"

"Not sure. She was also under police protection."

The words began to play in her head. The police department wasn't up to par this week. The mishandled evidence with the Jordan case, twice someone had gotten to her, and now Mrs. Hart. As she looked at his face, his eyes softened.

"What were you talking about earlier to Charli?"

She blushed. "You only heard part of the conversation. I…"

She felt her face turn a crimson red. She hated that. With her fair complexion, it was so easy to see when she blushed. She covered her face with her hands. He walked near her and pulled her back down onto the couch and kissed her face, pulling her hands away.

147

"Thanks, Lilee Parker, for bringing sunshine into my life."

***

It was an unusually slow night in the ER for a Sunday. Too soon for flu season and too late in the year for heat-related injuries. A few patients trickled into Atlanta General with minor scrapes and broken bones. So far, no serious car accidents and no shootings. Nick Woods sat at his station and waited for a call. An hour and a half had gone by without any runs.

Candice Hall walked over, a cute little nurse in her late twenties, to flirt with Nick, who was also single and around the same age.

"Hiya, Nick. Enjoying the slow night?"

He watched as she set a stack of charts down and picked up a pen to make a notation in one before closing it.

"Don't jinx me, Candice. You know it won't last."

She winked. "Duty calls. Got a wailing tot with a high fever."

He watched as she left. She was pretty with her dark brown hair piled high on top of her head. She was fit, and he liked the way her hips swung to the sides as she walked. As if sensing him staring, she turned around and winked again. He winked back. He knew she was available. She had sent all the right signals, but he was a little worried about mixing romance with work. In the past, that hadn't turned out so well.

The control panel lit up, and he listened. A haggard breathing sound was coming from a phone. The operator was asking all the standard questions, but nothing. He heard her yell, "Trace this call." Then she picked up a secure line and phoned Nick.

"We got a victim who is short of breath with no verbal response. Pay phone, and it's coming from…" She paused another moment and then announced, "605 Memorial Drive."

148

Nick closed his eyes. He hated these calls. A park at dark. Probably a hoax or some drug- or gang-related injury where the perp gets to the nearest pay phone. He mumbled, "Great!"

"I'm sorry. I couldn't read you?"

I'm on my way. ETA, ten minutes. Stay on this line. I want updates!"

"Affirm."

Nick motioned for Jake, who had just come back from a coffee run. "Got a live one. Memorial Drive, pay phone."

"Oh, shit. Not another one."

Soon they were out the door with Jake driving. The operator had informed them the person was no longer on the line. She had tried ringing back, but it was busy. "Police have already been dispatched and should arrive at the same time," she said.

It was a known fact around the medical community in any major city, that if there were an emergency, you would get a faster response screaming "fire" or "heart attack" than "robbery" or "intruder." Luckily not everyone believed this. Jake slammed on the brakes and backed the ambulance up toward a person lying on the ground by a pay phone, neither were surprised they were the first to arrive on the scene.

"Be careful, Nick. He could be high as a kite and armed."

Nick nodded and opened his door as Jake did the same. Both arrived behind the ambulance at the same time. Nick scanned the area. They appeared to be alone. Jake saw the dangling phone and knelt down. "Mister, where are you hurt?"

Suddenly the man opened his bloodshot eyes and began hitting Jake like some wild animal. Nick immediately stepped in and forced a needle into the man's neck. Instantly he stilled. "Shit, are you OK?"

Jake looked at his arm. "He tried to bite me!"

"Did he?"

Jake searched his arm and looked for any scratches or indentations. "No, thank God."

Nick let out a sigh of relief. "Let's load up his sorry ass. I'll get the IVs going inside. This place gives me the creeps." Jake stood and opened the back door and pulled out the stretcher. On the count of three, they lifted and put him on the stretcher and then wheeled him inside. Nick offered to drive since Jake seemed shaken.

"Yeah. I would much rather miss a vein on this loser versus crossing a lane driving."

Nick nodded and watched as Jake began tying their patient down where he wouldn't move and attack again. Satisfied Jake was safe, he backed up and closed the doors and secured them. Looking around he felt a chill go down his back at the thought that he was being watched. Quickly he shook it off, climbed in behind the wheel, turned on the sirens, and sped away. Out on the highway, he picked up his radio and called it in.

Jake took over and read out his vitals as a room was prepared and a doctor summoned. ETA was now five minutes.

The police had been called off from Memorial Drive, and an officer would be available at the hospital. This was standard with all cases that appeared to be brought on by drugs or alcohol. Nick pulled under the overhang used by emergency services, and two attendants greeted him. They opened the doors, Jake read off an update on the vitals, and then the man was whisked away. Nick walked around and watched as Jake stepped down from the truck. Once again Jake was looking over his body for bruises or cuts.

"Come on inside," Nick said. "Let's get under the light where we can see."

Candice walked by and saw the guys. She walked over and said, "Sorry, I did jinx you."

She looked at Jake. "Hey, you're bleeding."

"Aw, shit!"

"Wait, that isn't your blood. It's his," said Nick.

Jake shivered. "I'm gonna wipe down and change."

Candice watched him walk away. "That bad, huh?"

Nick stared hard into her eyes. He needed a break from it all, and he was looking at one fine piece of female specimen that was sure to give him what he needed. "I get off in ten minutes. What time does your shift end?"

"Sorry, Nick. My shift ends at eleven. I got another hour to go."

He nodded and looked around. The place was still pretty quiet. He stepped closer. "There's a supply closet down the hall."

She stepped back. "What kind of girl do you think I am, Nick Woods?"

He studied her face and finally responded, "One that will meet me in ten minutes."

She didn't respond but smiled as she turned away with a chart in her hands.

He watched as she walked through the swinging doors to the reception area and started talking to a nurse. He smiled and went to find Jake in the men's room. After seeing that his friend was going to be OK, he left him. Instead of taking a left out of the building, he took a right down the hallway. Finding the supply closet, he looked both ways and then entered. Seeing it empty, his heart sank and he began to wonder if he had read Candice all wrong. He had not. She opened the door and stepped inside, locking it behind her. Quickly she lifted her skirt and dropped her red lace underwear to the floor. "You get five minutes now, and I get one hour later when my shift ends. Deal?"

He let his hands respond for him. Luckily he got seven minutes, and then Candice quickly pulled her skirt down and pulled up her underwear. "See you outside at eleven oh five."

He smiled. "Count on it."

She winked again and then left.

Candice walked around light as a feather for the next thirty minutes. Her friend commented, "Must have been some break."

She smiled. "Oh, yeah."

"Well, we got work to do. Carjacking. Victim was shot multiple times before the gunman took off in his car."

"Where was this?"

"That's the scary part," Jeanice replied. "Two miles from here."

Candice shuddered. "We'll start, but the night shift will finish—if there's anything to finish."

Candice heard someone yell, "ETA, one minute!"

She washed her hands and then pulled on some gloves. Like clockwork an ambulance arrived one minute later, and its doors opened. Stepping forward, she heard a hush fall across the room. Wondering what everyone saw, she moved forward again and froze at the sight of Nick Woods lying on a stretcher covered in blood. She heard people calling his name. No response. She watched as the doctors began to work.

Jeanice tried to push her into action. "Snap out of it. Let's move."

She couldn't. She was stiff with fear. Two more nurses ran forward, and one took over as another tended to Candice. "What's wrong?"

She opened her mouth to speak, but no words formed. She watched as they continued to work on Nick as a nurse held her. She heard one of the doctors say, "We lost him. No use. Time of death: ten thirty-five. Shit!"

She whispered to Bonnie, who was holding her tight, "I think, I'm gonna fai…" The younger nurse caught her before she fell to the floor.

Chapter 19

A garage door opened and then lowered as Forest pulled his Mustang inside his secure garage. Lilee stepped out and then grabbed her small bag from the back seat.

"Stay here," Forest said. "I'll be right back."

She watched as Forest climbed two stairs and then unlocked a dead bolt. He entered and returned in two minutes. Once she was safely inside, he reset his alarm and bolted the door. She noticed he glanced toward his answering machine and saw the blinking red light. Deciding to give him some privacy, she asked, "Is the restroom this way?"

He looked up and nodded. "Yeah. Second door on your left."

She smiled and left him, carrying her small bag. She passed one room that appeared to be a study and then found the bathroom. Stepping in, she closed the door behind her and placed her bag on the counter. She found her toothpaste and toothbrush and began to brush.

As soon as she began, she realized she was muffling the sounds coming from the machine. She wanted to stop and step toward the door to listen but fought the urge. Soon she pulled out her ponytail elastic and brushed out her long blond hair. She wanted to change but hadn't packed much.

Settling on her gray T-shirt and black yoga pants, she quickly changed and then left the bathroom.

Forest had his back turned toward her as he dug around in his refrigerator. When he heard her approach, he turned around and asked, "Beer or wine?"

She smiled. "Whatever you're having."

"Beer it is."

She watched as he removed two and then used his leg to close the door. "I got some chips and salsa. Sound good?"

"Yes. Perfect."

She took the offered beer and watched as he pulled down a bowl, dumped the bag of chips inside, and then popped the salsa top.

"Let's take the couch. More comfortable."

She grabbed the bowl and followed him over to the living room. He slid the coffee table closer and then set the salsa down and took a seat. She set the chips down and sat close to him. He took a long sip from his beer. "Long day!"

"Yeah. I vaguely remember waking up to some clatter outside my window."

He smiled. "Was that really today?"

"No kidding!"

"Come here." He opened his arm and motioned for her to sit closer. She did, fitting her body snuggly up against his. Moments passed as neither said a word. Lilee leaned forward, grabbed another chip, and then took another sip of her beer.

He casually began rubbing her shoulder with his hand that was draped around her. It felt good. It had been so long since she'd been held like that. The last time she spent twenty minutes in Landon's arms had been months before the breakup. She snuggled closer. Soon she watched as he placed his beer on the coffee table and then leaned into her. When his mouth was within inches, he asked, "What is this I'm feeling, prosecutor?"

Her heart skipped a beat and then picked up speed. There was no doubt in her mind he could hear her heart pounding. Slowly he touched her face with his hand and then traced her delicate pink lips with his finger. "Do you feel what I feel, Ms. Parker?"

She parted her mouth as she let out a small gasp. His lips soon met hers and his hands wrapped up in her long hair. *Oh, I'm feeling it alright!* Heat surged through her body with his touch. Soon he was on top of her and she lay stretched out beneath him. He lowered his mouth and found her throat; all the while his hands moved over her body. He found her breast, playfully rubbed it, and coyly said, "No bra."

She felt her nipples harden at his touch as she let out another small gasp. He was driving her mad with his touches, taking his time exploring every inch of her body. Soon she felt her shirt raise and the warmth of his mouth on her as he tickled her with his tongue, teasing her. Reflexively she arched her back and he moved his hands down and placed them around her ass. Slowly he lowered his mouth and stopped at her navel. She tensed and then shivered from his touch. Lower he continued. With smooth hands, he found the top of her pants and pulled them down.

He stood up as he removed each pants leg and looked at her in a way that left no question as to his desire. He carefully lifted the hem of her shirt and pulled it over her head. She was now lying naked on his couch. In one swift move, Forest lifted his own T-shirt and then lowered his body down on top of her once again. He found her mouth as his hands explored below. Slowly he left in search of her throat and then found her firm chest once again.

She touched his hair and wrapped her legs around him as he continued to lower his mouth down her body once more. She arched and placed her arms back by her head as he parted her legs with his mouth and began to drive her further to the point of insanity. She cried out as he continued taking his time exploring and giving her what she wanted, as well as needed. She shivered and cried out over and over as he continued. Finally she reached for him. "Now. I want you inside me now!"

He stood and then picked her up, carrying her toward the bedroom. He turned on the light and then gently laid her down. He quickly unbuckled his belt, took off his jeans, and crawled onto the bed by her feet. Slowly he lowered his mouth to her ankle and began moving his way up with his mouth once more.

When she completely lost it, he raised himself up and entered her forcefully. She wrapped her legs around him and flipped him over onto his back. For the next several minutes he held on as she rocked back and forth and her body continued to spasm with each bolt that jolted her, leaving her wanting for more. She was alive and feeling a pleasure she had never experienced in her whole life. She couldn't get enough as her senses were heightened and the feel of pure ecstasy consumed her whole being.

Finally she slowed and then dropped to his chest. She panted, "Forest, I…I've never…" She blushed as she rose to meet his eyes. "Promise me, Forest, we'll do that again."

He stroked her back and laughed. "Oh, yeah. We'll do that again."

She smiled and then immediately rolled over as he cradled her to sleep.

***

When Ronny Jordan came home around one a.m., he was surprised to see Carly sitting in the living room. "What you doing up, Momma? Why ain't you in bed?"

"I couldn't sleep."

"It Johnny Rae?"

She didn't answer.

"Where iz he?"

"Not here."

He looked at the time on the microwave. "Iz after one. Iz he with that girl?"

Carly stood. "Her name is Marilynn, and I don't know. All I know is no good will come after midnight."

"What haz gotten into dat fool?"

"You. All was fine until you got locked up."

Ronny held his tongue. The last thing he wanted to do was make her more upset. Already she was going to be tired come six in the morning. He offered, "I go out and look for him."

She rolled her eyes and shook her head. "No. You don't know where to look, and I don't want two of my boys missing come morning when I have to go to work."

He thought about Ronny Jr. asleep in the back room. She was right. Finally he said, "Go on; go ta bed. I wait up and talk ta him."

She hesitated as he sat down in the recliner and leaned back. Slowly she turned and walked away. When she was out of sight, he mumbled, "Damn it, Johnny Rae. You fool!"

***

Marilynn sat up with a frown across her face. "Don't go, Johnny Rae. Please!"

"I got to. Your daddy come through that door and I'm a dead man."

Marilynn peeled her eyes off Johnny Rae and stared at the locked door. Even if her daddy did barge in, nothing was going on, but she knew she wouldn't be able to convince him otherwise. He was right. Her daddy would kill him. She looked back at Johnny Rae and watched as he opened the window to her small bedroom in her family's ground-floor apartment.

"I'll see you after school?"

He stopped and turned, "I got work tomorrow. We'll see."

"I'll get that paper from the counselor," she said.

"What paper?"

She narrowed her eyes and watched as a small smile spread across his face. "I know what paper. Come by around four. I'll be home."

She smiled and jumped up and ran over to kiss him once more. "Now go home. Straight home."

He pulled away and eased out the window. "OK."

"I mean it, Johnny Rae. Don't take the path by Memorial Drive at the park."

He smirked as an image of his friends drinking and smoking filled his head.

"Johnny Rae?"

He looked toward her.

"Promise me."

He met her eyes and grinned. "I won't go by the park."

She nodded, stepped back, and pulled the window closed. Through the glass pane, she watched as he waved and turned left, away from the park. As she closed the curtains, he turned and looked once more. When he saw that she had left and crawled back into bed, he turned back around and headed in the opposite direction. He shook his head as he thought, *Not the park, Marilynn, but there's something I got to finish—tonight.*

Chapter 20

Lilee slowly awoke the next morning in a strange room. She immediately thought of the night before and turned her head to find Forest. He wasn't there. She leaned forward and looked around his bedroom. Smelling coffee, she smiled. Just as she sat up, he walked in holding a cup of coffee, dressed for the day. She pouted. "Why are you dressed?"

He laughed and set her coffee down on the nightstand and then sat down beside her. His lips soon met hers, and he leaned her back for a deep kiss. Sitting back up, he traced her mouth with his finger and said, "We have to get going. Lots of things happened last night outside of this bedroom."

She smiled. He continued to move his hand down her throat and then lifted the sheet and cupped her breast with his hands. Just as he was about to lower his mouth to her, she placed her hands on him. "Oh, no. We aren't gonna start something you can't finish!"

He stopped and pulled the sheet back up. "Fair enough."

With a serious tone, she asked, "What happened last night?"

"They made an arrest at your house last night."

She tensed at his words. "At my house?"

"Yes. The person scaring you to death is not who any of us expected."

She was confused. "Who is it?"

"Kelley Wells' fourteen-year-old grandson, Kenny Wells."

A memory of the tall, skinny, brown-headed boy at the trial filled her memory. She remembered how angry he looked as she turned around and finally faced the family. He had stormed off without anyone in the family noticing him, but she had seen it. His mom's attention as well as his grandfather's had been focused on Kelley Wells, the victim. She mumbled, "Poor kid."

Forest was taken aback by her comment and repeated, "Poor kid? You're joking, right!"

She opened her mouth to speak but chose not to.

"Lilee, I understand. You feel responsible for his pain. But there's no excuse, none, for scaring you like that. Besides, there's something wrong with him if he can kill a cat and attack a police officer. He's filled with a lot of anger. He's messed up."

"You're right. But, he needs help."

Forest watched her and placed a loving hand along her cheek. "Lilee, there's no doubt in my mind or anyone else's that Ronny Jordan was guilty. But people can't start taking the law into their own hands. It would make the world a very dangerous place."

She was listening but didn't feel any better. He continued. "Also, Maggs wants to see you in his office at seven."

She glanced at her watch. "That's one hour. I don't have any more clothes."

"He knows. But he wants you to come as you are for a talk."

164

She tilted her head. "How do you know all of this?"

He smiled. "My uncle and I are very close."

She blushed. "Does he know I stayed over last night?"

"Oh, yeah. He wanted all the details."

"What?"

"Don't worry. I left nothing out."

She opened her mouth to protest but knew he was lying. She picked up a pillow and threw it at him. Next she got up naked, picked up her coffee, and waltzed to the bathroom, giving him a little dose of his own medicine. She smiled as she closed the door. *Two can play this game.* When she was about to turn the water on, Forest barged in and took her in his arms. "The hell with being on time."

***

At seven forty-five, Lilee arrived at City Hall. She leaned over, quickly gave Forest a kiss, and exited his Mustang. She smiled as she entered the building and handed her badge to the security guard. Her purse was scanned, and then she walked through the metal detector, retrieved her purse, and clipped her badge onto a belt loop of her jeans. "Thanks, Marvin."

He nodded. "Ms. Parker."

She didn't have to wait, as the elevator door opened immediately. She quickly sidestepped the others coming off and stepped on, pressing the number four. Luckily she went straight up without any other passengers. When the door opened, she immediately heard screaming from down the hall.

"Meredith, what's going on?" she asked as she stepped toward the secretary.

"Mr. Wells is here. He's lost it. They arrested his grandson last night at your house. He's demanding Maggs let him go and not press charges."

Lilee closed her eyes. All of this could have been avoided with a guilty verdict. The yelling escalated and she opened her eyes. "Has security been alerted?"

"Yes. Two are in there now, but he has no weapon. There's not a whole lot the old guy can do. He's sixty-eight."

"What about Mrs. Wells? Is she here too?"

"No. She's with her daughter, waiting to see the grandson at city lockup."

Lilee shook her head. "This just keeps getting worse!"

Just then a door opened down the hall and a red-faced Mr. Wells exited Maggs' office, flanked by two security officers. When he saw Lilee, he stopped and pointed his finger at her.

"You! This is your fault! None of this…this…" He grabbed his chest and swayed to the side. Then his legs gave out and he fell to the floor. Jeremy, the younger security guard, was able to break his fall before his head hit the wooden floor.

Lilee's eyes widened and she rushed forward, screaming to Meredith, "Call an ambulance. Now!"

Paul, the other security guard, yelled, "Clear this hall! We need to get him calm."

Lilee watched in horror as Mr. Wells' body jerked and then stilled. Someone placed a hand around Lilee's waist and guided her backward toward an open office. Turning around, she came face-to-face with Andy Kane, who wore a solemn expression.

"Wha…what are you doing here?"

166

He didn't answer as both turned back toward the hallway at the sound of more people. In a matter of seconds, the paramedic stationed in the building was running past them down the hall.

Andy pulled her away from the open door and turned her around to face him. "I've offered to represent the grandson, Kenny Wells."

Lilee peeled his hand off of her waist, stepped back, and stared at the tall man with his perfect wavy blond hair. "You can't be serious. You're the one who got Ronny Jordan off for near killing his grandmother."

He took a step back and crossed his arms, shaking his head. "Your department is the one that let Ronny Jordan walk, not me."

He continued. "Lilee, I'm offering my services for free."

She broke eye contact and turned and took the nearest chair. Running a hand through her hair, she spoke in a surprisingly calm voice. "Andy, the last person they want to see is you."

He laughed and then stepped forward and shut the door. Turning back toward her, he took the seat beside her. "Lilee, darling, it's you they don't want to see again. Not me."

"You arrogant bastard!" She rose to her feet, but he was quicker. He pulled her back down and stood over her. She found his notorious sexy blue eyes.

He leaned closer. "Lilee, I didn't know how else to get your attention. I've enjoyed seeing you every day in the courtroom. Now, this will give us another opportunity to work together."

He continued to lean closer until she felt paralyzed, like she was caught up in a trance. When he was an inch away, she reached up and pushed his chest—hard. "That's close enough, counselor."

He straightened, turned, and strolled back toward the door. Touching the knob, he glanced back over his shoulder. "We'll talk again soon, Lilee."

167

When he opened the door, another paramedic ran by pushing a stretcher. After he passed, Andy stepped out and left in the opposite direction. Charli appeared and entered the office, closing the door behind her.

"Lilee! Mr. Wells has collapsed in our hallway. Oh my God. This can't be happening!"

Lilee didn't respond as she looked down at her black boots.

Charli took the closest chair and lowered her voice. "And what the hell is Andy Kane doing here?"

Lilee looked up and met her friend's eyes. "He's offered to represent Kenny Wells for free."

"What? He can't do that. Can he?"

Lilee stood and opened the door just in time to see Mr. Wells being carried away. No one spoke and everyone watched as one paramedic held the elevator door while the other wheeled Mr. Wells inside. When the elevator door closed, Lilee looked back down the hall and found Daniel Maggs standing there with his hands on his hips. Seeing Lilee, and Charli appearing behind her, he commanded, "In my office, now!"

Lilee and Charli exchanged looks before walking down the hallway and into his office.

"Close the door."

Charli pulled the door closed and spoke. "Sir…"

"No one talk. Just sit."

Charli and Lilee found the closest chairs to the large oval table and sat while Maggs paced back and forth mumbling profanity under his breath. No one spoke, as directed, for the next five minutes. Finally Maggs pressed a button on his phone. "Send in Shultz."

"Yes, sir."

Lilee cringed inside. The last person she wanted in there right then was Maggs' number one go-to boy. *Damn, can it get any worse?* she thought.

Charli gave Lilee an inquisitive expression. Lilee shrugged. Then a door opened and Wes Schultz entered.

"Good. That didn't take long." Everyone watched as Maggs picked up a folder off his desk and handed it to Wes. "You're handling the Kenny Wells case."

Lilee opened her mouth to protest, but Maggs raised a hand to quiet her. He turned back toward Wes. "Don't go soft on the boy. He terrorized one of our own and knocked out a policeman as well as a hotel staff waiter." He raised his voice. "This department will not go easy on Kenny Wells. Justice is not served by revenge, and it's our job to teach him that."

Maggs looked back at Lilee. "Do we all understand?"

In a voice that sounded soft, too soft, Lilee responded first. "Yes, sir."

The other two quickly agreed, and Wes was dismissed.

Daniel Maggs relaxed his arms from his hips and his face softened. "Lilee, I was worried about you. I'm glad you're OK." He walked over toward the table, took a seat, placed his hands under his chin, and stared at her. He asked, "You are OK, aren't you?"

Lilee held her head high and found her voice. "I am. Thank you, sir."

Maggs was the first to break eye contact as he opened a file folder in front of him. He said, "With much regret, I've opened a full-scale investigation into the mishandling of the case against Ronny Jordan."

Lilee's eyes widened and she held her breath. Maggs looked up and faced Lilee. "The investigation will start within the police department, and, hopefully, it'll stop there."

Lilee slowly closed her eyes and took a breath. Maggs took off his glasses and set them on the table. He added, "However, we missed it and ended up dropping the ball. We lost the case, and a guilty man walked free."

Lilee opened her eyes and felt his hard stare bearing down on her. She opened her mouth to speak but stopped when she heard Charli.

"Mr. Maggs, we missed it because we're understaffed and overworked. It's as simple as that."

Lilee shot her friend a look, but Charli continued with her head held high and her shoulders squared as she faced Maggs. "Please think about it before you speak, sir." She let a silent moment pass for her comment to sink in, striking a nerve. Lilee looked at Maggs' expression, but it hadn't changed to reveal his thoughts.

Charli continued. "You denied our office when we all requested more help. We've logged in over eighty hours a week for the last four months. Is it any wonder we didn't have the time or people to go in and follow up on all police statements and records? When it's crunch time, we can't spend time double checking and second guessing everyone on the team. We had to trust everyone was doing their job, and correctly."

Daniel Maggs broke eye contact and looked down at the folder in front of him. She was right. They were understaffed. The previous week, Wes Schultz, his number one prosecutor, had said the same thing. Slowly he closed the file and put his glasses back on.

Both ladies eyed him, waiting for his reply. Finally he pushed his chair back and stood. "Ladies, you've given me a lot to consider. Report back here at eight a.m. on Wednesday."

Lilee stood as Charli did the same. "But, sir…" Charli began.

Maggs looked at Lilee and then to Charli. "Hopefully on Wednesday, we'll have enough to move forward on the Hart case, and I want my best rested and ready for the challenge. So, go home until Wednesday."

Charli's eyes widened and a small smile escaped. "I...I thought Wes was going to get that case?"

"Wes will have his hands full. Now do you want this case or not? Or do I need to give it to someone else?" he barked loudly.

Lilee answered first. "No, sir. We'll be ready." Lilee stepped out from behind the table and quickly walked toward the door with Charli right behind her.

"Good-bye, sir," Charli said as she closed the door.

Both ladies looked at one another and had to quickly cover their mouths from laughter. As they walked, Lilee whispered, "When did you grow a set of balls, Charli?"

"Ha, ha. Very funny. I...I was just tired of it all; that's it. Time to stand up to him. He had it coming!"

Lilee smiled.

Charli looked closely at her friend and stopped walking. "Looks like you're going to be seeing a lot more of this Detective Styles."

Lilee's eyes sparkled. "God, I hope so! Come on. Let's go downstairs and get a coffee. We need to talk!"

Wes Schultz rounded the corner and bumped into them, holding a stack of files. "Ladies. In a hurry?"

Lilee nodded and eased Charli forward toward an elevator that had just opened up. When she turned she saw a frown on Wes' face. "We need to talk, Lilee."

The elevator door closed with no response.

Chapter 21

Christa Hart lay sleeping. Her body had taken another hard hit by some-one who wanted her dead. Andrea Raines sat quietly by her side and waited on her dear friend to wake up once more. An hour had passed since Dr. Griffin had shown up with an update. No one could be sure when or if Christa Hart would ever wake up again. A tear rolled down her cheek as she watched her friend's small chest rise and fall and lis-tened to the humming of the machine beside her. The boys had left ear-lier, after Dr. Griffin gave the grim news. Both boys were physically upset. Now Andrea was alone, watching her friend fight for her life.

She heard a noise from behind and turned toward the door to see who it was. Standing in a white coat was her husband, Derrick. "How are you doing?"

She was still mad at her husband for keeping a secret from her. William Hart had cheated on her best friend, and he had known about it. *Not only did he cheat, but he was having an ongoing affair, something completely different from…* She pushed the awful night out of her mind.

Andrea broke eye contact and then turned away. Not deterred, Derrick closed the door behind him, walked over beside her, placed a hand on her shoulder, and waited. They hadn't spoken since the detectives had revealed William Hart's infidelity. Afterward, Derrick had gone back into the hospital without her and remained on call all night.

Another minute of silence went by before Derrick offered, "Andrea, I'm off until Wednesday. Let's go home."

No reply.

Another minute went by, and he continued. "You need to get ready for tonight's service."

She turned and faced him. "How long did you know?"

He shook his head. "Not here. We'll talk at home."

She turned back around and faced her dear friend. "I'm not going tonight."

Derrick closed his eyes and then took the chair beside her. "Andrea, we have to go."

She shot her husband a fierce look. "No. I don't have to go. She needs me here, needs me more than someone who…who…" Unable to continue, she closed her eyes and bowed her head.

He reached out for her, and she recoiled at his touch. "No. Don't touch me."

Derrick stood suddenly, knocking the chair over. It crashed to the floor with a loud bang.

The door flew open and an officer entered with his hand on his weapon and demanded, "What's going on in here?"

Derrick looked at the chair and then to Andrea. Andrea slowly stood and faced the Officer. "My mistake. I accidentally knocked the chair over. I…I felt faint."

The officer relaxed and nodded. He took a step forward, picked up the chair, and studied Christa Hart's monitor. When nothing else was said, he looked at the doctor.

Derrick reached out and grabbed his wife's elbow. "Keep an eye on Mrs. Hart. I need to take my wife home. She's tired."

The middle-aged officer looked at Andrea, and his face softened. "Take care, Mrs. Raines. Someone will contact you if there's any change." He looked up and met Derrick's eyes. "Doctor." With that, he left.

Andrea looked once more at her friend and then squeezed her hand. "I'll be back later, my friend. Hang in there. You have a lot to live for. Your boys need you. I...I need you!"

Derrick placed his free arm around Andrea for support, but she felt a chill. Slowly she let go of Christa's hand and turned to leave, with Derrick still hovering close and his other hand still holding her arm tightly. When they were at the closed door, she stopped and stared into his eyes. "Derrick, please let me go. I can walk out of here on my own."

He studied her face as his eyebrows creased. "Fine."

He opened the door and Andrea walked out and nodded at the officer who had interrupted them earlier. "Dr. and Mrs. Raines. Drive carefully."

Andrea didn't respond. She just patted him on the arm and walked on by. Derrick scanned the hallway and saw Marla Kay Abbott standing at the nurses' station staring at them intently. Even from this distance, Derrick saw that she was shaken and upset. He allowed a small smile to form to acknowledge that he understood her pain and let her know she wasn't alone. Seeing his gesture, Marla Kay closed her eyes and half smiled.

A moment passed and she opened her eyes, just as Andrea stopped and turned around. Quickly, Marla Kay broke eye contact and looked down at the chart she held. Derrick faced Andrea. She studied his face and then glanced back down the hallway at the group of nurses. Slowly she turned back around and pressed the large silver button that opened the doors to the ICU. Derrick followed and Marla Kay glanced up once more, only to see the double doors closing and an armed policeman looking her way. She turned and left with her chart.

Tim and Todd Hart were seated on the leather couches when the double doors swung open. Todd nodded to Derrick and Andrea as Tim glanced down the long hallway and saw Marla Kay standing at the nurses' station. Their eyes met just before the double doors closed. Tim looked back at the elevators just as the Raineses stepped inside and the doors closed behind them.

Todd stood. "I'm gonna go sit with mother. I don't want her alone when she wakes up."

Tim nodded.

"Are you coming?"

"No. We'll take turns," Tim said. "You're right. She doesn't need to wake up alone."

"If you go out, bring me back something to eat."

"Yeah, I will."

Tim watched as his brother hit the metal button and the doors swung open once again. Tim searched for Marla Kay, but she was gone. The doors closed, and Tim set the magazine he was holding back on the table just as two young teenagers stepped off the elevator. He knew them. They were one of the nurses' children. Memories came flooding back as he thought about all the visits he and Todd had made to the hospital growing up.

Soon an image of Jenna's pretty young face came into sight. She was older by two years, but he didn't care. She was fourteen at the time, and he was twelve. Her older sister had worked for his dad, and they were introduced. For an entire summer they had met for lunch, both dressed in hospital volunteer clothing. She was a candy striper, and she was beautiful with her long dark hair pulled back under her cap. Todd hadn't volunteered that summer, so there had been no competition like there generally was between them in junior high.

The young teenage girl laughed at something her brother said as they waited on their mom. Her laughter brought back a time when he and Jenna were running around playing hide and seek late one night after visitors' hours. She squealed with laughter when he caught her, and she ran down the hall and disappeared into a vacant room. He followed, but when he got to the door he looked both ways, he saw no one. He entered the room.

Jenna had bounced up on the bed and lay down. "Dr. Hart, I'm not feeling well. How about an exam?" The memory was so clear, as she began to unbutton her crisp white uniform.

He stepped forward and asked, "Where does it hurt?"

She picked up his hand, guided it to her chest, and placed it on her firm breast. He was shaking, and she had taken her other hand and placed it on top of his. "Do you feel my heartbeat? It's beating so fast! Kiss me." He took another timid step forward and leaned down and met her lips. Their first kiss was warm and soft, a memory that was so strong even to this day.

She had reached up and pulled him down on top of her. He complied. Just as he stretched his body out covering hers, the door swung open. They had been caught. Marla Kay yelled, "Get off my sister, Tim Hart! And stay the hell away from her!"

Tim eased back on the leather couch and covered his face with his hands at the memory. He was in love with her. Probably would always be in love with Jenna Abbott. Even after all these years and everything that had happened.

"Tim."

At the sound of Marla Kay's voice, he removed his hands from his face, opened his eyes, and found Jenna's sister once more.

"Marla Kay."

"I just wanted to say that I'm sorry. For everything. Please, allow me to say good-bye to your father." She sat down and grabbed his hand. "I want to come to the funeral tomorrow, please."

Tim stared into her dark green eyes. She looked so different now. Almost broken. After a moment, he pulled his hand away from hers. "I'll talk to my brother. Can't make you any promises, though."

She narrowed her eyes. "That's not fair. You've never corrected him. He thinks…"

"I know what he thinks." He stood and continued. "I said I would talk to him."

Tim broke eye contact and walked away.

Marla Kay could only sit and watch as he stepped onto the elevator and left.

***

Dr. Raines was five steps from the exit door when he heard his name and turned.

"Sorry, Dr. Raines," a nurse apologized as she jogged toward him.

"What do you have, Ms. Green?"

"Derrick, no!" he heard Andrea say from behind.

The nurse hesitated, but not for long once she saw the look on Dr. Raines' face. He was expecting an answer. "Chest pains and an elevated heart rate. You're needed in the ER."

"Start the IVs and monitor. I'll be there in two."

He quickly turned to face Andrea. "We're understaffed. William's gone, remember?" He saw the look of disgust appear on her face and turned away. After taking two steps, he suddenly stopped and turned around. "I'm sorry. That was insensitive. We both know how much he meant to you." He watched as color drained from her face and then turned and jogged off through the double doors to the ER.

Andrea watched in disbelief and covered her mouth at the realization that he knew; he knew all along. Frantically she stepped through the revolving door. Outside, she ran. Finding their Lincoln Navigator, she quickly hit the unlock button and stepped inside, slamming the door behind her. She hugged the steering wheel as tears poured through the floodgate and the guilt came charging back.

It had only been once, so many years ago—a mistake. She was so drunk. But was William? She honestly didn't know the answer to that. Shaking her head, she squinted her eyes shut. It didn't mean anything. It was a stupid, stupid mistake. Time slowed as Andrea held the wheel tight and tried to relax. After several minutes, she slowly pulled herself back together and asked herself, *How? How does Derrick know?* Suddenly she felt sick. *If Derrick knows, does Christa?*

"No. She couldn't possibly know. Could she?"

Finally Andrea pulled herself together enough to insert the key and fire up the engine to leave.

Chapter 22

Ronny Jordan pulled into a near empty parking lot driving his red 2002 Firebird. Girls, Girls, Girls wasn't as crowed at ten in the morning as it was around midnight. He locked his vehicle and his feet made crunching sounds as his large body crossed the gravel parking lot. Opening the front door, he was instantly greeted by Buzz, the daytime bouncer. Buzz had been given the name after Buzz Light Year, who he looked exactly alike.

"Little early for you. You coming to see some more action?" Buzz winked at Ronny.

Ronny chuckled. "Nah. Gotta see da boss. He still here?"

"Yep." Buzz held up a small radio and pressed a button. "Jordan's here to see the boss."

A moment passed before a voice answered and Buzz nodded. "Five minutes. Enjoy the show."

Ronny smiled and walked through another set of double doors. The familiar smoke and music greeted him and lights bounced around the ceiling and walls as three ladies up on stage did their thing. Ronny looked around and took a quick head count: six men and one woman seated around various tables. He turned toward the bar and found Julia pouring a shot for a middle-aged man wearing a suit. She smiled as she took his money.

"Ronny! What can I get you?"

"You."

She smiled and batted her eyes. Her blue silk blouse was tight and very low cut, revealing a nice rack. Julia was the only female on staff allowed to wear clothing if she chose to, which she always did. She had known the boss man since she was eight, when she had moved in next door to him. They had grown up together. When times got hard, he provided her a job—a well-paying job. Ronny always thought there was more to it but couldn't be sure.

"Unless da boss man wouldz kill me for asking?" he added.

She coyly replied, "Maybe, but he'll never know. I'll keep it our little secret."

She turned to remove a clean glass from the shelf and poured him a beer on tap. She handed it to him and then was off to wait on another customer. Ronny took his beer, wondered over to an empty table, and sat down. The girls had disappeared and the lights had dimmed. A new show was about to begin. Ronny heard whistles and clapping and looked around at the few customers. Music began, the lights brightened, and Ronny faced the front and got comfortable in his chair at the sight of one of his favorite dancers taking the stage.

Amber couldn't have been more than twenty, but she had moves that rocked the room as if she'd been doing it for years. Her long white legs waltzed across the stage to the music and she turned, releasing a clip from her long blond hair and shaking the long ringlets as they fell across her bare shoulders. Her tight red skirt was short, and her small top hugged her full chest. She saw Ronny and winked, and he felt a bolt of lightning shoot across his body.

She walked forward and stopped right in front of him. She turned with the music and bent over, removing her skirt in one swift move. Her G-string was red, matching her exotic outfit. Whistles went up once more as Ronny smiled and relaxed. She smoothly stood back up and then faced him once again, ripping off her top to expose her full, creamy white breasts. She rocked her hips and then covered her chest in a playful move. Ronny began sweating through his thin T-shirt. As if noticing, she smiled and spun around, rocking her hips and slowly touching her toes.

"Boss man will see you now."

Ronny jumped at Julia's voice. He turned to face her, and she laughed at his expression. "Down, boy. You're here to see the boss man, remember?"

Ronny stood up without commenting and turned once more to find Amber blowing him a kiss. He closed his eyes, shook his head, and walked toward the back room.

"Ronny! Have a seat."

Ronny stepped forward as a young brunette got up off the floor and pulled on a red silk robe. She walked by Ronny and winked, then closed the door behind her, leaving Ronny alone with the boss man.

The large white man, who everyone called Stone Wall, took a seat behind his desk and opened his large hands, showing that they were empty. "Got my money today, Ronny?"

Ronny put a hand in his pocket and retrieved several large bills rolled together. "Got haf. Should get da other haf tonight."

Stone Wall didn't smile. "Half? Why only half? Didn't the guy pay you on delivery?"

Ronny swallowed. "Not all of it. He promised to give da rest after he delivered the goods to da buyer."

Stone Wall looked shocked and started laughing. "You're shitting me, aren't you? Pulling my chain?"

Ronny felt beads of sweat forming again around his large frame. He had taken a chance with this new buyer because the deal was so large, bringing in more money for him, money that he desperately needed to pay some bills. Now, looking at Stone Wall, he no longer felt like his decision was a smart one. He had been wrong to give the goods without full payment.

"I see em at two, then I'll come straight over. I's promise."

Stone Wall's hand made a fist and then he slowly released his fingers and pointed at Ronny. "You made a mistake. You didn't follow the rules."

"Stone Wall, I's…"

He raised his hand for Ronny to stop speaking. He grabbed a pen and then a notebook. "Describe him."

"Um, white, skinny, young twenties."

"Name, hair, height."

"Goes by da name Bones. Um, black hair, 'round five eight."

"And where did you meet him again?"

"City lockup. He waz my cell mate for da week."

Stone Wall threw his pen at Ronny. "Better have my money, Ronny. If not…" He made a gesture of a gun pulling the trigger with his hand toward Ronny and smiled. "Welcome to the big leagues, Ronny. Sure hope you're man enough to play."

Ronny swallowed again and then stood. Carefully he turned, hoping a bullet wouldn't find the back of his skull. He grimaced as he took a step toward the door. Just as he placed a hand on the knob, he heard Stone Wall's voice and jumped.

"Your shift starts at three. I'll see you then."

Ronny relaxed his shoulder, opened the door, and left. Closing the door behind him, he leaned up against it and closed his eyes. If Bones failed to show, he had one hour to find him. Slowly he opened his eyes once more and pushed off the door. The noise suddenly hit his senses again as he looked around the room and noticed more people—the lunch crowd. Without giving any of the ladies a second thought, he took the side exit door and left.

***

Andrea Raines drove Derrick's black Lincoln Navigator through the open iron gates. The girls were home, and they hadn't thought to close it. *I need to speak to Donny and Michelle about that,* she thought. She pressed a button on her visor and watched as the gates closed. She pulled into the garage and shut the engine off, got out of the car, climbed the stairs, and opened the unlocked door.

"Unbelievable. Has everyone lost their minds? Mekenzie! Kimmy!"

No answer. Her heart missed a beat, and then panic began to set in. Running she found the staircase and climbed, yelling out once more, "Mekenzie, Kimmy! Girls!"

Reaching the top, she found an empty, quiet hallway. She ran toward Kimmy's room, the first one on the left, and peered inside. No one. Kimmy's overnight bag lay on her bed with clothing draped all around it. Andrea pushed off the doorframe and found Mekenzie's room. Empty also. Her overnight bag lay on the floor, and her bed looked like some-one had been jumping on it, with pillows tossed around and folds and lines in the comforter.

She turned and headed back down the hallway passing the guest suite, which was also empty. She looked back and found the double doors to the girls' game room closed. *Why is it so quiet?* she thought.

Taking another step she took a deep breath and pushed the doors open, finding her twelve- and fourteen-year-old dancing with headphones. Her breath caught, and she backed up against the wall at the sight of her girls safe and sound.

Mekenzie, the oldest, saw her first. She removed her headphones and took a step forward. "Mom, are you OK?"

Andrea closed her eyes and concentrated on breathing. Her girls were safe. No one had cut them up like William.

"I'm sorry, Mom. Were you calling for us?"

Andrea slowly opened her eyes and tried not to lose her composure. "Girls, the gate was open and the door was unlocked."

Kimmy ran forward and hugged her mom. "I'm sorry, Mom. We weren't thinking."

Mekenzie joined them, and they all three held each other. The embrace lasted a mere few seconds—far too short for Andrea. "Just...just be more cautious, please."

Kimmy tried to reassure her. "Yes. Promise, Mom."

"Have ya'll eaten?"

"Yes, ma'am. Mrs. Hughes stopped at a drive thru," responded Mekenzie.

Andrea cocked her head to the side and made a face. "And you ate it?"

Mekenzie, who was tiny, way too tiny for Andrea's liking, answered, "Yes. I was actually hungry for once."

"I didn't. I made a sandwich when we got home," added Kimmy.

"Oh, well. I'm going to take a hot bath and then lie down for a while. Holler if you need something."

"Mom?"

Andrea spun around and faced Mekenzie, who wore no makeup and had her hair pulled back into a ponytail. "Do we need to go tonight? Um, we talked it over. We would rather not."

She studied her two beautiful girls as they waited with unreadable expressions on their faces. *Should they?* She thought.

Kimmy interrupted her thoughts. "We plan to go tomorrow, Mom. Just not tonight. It's too creepy getting so close to his, um…his body."

Andrea nodded and closed her eyes and took a deep breath. She reached out and placed a hand on each of their arms. "No. Tomorrow's attendance will be enough. I'll make a call."

"Seriously, Mom? We're fine by ourselves," Mekenzie said in a voice she hoped wasn't sarcastic.

Andrea removed her hands and turned and left. She answered, "I'll think about it," from halfway down the hall.

Andrea checked the doors once more and then made her way into the master suite, located at the back of their large home on the main floor. She closed the bedroom door and stripped down as she walked into the master bath. She closed the drain and adjusted the water to the right temperature for a hot bath.

187

As she waited for the tub to fill, she collected her clothing and placed it in the large hamper. When she turned around, she caught sight of her bruised buttocks in the floor-length mirror and shook her head. *Why don't I remember falling so hard at the Hart house? It must have been an ugly fall.* She turned away, walked back toward the vanity, and opened a drawer.

She found a clip and a brush and quickly brushed her auburn hair and wrapped it up, securing it for her bath. Next she turned and stepped into her oversize garden tub and eased into the hot water. She lay back and closed her eyes. It had been a long day, too long. Christa had almost died, her girls had scared her, and her husband had divulged information he had been carrying around for years. *Damn,* she thought as she lifted and slightly hit her head against the tub.

It had been almost four years ago, and she had blocked it all out so well. She remembered how Christa had invited her over for an after work drink on a Friday. They were in the mood to celebrate after landing one of their biggest jobs yet. The housekeeper had made them a pitcher of frozen margaritas, and they took their first tall glasses out to the pool area. It was a warm summer night, and, after the third glass, they decided to go swimming. The twins were gone, William was at work as usual, the maid had left, and they thought nothing of stripping down to their underwear and taking a swim in the secluded backyard.

Eventually they ended up grabbing a bottle of wine and drinking together in the hot tub. That was the part that got all too fuzzy, and she couldn't remember anything past that point.

The next morning when she woke, she and William were lying beside one another naked in a bed in the guesthouse by the pool. She was mortified and quickly sat up. She had never blacked out from drinking before. Her movements woke William, and he just smiled at her and tried to pull her back down. Time began to speed up as she searched for her clothing and dressed. William didn't say anything. He just watched her, amused by her actions.

"Where is Christa?"

"In the house. I'm at the hospital, on call."

"I…I don't remember anything, William. This…this can't be happening."

"Andrea, calm down."

She shot him a look that could kill. "Calm down? No! This didn't happen!"

"Andrea."

Ignoring him, she turned and fled the guesthouse.

Andrea opened her eyes and stared at the ceiling, her mind lingering on his expression. He had looked truly hurt as she ran away. They had only talked about it once, on a Saturday afternoon two weeks after it happened. They had a heated argument, and she managed to avoid William for at least four months following the event. When they did see each other for the first time at a planned golf outing, he had ignored her. Funny thing was, when she returned home that night, she felt jealous. Derrick, who was in a really good mood after a nice, long day on the golf course, had treated Andrea like she was the only woman in the universe.

She shook her head. All along he knew. He knew! She closed her eyes, held her breath, and submerged her entire body under the water.

Chapter 23

Kelley Wells stood by her husband's side trying to concentrate on what the doctor was telling them.

"Stress. He needs to rest and avoid stress or the next time this happens, we might not be so lucky."

"Thank you, doctor. So, can I go home?"

Derrick Raines eyed Mr. Wells sharply. "No, sir. Sorry. I want to keep you overnight, run some more tests, and closely monitor you."

"Wha…what about tomorrow?"

Kelley Wells interrupted. "Henry, dear, listen to the doctor."

Derrick turned toward Henry Wells. "Your wife is right. You're not out of the woods yet. Rest. We'll look at your numbers again tomorrow and go from there."

Kelley squeezed her husband's hand and then leaned in to kiss him on the cheek and whisper in his ear. Derrick watched as Henry nodded and then began to settle back down in his bed.

"I will see you both in the morning. Excuse me."

"Thank you, Dr. Raines," Kelley said.

He nodded and walked out, closing the door behind him.

"Derrick?"

He looked up at the sound of her voice.

"We need to talk. Can you meet me later?"

His eyes found hers, and his heart missed a beat. He quickly looked around and saw no one. They were alone.

"I can. Twenty minutes?"

She nodded. "The usual," she said and then turned and headed back down the empty hallway.

***

Lilee sat outside on her back porch with Charli drinking beer and eating take-out. The girls had spent an hour chatting over coffee and then decided to spend the rest of the day at Lilee's place. The day was sunny, and the warm rays felt great as they both sat in short sleeves. Charli had shed her navy jacket and heels and had both of her long, sexy legs propped up on the coffee table with her navy skirt raised high on her thighs. "We so needed this!"

"No shit. Do you think Maggs will listen though and hire more people?"

Charli set her empty plate down and turned toward her friend. "I hope so, because my husband is starting to complain."

"Oh?"

192

"Yeah. The topic has come up too many times over the last two months."

Lilee took a swig of her beer. She'd had too many of those conversations with Landon. Relationships were hard anyway, and it didn't help having eighty-hour work weeks. "I'm sorry, Charli."

Charli picked up her beer. Rolling it around in both hands, she asked, "Do you ever think about kids and how we could possibly juggle them with our job? I mean, my mom was the best, and she always had time for me. I just...I just think I can't possibly give that to my own kids on this path I've taken."

Lilee took another swig and stared out across her backyard. She had asked herself that question too many times to count. If she had to be honest with herself, she was the one who drove Landon away. She could commit to marriage, but nothing else—at least, not yet. Landon said he would be patient, but his patience ran thin after too many long nights. Too many mornings had gone by with her leaving again before he even stirred. She looked at her friend. She was the last one to ask for advice.

Charli looked into Lilee's eyes and finally smirked. "We're a sad case sometimes, my friend."

Lilee shook her head. "Charli, you're twenty-six. You have your entire thirties to slow down and have babies."

She smiled. "Yeah, but it's my husband that needs me now."

Moments went by as Lilee pondered her statement. Thinking of Landon, she replied, "I know. I know what you mean."

Charli stood. "Well, you know what, I think I'm gonna surprise him at work. I...I haven't done that in...oh, I can't remember the last time."

"Good. That's smart, Charli." Lilee stood as well and collected the plates. Charli picked up her jacket and heels and the two empty beer bottles and followed Lilee back inside.

After they discarded the plates and trash, Lilee turned and saw her friend holding her purse, ready to leave. "Have fun at the office."

She gave a coy smile. "I will. Hey, what about dinner? Well, maybe tomorrow night would work better. Invite the good-looking detective, and we can all go downtown."

An image of Charli and Mark and her and Forest sitting together at a table with a bottle of wine and candlelight sharing an evening of laughter filled her mind. "I think I would like that very much, but, you know, check with Mark first before I ask Forest."

"Yeah. Good idea. He might have some business dinner. But hey, at least I will be able to attend for once."

Lilee walked over to the front door and opened it. "You and Mark are going to be just fine, Charli."

She walked outside and turned. "You really think so?"

Lilee forced a smile. "Absolutely. Now go, surprise your husband."

Charli smiled and literally bounced down the few steps to her sports car. As she cranked it up, she lowered the top, removed her hair clip, and yelled, "It feels good to cut loose in the middle of the day! Woo hoo!"

Lilee smiled and waved and then went back inside and closed the door—without locking it or setting the alarm.

Chapter 24

At 12:35 p.m., a nurse appeared with a chart to check Henry Wells' vitals once more. His wife sat by his side, patiently waiting for a report.

"All looks real good, Mr. Wells," said Becky with a smile.

"See there, Kelley? Now why don't you go and get something to eat. It's not good for you to be skipping meals like this."

Becky turned to Kelley and added, "Your husband's right. I'll keep an eye on him. Besides, I think he could use a nap as well."

Kelley nodded and the kind nurse squeezed her hand and left. Kelley leaned closely in to Henry's sweet face. "OK. I will leave. I'm gonna check with Doris and see if there's any news with Kenny."

Henry tensed, and she saw his brows crease. She quickly laid her hand on his forehead and whispered, "Everything's gonna be fine, Henry. We…we have to believe that and I…I can't lose you. Please try to stay calm and rest. Please."

He closed his eyes, and Kelley leaned in closer for a tender kiss. When she leaned back, he opened his eyes and nodded. She smiled and left without another word spoken.

Henry looked at the clock. His nurse probably wouldn't come back until closer to three, the end of her shift. Carefully he raised up and studied the IV attached to his hand—the only thing tying him to the hospital. Earlier they had removed the gadgets around his heart that attached to a machine, a machine that would have sounded an alarm if he had disconnected. He looked at the IV bag hanging on the metal stand. No alarm would sound if he removed the IV, which he quickly did, gritting his teeth as he pulled it out with his free hand.

Taking a deep breath, Henry eased both his legs over the side of the bed and gently stood, holding onto the railings for support. He stood for a full minute before making a step. *I feel better. I can do this*, he thought. Slowly he took a step and then another and let go of the steel railing. He opened the small closet, retrieved his clothing, and began to dress carefully. Ten minutes later, Henry Wells left the hospital undetected. He had a plan.

***

Eight miles from the hospital, Marla Kay's yellow sports car sat parked under a large oak tree in a secluded spot along a small, winding road at a large park. The twenty-five acres were popular with families on weekends, especially the large, open area and small pond. Walking trails and bike paths had been made for the city dwellers to enjoy the outdoors on.

Few cars traveled the long, narrow road that zigzagged through the park. Most families chose to park at the entrance by the play area and pond. On a weekday, one could park at any of the many hidden small parking lots throughout and not be noticed for a good hour or two.

Beside Marla Kay's car sat Derrick's dark, four-door BMW. The dark tint on its windows made it difficult for anyone driving by to notice whether it was vacant. Today it was occupied. At twelve forty-five, Marla Kay carefully lifted herself off of Derrick and onto the seat beside him. "I like your Navigator better; more room."

Derrick quickly pulled up his pants and raised the seat back to the forward position. "I know. Been a little crazy the last few days. Lots of car swapping."

His shirt remained folded neatly along the backseat. As he turned to get it, Marla Kay stopped him with her hand. "Wait. I want to talk."

"OK. We can do that with me dressed, though."

She searched his green eyes trying to read him. It was so hard. Marla Kay had learned over the last several years that there were several layers to Derrick Raines. Slowly she had peeled back all of them to the point where she finally felt like she knew him. He was ambitious, a great surgeon and friend, and loyal to his children and wife, until he made a move toward her, changing their friendship into an affair.

She had changed him, and it wasn't for the best. She had finally come to realize that over the last few days. The Derrick Raines she met eight years earlier when they were just friends, best of friends, was now different. If she was to be honest with herself, she was the reason he'd changed.

Marla Kay watched as he dressed and then turned back toward her and gestured for her to continue.

"What are we doing? We've been sleeping together for over three years now, ever since…"

"I found out my wife slept with my colleague," he interrupted.

Marla Kay touched his hand. "William Hart was more than just a colleague. He was our friend."

Derrick smirked as he shook his head and pulled his hand away. "I don't know how you can still call him a friend after everything he put you through."

"It wasn't entirely his fault. We were put in a difficult position."

"Yes. I guess you were. But it doesn't compare to having a one-night stand with my wife."

Marla Kay reached out and put a hand on his face, tracing his lips with her finger. "Why are you still with her, if what we have is so great?"

Derrick looked away from her dark green eyes and faced the thick shrubs and trees in front of his car. He had asked himself the same question over and over. Why was it he couldn't walk out on Andrea? Besides his daughters, what was it that kept him staying in a marriage that was full of betrayal?

He turned back toward Marla Kay. He had so willingly given her up to the detectives. Yes, the rumors were there, but he didn't have to do what he did. Why then? Whether or not he wanted to admit it, he was still so very angry with William Hart for sleeping with his wife. So he dangled Marla Kay's name to bring shame to William Hart's legacy. Derrick was a coward. He should have confronted William years ago, but he hadn't. He'd just pretended, along with his wife, that it never happened.

Marla Kay's dark hair had fallen from her clip and hung loosely over her bare shoulders. Her olive skin was so smooth and young. He touched her neck and slowly lowered his hand, caressing her body playfully. When he ran a finger under her black silk bra, she closed her eyes and inhaled. "Derrick, don't. We need to talk about…"

He reached up and grabbed her with his free hand and pulled her onto him once more. She stopped talking as he removed her bra and pulled it swiftly away from her body. Her hand found his shirt and quickly pulled it back off, ripping one of the buttons. He lowered his seat once more. No more questions were asked and no clear answers given.

Chapter 25

A hand raised and knocked twice. A voice answered. Soon the door swung open to reveal a lovely older woman wearing black slacks and a green silk blouse standing and filing papers in a silver metal file cabinet.

"Marilynn. Come in dear, and close the door."

Timidly she stepped forward in her corduroy skirt and short-sleeve sweater. Today, students were allowed to wear a school-appropriate outfit if they donated one dollar to charity.

"You look nice, Marilynn."

"Thank you, Ms. Jones."

The petite lady with grayish blond hair smiled. "It's nice to leave the uniform at home for one day, isn't it?"

"Yes, ma'am."

"Well, it was a good idea, Marilynn. The honor society has raised four thousand dollars so far, and that's not counting contributions coming in from the outside."

Marilynn smiled and blushed slightly. "Thank you, Ms. Jones. But it wasn't totally my idea. Other schools have done the same thing around the country."

"Well, that might be, but you were the one to convince the principal to move forward, a task we both know can be difficult. Now, take a seat and tell me what's on your mind."

Marilynn dropped her purse on the floor and took the offered seat. She searched for the right words but for some reason couldn't form a complete sentence in her head.

Beverly Jones set a file down, walked around her desk, and quickly sat down. When Marilynn hesitated, she began to worry and asked in a concerned voice, "Is everything OK, Marilynn?"

Marilynn saw the look and concern and closed her eyes. She opened them and smiled with a little laugh. "I'm not pregnant, Ms. Jones. Relax!"

Beverly opened her mouth and quickly closed it. Her face flushed and then she patted her hair around her clip and smiled.

"Ms. Jones, it does concern my boyfriend though."

"Oh?"

Marilynn forced a smile. Ms. Jones knew Johnny Rae and wasn't pleased when he dropped out of school. She had cautioned Marilynn about her choices and sticking with the plan. Graduation was just around the corner. "Johnny Rae would like to take his GED."

Instant relief washed over Beverly's face, and a genuine smile appeared. "That's the best news I've heard all day, Marilynn! It even trumps the money we raised."

It was Marilynn's turn to smile and blush. "Yeah, it does, doesn't it?"

Quickly Ms. Jones stood and walked over to grab a stapled handout out of a clear holder mounted to the wall. She talked as she walked back over and sat on the corner of her desk, right in front of Marilynn. "Now, this handout has all the information with step-by-step instructions. Also, the fee can be waived by the school. I'll just fill out a sheet of paper when you return the handout complete and attach it and put it in the mail. Simple as that."

"Thanks, Ms. Jones," Marilynn said, taking the handout and standing. "I need to get going. I got an exam next period, and I want to look over my notes once more."

Ms. Jones nodded. "OK then, I'll see you at the meeting later on."

As Marilynn turned and walked toward the door, she stopped when she heard Ms. Jones speak once more.

"Marilynn, make sure Johnny Rae is the one to fill out those papers. You can help, but it's important for him to take that step."

Marilynn turned and the kind woman stepped forward. "The chances will be higher for him to show up for the test, if he completes it himself."

Marilynn nodded. She understood. She left without another word spoken, closing the door behind her.

***

Five blocks from the high school, two miles from the hospital, and ten miles from the park, City Hall bustled with people on a Monday afternoon. The parking lot across the street was full as people wearing suits and ties plotted, planned, and tossed ideas around for the week's agenda in the building across the street. Business as usual. On the fourth floor, Daniel Maggs, the well-thought-of, popular district attorney, sat at his desk and combed over an open file, unaware of the man sitting in a pickup, filled with rage and revenge, staring through his back windshield at his office window.

The man turned, opened his glove box, and removed the bullets. Taking the hunting rifle off the back windshield, he set it in his lap and began loading the high-powered chunk of solid lead. The district attorney and his team had failed—miserably. Now, the time had come to settle the score. Picking up a pair of camouflage binoculars, he turned back around and found Maggs through their small lens.

Maggs lifted the phone and held it to his face. "What? No. Too low." A moment passed and then he yelled, "Just get it done, alright?"

He slammed the phone down and heard a tap at his closed door. "Come in."

Maggs stood as the door opened to reveal Wes Schultz. "I got that file. It wasn't easy, but they folded."

Maggs took the folder, opened it, and began to read. Schultz's phone vibrated in his coat pocket. "Gotta take it. Excuse me."

Maggs waved a hand but kept reading as Schultz carried on a conversation on the other side of the room. When he heard Schultz call his name, he put a finger on a sentence and looked up.

"That's the court. Bail arraignment is set at two thirty for Kenny Wells."

Maggs asked, "What took so long?"

"Busy day. Look I better get on down there. Looks like the Wells family has accepted help from Andy Kane."

Maggs closed the folder and slid it across his desk. "Great. The family can no longer trust us, but they trust the likes of Andy Kane. Unbelievable!"

"Yeah. Look, I'm clear at four. We can meet back then."

Maggs said, "Make it four thirty." Then he turned and walked toward his glass window as Schultz left the room. The day had turned nice with blue skies, the complete opposite of the rain shower and fog from earlier that morning. He looked down at the sidewalk below and saw one of his staff members check the street and then run across the road, down a sidewalk, and into a coffee shop. "I think I could use a latte."

He smiled. He had promised his wife that he would cut back on the caffeine after lunch. Lately he had trouble sleeping, and his wife had blamed it all on the caffeine. He knew different, though. It was the Wells case that had kept him up for the last few days. On top of that, it was too much work to do, and he was carrying too much of it home. *Charli was right,* he thought. *We are understaffed.*

He reached into his pocket to retrieve his cell phone to call Linda and make his coffee request. He smirked at the thought of her expression when he asked her to place an order for him as well. She would think Maggs truly did have eyes and ears everywhere, just like the rumors he was well aware of that floated around the office.

The man in the old pickup saw the smirk through the scope and frowned. "Time to die, you bastard," he said and pulled the trigger. Maggs vanished from the window. The man lowered the rifle and closed the back glass. Settling back into the seat, he put the truck in first gear and pulled forward, took a sharp right, and was soon out of the parking lot. He lowered his cap as he quickly pulled away. People had hunched down panicked at the sound of the piercing noise. By the time security came out of City Hall, he was out of sight one block away, speeding toward the nearby exit to the interstate.

After traveling five miles on the interstate, he exited and pulled into a busy twenty-four-hour truck stop. He quickly got out of the truck leaving the rifle, keys, and no prints. Walking across the parking lot, he reached into his pocket and retrieved his keys. Unlocking the car, he got in and sped away.

Chapter 26

Forest was sitting in his office only two blocks away when he heard that a shot had been fired at City Hall. He immediately jumped up from his desk, ran out of his office and down the hall, and took the stairs. It only took five minutes for Forest to arrive at his uncle's office, which was surrounded by policemen.

"Where is he?"

Officer Carter turned away from another officer and looked at Forest. "Inside. He's fine; just shaken up."

Forest pushed through and found Maggs sitting at his desk with his head in his hands.

"Daniel!" Forest jogged over and placed a hand on his shoulder and knelt to look at him at eye level. In a tender voice, he asked, "What happened?"

Maggs looked up at Forest and opened his mouth to speak, but no words formed. Forest leaned closer. "It's gonna be alright. You're alive, thank God."

"Forest, I...I dropped my phone and...and I bent over. All I remember is glass shattering to pieces around me."

Forest noticed his jacket had been removed, and he had one small cut on his forehead, probably from the glass. He looked over toward the window and grimaced. "Who the hell did this?"

"Detective Styles."

Forest squeezed Maggs' shoulder and stood to face Officer Carter. "What do you have?" he asked as he walked toward him.

"Security camera picked up an old blue Ford pickup tearing out of the parking lot across the street at the time of the shot."

"Good. What else?"

"Got two witnesses who claim the driver was a male wearing a dark long-sleeve shirt and a hunting cap."

Forrest commanded, "Put out an alert, and get the photos circulated from the security cameras."

"Already on it. Photo will be transmitted within five minutes to every officer within fifty miles of here."

"Good job!" Forest turned and walked back toward Maggs. "I need your gut feeling here, Daniel. Who do we look at first? And then your top five."

Maggs looked around the room at the officers at work. One snapped pictures of the window, and men were carrying on with each other and writing things down. "I...I can't think. I..."

"Maggs! Are you OK?" Wes Schultz asked, running into the office. Forest took a step to give them some room. A quick emotional exchange was made and then Forest interrupted. "Wes, who did this? Who are we looking at?"

Schultz spun around and faced Forest. "I…I would look at Henry Wells first."

Maggs started to protest. "He had a heart attack this morning. I don't think…"

"What's he talking about?" Forest asked, staring at Schultz for an answer.

"This morning Henry Wells was in here, tearing up the place and screaming accusations. He was very upset about his grandson being arrested, and then he collapsed."

"But he had a heart attack. He couldn't have done this!" Maggs stood too quickly and lost his balance. Schultz grabbed him and gently pushed him back into his chair.

"Daniel, I talked to the hospital earlier. He didn't have a heart attack. He's fine."

"What? Why didn't someone tell me this?"

"I'm sorry," Schultz said. "I thought someone had told you."

Forest asked, "What hospital is he at?"

"General."

"Officer Carter, call General and see if Henry Wells is still a patient. I want a visual on the man, not just looking at his name on a computer screen."

"Yes, sir."

Forest looked back at Schultz and Maggs and then asked, "Wes, who else do we need to be looking at?"

He rubbed his face quickly and then took a pen and paper off the desk and began writing down names. When he was done, he shoved the list at Forest. "Start with these."

"Officer Brown," Forest said, "get this list out, and I want confirmation on the whereabouts of all city prosecutors."

Brown walked away from another officer toward Forest and took the list. Forest watched him leave and then looked back at Maggs. "Where's Lilee?"

"I don't know. I sent her and Charli Pepper home till Wednesday," Maggs said with a worried expression.

"Detective Styles."

Forest turned to the door and saw Officer Carter. "Sir, Henry Wells is missing from the hospital. The last he was seen was at twelve thirty, when a nurse made her rounds."

"Shit. People, we need to find Lilee Parker and Charli Pepper now!"

Officer Carter picked up his radio and began speaking. Forest turned away and looked back toward Maggs. "I'm going to find Lilee. Are you OK? Has Marge been called?"

He nodded. "She was at the mall. She's already been picked up by an officer."

"Good," Forest said, squeezing his shoulder once more before he left.

***

Lilee was running in the grass along the empty street that ran through her neighborhood. It was quiet with few cars passing by. She had chosen the neighborhood because the houses were on large blocks of land and the neighbors weren't so close. There were no community parks or sidewalks, just homes with white fences and a few horses. In total, there were only about twenty homes. She smiled as she passed a horse standing along the fence watching her. She felt free and at peace.

She couldn't believe she had the day off and was running during normal business hours on a clear, sunny day. After last night with Forest, she felt a renewed spirit that made her feel alive. Yes, her life with Landon was officially over. She smiled again. It was because of Forest; he made her smile. *Took you long enough, Lilee Parker,* she told herself. *Long time coming.* She picked up her pace and started the last mile stretch. This mile was her favorite. There were only two homes on this stretch, and white fences, dogwoods, oaks, and magnolias filled the narrow lane. It was calm and peaceful.

She continued on past the sharp turn that led into thick shrubs and trees. The land hadn't been sold yet, so no trees had been cleared for new homes. Suddenly a cloud rolled over the sun, and the branches and leaves began to move as she felt a light wind. *Soon the leaves will fall and all would look bare through winter,* she thought. Lilee felt another gust of wind and looked up at the sky. *So much for the sunshine.* Suddenly she felt a chill run down her back as she watched the leaves shake and the tree limbs sway. She felt spooked. As if Forest was standing right beside her, she clearly heard him say, "Don't take chances, Lilee."

She stopped dead in her tracks as she heard a noise. She turned and realized she had drifted into the road as she'd rounded the sharp turn. Realizing it was the sound of a car, she ran toward the trees. Feeling slightly paranoid, she ran further and ducked inside the brush just as a dark vehicle rounded the corner, passed her by, and continued on.

She stood there for a moment. "Oh my gosh, Lilee. You're losing it!" She took a step forward but stopped again. Still feeling a chill, she unwrapped her windbreaker from around her waist and pulled it on. Just as she put her hands in her pockets, she felt her phone vibrate. She pulled it out and saw a message, "Ten Missed Calls," across the small screen. She moved her finger across the screen, unlocking her phone. She pressed her call log and saw Forest's name appear last. She pressed the screen.

"Lilee, where are you?"

Something about the tone in his voice scared her as she eased closer to the trees further away from the car that had passed by earlier. She clutched the phone tighter as she spoke. "I'm home. Um, well, running. By my home."

"Where exactly, Lilee?"

She looked around frantically. She was alone, right? There was no one in these woods. She backed away from the trees and muttered, "Um, in the bushes."

"How far, Lilee, from the house?"

"You're scaring me!"

She heard a noise and jumped as she realized a car was coming from behind. She turned and then froze when she saw who was driving the car.

Chapter 27

For the rest of the day Marilynn continued on with her classes, took her exam, and met back with Ms. Jones during activity period, the last class of the day. Praises were passed around for their fundraiser success and new plans were created as Ms. Jones presided over the Honor Society Club. Soon the bell rang and everyone jumped up saying their good-byes.

Marilynn, deep in thought, had only heard half of the conversation discussed among the twelve members and Ms. Jones. Suddenly Marilynn found herself alone with Ms. Jones speaking.

"What do you think, Marilynn?"

Marilynn looked up and saw Ms. Jones stacking handouts together and straightening up the room.

"I'm sorry, Ms. Jones. What did you say?"

Beverly Jones turned around and set the handouts down. "What's on your mind, Marilynn? Did you do well on your exam?"

She smiled. "Yes, ma'am. I'm sure I made an A. I only struggled with one of the questions."

Beverly smiled. "What class?"

"Calculus."

"Very good, Marilynn. So if it's not a math exam on your mind, what is it? Johnny Rae's GED?"

Marilynn lied. "Yes, ma'am. Sorry. I'm just a little distracted and excited about his big decision."

Beverly nodded. "I understand. When you see him, tell him I said hello and not to be a stranger. I'll do all I can, Marilynn, to help him."

"Yes, ma'am. Thank you. Um, I need to get going. Thanks for the papers, and I hope to bring them back tomorrow, completed."

"Good. See you tomorrow."

Marilynn picked her heavy backpack up off the floor and grabbed her purse. She didn't need to go to her locker. She had everything already, so she opened the exit door leading to the student parking lot. Finding her car, she inserted the key and unlocked it. Climbing in behind the wheel, she paused before starting the engine. *What is it?* she thought. *Why can't I shake this feeling that something bad is gonna happen to Johnny Rae?* She gripped the steering wheel tighter. These last few months had been hard on Johnny Rae, and he seemed distant since the trial had ended. Finally, after more thought, she shook her head and turned the switch. Nothing.

"Damn it! This is the last thing I need." Looking around the dash, she noticed that her headlight button was still pulled. Closing her eyes, she realized she had failed to push it back in to turn her lights off. It was raining that morning, and she had used her headlights. "Damn! Not a good time for a dead battery."

She looked around the near-empty parking lot and then got out of her old car, wishing it was a newer model that dinged when you left your lights on. Scanning the area, she saw a group of guys standing around a pickup. *Surely one of them will have a jumper cable*, she thought. She took two steps and stopped. *Not a good idea, Marilynn*, she thought. *Those boys are trouble.*

Quickly she turned around and headed back toward the building in search of security. Being an extra fifteen minutes late to meet Johnny Rae would be worth it. She smiled. Book smart was only part of it. Street smart was much more important where she came from.

***

Dr. Raines had been paged, and he was angry. He had called earlier to inform Andrea that Christa had woken up, and he was on his way home. They would go to the hospital together and then on to the visiting hours at the funeral home for William Hart. Now he was going back to the hospital alone, and he wasn't going to be able to get a shower before the service.

Thinking of Marla Kay, he shook his head and decided that a quick five-minute shower at the hospital was needed. Even though Andrea had hurt him, he never wanted her to find out about Marla Kay. Thoughts of Andrea hugging him closely that night for support made him cringe with the thought she would be able to smell Marla Kay's perfume. Looking down, he ran a hand over his shirt. He had lost a button.

"Damn it!" he cussed aloud as he sped into the hospital parking lot. He was probably more mad that no one had given him any information over the phone, other than "It concerns Henry Wells," his last patient of the day. He had been practicing medicine for a long time, and there was never time for doubt or second-guessing, just no room for it if you wanted to be the best. Still he began to run through a checklist in his head of all the steps of the procedures he had performed that day. He got out of his car, finally satisfied he hadn't missed anything or made an error in judgment.

He walked quickly into the hospital and immediately stepped onto the elevator to go straight to the doctors' lounge. He opened his locker, discarded his clothing, grabbed a pair of scrubs, and headed toward the showers. The shower took three minutes, not five. Seven minutes later he walked out wearing fresh scrubs and a white coat, stepped onto the elevator once more, and pressed level five.

When the doors opened, an officer and Dr. Jerry Thomas immediately greeted him.

"Gentlemen, what's this about?"

Dr. Thomas spoke first. "Henry Wells is missing, and he's a key suspect in an ongoing investigation."

Derrick relaxed. This he could deal with. "OK, gentlemen. What can I do?"

"I'm Officer Carter," the officer said extending his hand. Derrick shook it.

"We wanted to hear from you about Mr. Wells' state of mind when you last saw him."

Derrick placed his hands on his hips and thought for a moment before answering. "Anxious. Wanting to go home. He clearly didn't want to be here."

"Did he give you any indication that he was going to leave without your consent?"

"You mean like sneak out of here? No, he didn't."

Derrick turned to Dr. Thomas. "Jerry, how does this concern you?"

Officer Carter said, "Well, I guess that answers that question."

Derrick looked at the officer, but Dr. Thomas answered, "Henry Wells came and saw me a month ago. He has stage four cancer, inoperable."

Suddenly it was like a stack of bricks crashed upon his chest. As a doctor, he never could get used to those few words. "Damn. Cancer. He didn't say."

"No, he wouldn't. He didn't want anyone to know."

Officer Carter looked confused. "How could you not know about the cancer? I mean, wasn't it in his chart or…"

Derrick smiled and tilted his head. He let a moment pass and then answered. "He came in through the ER. The only information we had was from his wife, and yes, there were some numbers that didn't look right, and that's why I didn't release him. I had ordered more tests."

Dr. Thomas added, "All the information would have come to light by the end of the day. Sometimes it takes a little longer for the paperwork to catch up, but it does."

Derrick looked at the other doctor and then back to the officer. "Does his wife know?"

"We haven't said anything to her about the cancer, but she has been notified that he left the hospital without permission."

Derrick nodded and turned toward Dr. Thomas. "How long does Mr. Wells have?"

"A month ago, three to five months," Dr. Thomas stated with a frown.

Officer Carter spoke. "Thank you, gentlemen. I won't take any more of your time. If he does come back, treat him with caution and contact us immediately."

"We will," replied Dr. Thomas.

Derrick watched as the officer left and then turned back toward Jerry, who was already apologizing. "I'm sorry, Derrick, to drag you back in here."

Derrick forced a smile. "Don't be. But I do need to get home and get Andrea for William's service."

"Of course. Give my best to his sons. I'm on call tonight."

Derrick nodded and left.

Chapter 28

The black Mustang rounded the corner fast and came to an abrupt halt, and Detective Forest Styles jumped out and ran toward Lilee. "Are you OK?"

Lilee was still clutching her phone tightly and searching the area around her. Finally she answered, "Yes. Now tell me what's going on, damn it!"

Forest reached out and hugged her and then began leading her to his car. "I will, but we need to get out of here."

Lilee allowed herself to be led to the car and gently pushed inside, and then Forest ran around to the driver's side. He quickly got in and shifted into first gear. Without further explanation, Forest looked both ways and then did a three sixty, pulling into the grass and taking Lilee in the opposite direction from her home.

"Wait! Why aren't we going home?"

"Sorry, but we haven't secured it." Forest's phone rang and he added, "Excuse me, but I have to take this."

Lilee just watched in disbelief as he pulled out his cell phone as they drove further away from her home. As he talked she looked down at her legs and realized she was shaking. She had chosen shorts for her run, and now, with the weather changing and the unexplained events, she was cold.

She looked back at Forest and heard the words "cancer" and "time bomb." She noticed how his body tensed and he seemed worried. When Forest slowed down, she looked up ahead and saw an oncoming police car with sirens. Forest eased to the shoulder as the police car did the same and then turned off its sirens. Forest ended his call and turned to Lilee.

"I'm sorry to frighten you like that. Look, a lot has happened today. A shot was fired at Maggs, but he's fine."

"Wh…what? When did this happen?"

"Earlier this afternoon. Everyone in your office had been accounted for except you. I was worried that something had…"

She reached out and touched his arm. "I'm right here. I'm fine."

He forced a smile and placed a hand on top of hers. A moment passed as they looked into each other's eyes. Finally he said, "Henry Wells left the hospital, and he's missing."

An odd laugh emerged from Lilee's lips. "You suspect Henry Wells?"

Forest studied her face and then met her green eyes once more. "Henry has cancer. He doesn't have long to live."

Lilee grabbed her chest and shook her head. "That poor family; his wife. But Forest, I don't think Henry has it in him to kill anyone. I mean, he might be angry, but taking a life…no. I don't think it was him."

Forest sighed. "Stay here. I need to talk to the officer."

Lilee didn't respond as he left, shutting the door behind him. Forest took a few steps, looking around at his surroundings as he spoke. She watched his body language as they exchanged words; he was tense and on edge. Finally he nodded and then turned back toward her and climbed in the car.

"Officer Johnson is going to your place to check things out. I will feel better if you let me take you to Charli Pepper's house. It's secure, and we have a unit there."

Feeling she had no choice, she agreed. Forest placed a hand on hers and then leaned in and kissed her tenderly. When he pulled away, he said, "I'm sorry. We have to move."

Lilee leaned forward, kissed him back quickly on the lips, and then pulled away an inch and whispered, "Fine. But I want to stay with you tonight."

Forest smiled. "I wouldn't have it any other way."

***

At 3:45, Ronny Jordan arrived home in a panic. Bones hadn't showed up with the money. He paced back and forth, running a hand over his head and mumbling under his breath. Johnny Rae walked out of his small bedroom and found his brother.

"What's wrong?"

Ronny turned. He'd thought he was home alone. He shook his head and continued to pace with both hands on his head.

"Bro, what now?"

Ronny stopped and faced his younger brother. "I…I screwed up."

Johnny Rae's face drained of color. This was bad. His whole life, he'd never heard his brother utter those words. Something was wrong, bad wrong.

"Wherz Momma and da baby?"

Johnny Rae stepped closer to his brother and responded, "Buying groceries."

Ronny stared hard into the face of his brother, who was almost his height. Johnny Rae had given up high school to get a job when he had landed in the cell. Now, he had let him down once more. Shame washed over Ronny, and he turned away.

"What can I do to help?"

Ronny's shoulder's sagged and he bowed his head at his brother's words. He felt Johnny Rae's hand on his shoulder and turned back around and embraced him. He held tight to him and whispered, "I's gotz ta go away again. I…I's sorry."

Johnny Rae pushed away and jerked his brother's shoulders as he grabbed him and shook him hard. "What do you mean, go away?"

Ronny's eyes grew moist. "I gotz ta, bro. It won't be safe with me here."

"What the hell you do?"

Ronny shook his head. "I's sorry."

"Sorry! You're sorry? You put Momma and Junior in danger, and you're sorry!"

"I…I's didn't…"

"What did you do, damn it?"

Silence. Then Johnny Rae turned mean. "Tell me, or I'll kill you myself!"

Ronny saw the fire in his brother's eyes. He knew he didn't mean the words; he was just so hurt and angry at him. "I's made a run and gotz no pay. I can't find da dude for da cash. They come for me now."

Johnny Rae staggered backward. "You didn't. How could you! You promised us, no drugs, never!"

"Johnny Rae, I's…"

Johnny Rae punched his brother away. "No. You preached and preached to me, and then you do this! Get out! Get out of here, and don't come back. I never want to see you again!"

The words stung as they hit Ronny with the full force of another punch. He had nothing more he could say. Johnny Rae was right. He had been a terrible role model for his younger brother. Shame filled him once again, and he quickly turned away once more.

Outside a car pulled along the street and the engine was cut. The man stared out the window at the small frame house contemplating his next move. He was tired. The cancer was slowly eating him alive. Henry Wells touched his gun. He wanted justice. A man had beat his wife and left her for dead. His grandson was locked up, and he was dying while Ronny Jordan walked the streets a free man. Henry felt a tear roll down his cheek as he loaded his gun.

Inside, Ronny was shoving clothing into a bag while Johnny Rae watched from an open doorway. Neither spoke. When Ronny zipped the bag, he turned around and faced his brother once again.

"I's sorry. I's never meant to let you down."

Johnny Rae didn't respond as he eased away from the doorframe and walked to his room, slamming the door. Ronny took a deep breath and then picked up his bag and walked back into the small living room. He wanted to leave a note for him momma, but time was not on his side. The longer he stayed, the more danger his family was in. Besides, what could he possibly say in a note that would make his momma understand? He shook his head as he gripped his bag tighter and headed for the front door.

As Ronny grabbed the small antique doorknob, he looked around once more. Ronny Junior's toys lay in the corner along with one of his blankets. He took his hand off the door, walked over to the blanket, and picked it up. He brought the blanket to his nose and inhaled. It smelled of him. Finally, after a moment, he opened his eyes and dropped it back to the floor. Quickly he turned and walked four giant steps to the front door, opened it, and stepped outside, closing it behind him.

Henry Wells watched as the front door open and revealed Ronny Jordan. Slowly he lifted his gun and aimed as Ronny walked over to his red Firebird. With shaky hands he watched as Ronny turned his back and popped his trunk, throwing his bag inside. He took a breath and then prepared to squeeze the trigger. Suddenly a car sped by at lightning speed and slowed just a moment, long enough for a person to unload several rounds of an automatic into the back of Ronny Jordan. Speechless, he watched as the young man who had beaten his wife fell to the ground dead.

Henry dropped his loaded gun and stared ahead at the dark four-door Lincoln as it quickly disappeared around a corner. He heard screaming from his left and turned. A younger man was running down the steps, yelling Ronny's name. Henry fumbled at the keys in the ignition as he tried to crank his vehicle.

Just as the engine turned, another car drove past and pulled into the gravel driveway. The young girl driving the old Oldsmobile turned and saw him. Panicked, he forced the car into gear and mashed the gas pedal, spinning gravel as he drove away.

Marilynn jumped out of her car and ran to Johnny Rae, who was on the ground cradling his brother.

"No! Ronny, no! I didn't mean it. I'm sorry. I don't want you to go!"

Marilynn watched as the blood continued to pour out of Ronny. There was no hope. Johnny Rae was holding his stomach trying to stop the bleeding, but it was no use. Ronny was dying. Too many bullet wounds and too much blood loss. Slowly he closed his eyes and faded away. Marilynn reached out toward Johnny Rae, but he wouldn't let go of his brother. Tears filled her eyes as she sat helpless, watching the love of her life scream out in pain.

Soon they heard policemen running toward them yelling with guns in the air. Marilynn rocked back onto her bottom and held her hands in the air. "I saw who did it. It was an old man driving a brown four-door car."

The officer carefully lowered his gun and helped Marilynn to her feet. "I need you to come with me, please."

Marilynn turned back just in time to see Johnny Rae push away an officer. "No. Don't touch him! Leave us!"

The officer took a step back and faced Marilynn. She pleaded with her eyes for him to give Johnny Rae some space. The officer shook his head and threw his hands up in the air in disgust. Next he got out a notepad. "OK, miss, what's your name and what exactly did you see?"

Chapter 29

Trevor Watts drove the sedan as Forest rode shotgun to the funeral home. The captain had advised them to continue on with the Hart case. Now that a witness had placed Henry Wells at the home of Ronny Jordan, it appeared Henry Wells was indeed their man. The only thing puzzling at the moment was the inconsistency with the automobiles. A blue truck had been seen at Maggs' office, not the four-door car that was spotted outside the Jordan home registered to Henry Wells.

Forest raked a hand through his hair and tried to relax. Every lawman had been alerted to Henry Wells' brown Chrysler and the blue Ford. He had just spoken to Lilee, and she was still safely tucked away at the Pepper home under police watch.

"Rough day. You gonna make it tonight?"

Forest looked at his partner. "Yeah. I'll feel better once we get our hands on Henry Wells and that blue truck."

He chuckled. "Yeah, me too."

Trevor pulled into the funeral home and found a parking spot. Together they got out and scanned the parking lot to wait and watch.

Inside, Tim and Todd Hart were dressed in black suits and standing by an open casket greeting visitors when Derrick and Andrea arrived a little after six. A long line of mourners had turned out to show their respect to a gifted surgeon, father, husband, and friend. Derrick looked around and found people engaged in small talk as everyone inched forward slowly. Andrea, as expected, was holding his arm tight. She hated funerals. Ever since the passing of her parents, they had been extra hard on her. He reached out and embraced her arm with his free hand. She looked up and smiled.

A few minutes turned into thirty, forty-five, and then an hour before Derrick and Andrea made their way over to Tim and Todd. Andrea didn't shake hands. She reached out and gave each a tight, long hug.

"Your father loved you two very much. I'm...I'm so very sorry for your loss. If there's anything we can do, please, please just call."

Derrick shook each of their hands. "My wife is right. Please let us know if there's anything you need. Day or night, we're just a phone call away."

Todd spoke. "Thank you, Derrick, Andrea. Both of you meant a lot to our parents. Um, still do...to, um, my mom."

Andrea smiled and nodded. "Yes. Christa means the world to me too. I will be right by her side, every step of the way."

Tim reached out and gave Andrea another hug. "We appreciate that so much. It's going to be a long road."

Andrea squeezed him tight and then gradually pulled back. She touched his sweet face and then turned and made another step toward the open coffin. Derrick watched her and took a step as well. Then he placed one of his arms under her arm for support.

She whispered, "He's gone."

She reached out and placed a hand on his chest and then quickly jerked it away. She grabbed Derrick's arm for support and took a deep breath.

226

Derrick remained silent. He had no words. Carefully he stepped back and guided his wife away.

Forest and Trevor were still watching the crowd when they saw the Raineses exit. Forest nodded politely and watched them carefully as they left.

"Lots of people here tonight," Trevor remarked. "Do you think our guy is here?"

Forest turned and looked up at Trevor. "I don't know. Maybe. My gut isn't telling me anything."

Trevor smirked. "My gut instinct ended ten years ago. I think it's tired and ready for me to retire."

Forest didn't answer as he studied the crowd and watched the exchanges between the guests and the twins. "I don't know, but there's something about Tim and Todd. But I don't think they were involved."

"Oh?"

"Yeah. Don't know why, but there's something else going on here. We aren't seeing it."

"Oh, is that why we don't have an arrest yet?" Trevor asked.

Forest peeled his eyes off the twins, looked at his partner again, and smiled. Another officer walked over and interrupted. "Detective Styles."

Forest turned. "Yeah. What's up?"

"Just wanted you to know they found Henry Wells' car abandoned at a park."

"Where?"

"About fifteen miles away from Ronny Jordan's house. No sign of Wells, but there was a note."

"What kind of note?"

"Looks to be a suicide note. They're searching the area now."

Trevor looked at his watch and asked, "How long ago was this?"

"Ten minutes at the most. I wanted to inform you right away, with Mr. Maggs being your uncle and all."

Forest nodded. "Thank you for that. Find an automatic weapon?"

"No sir, but there's more, sir."

Forest nodded. "Go on."

"A pickup matching the description of the one spotted at City Hall was found outside a twenty-four-hour truck stop, just a few miles from downtown. The owner was contacted. He was asleep after working the night shift at the power plant. His wife apparently was home all day as well and swears her husband never left home today. Apparently the pickup had been stolen out of his barn. He keeps his hunting rifle inside, along with the keys."

Trevor looked at his partner. "Who leaves their keys in the ignition now days?"

"They lived on a five-acre farm. Never had any trouble before."

Forest replied, "Thank you for the update, officer."

"Yes sir. I'm needed. Excuse me."

Forest watched him walk away and then he turned toward Trevor. "How do you think Henry Wells got a hold of a weapon of that caliber?"

"I don't know. Henry Wells definitely had a lot of anger. Ronny Jordan never saw him coming."

"No. I'm sure he felt no fear from the Wells family."

"How's Ms. Parker?"

Forest replied, "She's fine."

"I heard she will handle the Hart case when we're ready."

"Yes. She told me."

Trevor smiled. "Good. I think that's a good thing."

Over the next two hours, more news came in about the blue truck. A connection had been made between Henry Wells and Doug Nelson, the owner of the Ford pickup. Apparently they belonged to the same hunting club. Now they just needed to find the body of Henry Wells and the weapon used on Ronny Jordan, and the case would be wrapped up nice and tidy.

"Now, if we can just get a break with this Hart case, we'll be alright."

Forest looked around and studied the faces of the people exiting the building. No one appeared overly suspicious. Just a long, tiresome night surrounded by death and sorrow. He answered, "Yeah, if only. Let's call it a night."

Forest said his good-byes to Trevor, and they agreed to meet at seven a.m. back at the office to dig some more on the Hart case. Once he left the station in his Mustang, it took him about twenty minutes to drive across town to Mark and Charli Pepper's home, where Lilee was staying. Two officers stood outside, still airing on the side of caution until a confirmation that Henry Wells had been found.

Forest pulled up in his Mustang and greeted the two men on shift. "Gentlemen. Anything new?"

"No, Detective Styles. They got divers in the lake, but no body has been discovered."

"The lake?"

"Yes, sir. There's a one-acre lake at Smith's Park."

Forest was taken aback. "I didn't know there was a lake there."

"It's toward the back, away from the parking. It's hidden."

Forest nodded and then headed up the three stairs and rang the doorbell.

A minute passed and Mark Pepper arrived at the double oak door holding a glass of wine. "I'm Detective Forest Styles."

Mark smiled and opened the door wider as Lilee appeared in the background wearing sweatpants and a T-shirt. Her hair was damp and she wasn't wearing any makeup. She looked beautiful as she smiled back at him. Forest returned the smile and Mark invited him in. Mark extended his hand, and quick introductions were made.

"Come on in the kitchen. We're just finishing up the dishes."

Forest followed Lilee down the hall as Mark closed and locked the door behind him.

"Officer Nelley informed us earlier they found Wells' car and what appears to be a suicide note."

Forest turned back toward Mark. "Yeah. Hopefully this will end tonight and the ladies can get back to their normal routines tomorrow."

Charli set her hand towel down and announced, "Good. Because us four have reservations tomorrow at Mario's downtown at seven."

Lilee opened her mouth to speak but stopped when Forest turned to her and replied, "Sounds great. Look forward to it."

She smiled, placed a hand on Forest's chest, and leaned close. "I didn't have a chance to ask you earlier."

He touched her hand and replied, "I will have a busy day tomorrow, but diner at seven sounds great."

"So what's the latest with the Hart case? Any leads?" asked Mark.

Forest peeled his eyes off Lilee and turned to Mark, who was now rinsing his wine glass.

"Off the record?"

Mark nodded and Forest continued. "Frustrating as hell. We have a few leads we're checking on, but other than that, we're still digging."

Charli said, "The papers are claiming it was some kind of hit. They weren't robbed."

"No. They weren't. It was personal."

Forest received an incoming call. "Excuse me."

Charli, Lilee, and Mark watched as Forest stepped away into the family room adjacent to the kitchen to take his call.

Lilee looked back at Charli. "Wednesday might be an easy day after all."

Mark laughed. "Yeah, right. Maggs will just throw another case at you. Then when there is a lead, you'll have two cases."

Lilee heard the underlying bitterness in his voice. She knew he was unpleased with their workload and hours and tried to downplay it. "I

231

don't know. Your wife laid into Maggs pretty good today. I think we'll see some changes around the office."

Mark dried his glass and set it behind the glass cabinet door. "I'll believe it when I see it."

Charli looked at Lilee, and Lilee forced a smile to reassure her.

"Lilee is right. There might be a lot of changes coming. After all, Maggs did have a near-death experience today," commented Charli.

Forest walked back into the kitchen. "Henry Wells is dead. Looks self-inflicted."

Lilee closed her eyes and shook her head.

Charli asked, "So it's over. No more security?"

Forest looked at Mark. "We'll keep the officer on watch through the night, just until things are verified tomorrow and the case is closed."

"Good idea," Mark said and walked over and grabbed Charli around the waist and continued, "I don't want to take chances with my wife."

Charli kissed him as Lilee announced, "Well, I think it's time for us two to leave, and we'll see you guys tomorrow night."

Charli pulled away from Mark and both followed Forest and Lilee to the door.

"Nice to meet you, Mark."

"Yes. We'll see you tomorrow."

Forest reached out and grabbed Lilee's hand and together they walked toward his Mustang. He nodded at the officer sitting inside the patrol car and then opened the passenger door for Lilee. Soon they were off headed toward his place for the night.

232

Chapter 30

At nine thirty, Derrick paced back and forth in his study as Andrea said good night to their teenage daughters upstairs. He was restless and felt as if his life was at an impasse. Andrea was always there, right beside him supporting his every move. She had never wavered, no matter how many times he had stood her and the girls up for one event after another. She was a rock.

Derrick took a seat on his fine leather chair and forced his mind to go back in time to the moment he discovered his wife's one night of infidelity. He had overhead them in a heated argument in their very own kitchen. He was supposed to be outside with Christa but decided to help Andrea in the kitchen, which was completely out of character for him. William had stepped away to use the facilities, but he had met up with Andrea in the kitchen instead. Derrick had heard their hurtful words and left immediately undetected. Now, he forced himself to remember the tone in Andrea's voice. She had been upset.

"Derrick?"

He turned and found his wife standing in the hallway looking in. She looked tired, almost broken. He raked a hand through his perfect hair and stood. "Andrea."

She timidly took a step and then another and entered, closing the door behind her. Her eyes were red and puffy. She wrapped both arms around her body and then gently spoke, choosing her words carefully. "It was a mistake, one I've lived with for too many years now. I want it to be over. I want to move on. So just tell me, can you move on with me or…" She stopped as her voice broke.

He didn't answer. He just watched as she placed both her hands over her face. She wiped her tears, crossed her arms, held her shoulders tight, and bowed her head. Her red hair swung down, covering the tops of her shoulders. He could see her pain and shame—something he had never seen before. But why would he? She'd never known he knew all along. He remained silent, waiting for her to continue.

Soon she looked up and spoke with detest. "William is dead now and… and I'm tired. I'm so tired of trying to forget. I was drunk, and I'm not using that as an excuse. But the fact is…" she stopped and looked intently into his eyes. When he didn't interrupt, she said, "He wasn't, and that…that is…"

"Is unforgivable and inexcusable," he heard himself say.

She opened her mouth to continue but closed her lips and nodded. Another moment passed and then she yelled, "I hate him for it! I honestly hate him, and I'm glad he's dead!"

Quickly she placed a hand over her mouth, realizing she'd said how she had felt aloud, making it real now. She watched in shock as Derrick walked toward her and placed his hand on the side of her face, pushing her hair away and pulling her into his arms. He held her tightly and caressed her back as she cried on his shoulder. Minutes went by as neither spoke. She just held him back and continued to cry. Finally, when her sobs stopped, he gently picked her up into his arms and carried her to bed.

Derrick laid his wife down carefully, tucked the covers around her, and then stood above her without a word. Slowly he turned and walked toward the door. Just as he walked out, she found her voice. "Derrick."

He slowly turned and waited, but she had no more words. A long minute passed as they held each other's stare. Finally he spoke. "Andrea, tomorrow's a new day. A fresh start."

Her forehead creased at his words as she tried to decipher his true meaning. When she saw him smile, she smiled back and closed her eyes.

***

Marla Kay arrived home at eleven thirty after what seemed like the longest shift of her life. When she entered the home, she found Jenna still awake sitting in the living room surrounded by darkness. She flipped a switch and watched as Jenna turned toward her.

"Hi."

"Hi yourself. What are you doing sitting in the dark so late?"

Jenna stretched out her legs and then quickly stood. "I couldn't sleep."

"How's Rosemary?"

"Fine. She ate well tonight and went on to bed around seven thirty."

"Good, but that means she'll be up around five thirty, so you better get some sleep."

Jenna raked a hand through her long, dark hair. Something was clearly on her mind.

Marla Kay walked over and placed a hand on her arm. "Spill it and maybe you'll sleep."

They locked eyes. "I…I called Tim tonight."

Marla Kay stepped back and crossed her arms. "Why did you do that?"

Jenna narrowed her eyes and explained, "Because he just lost his father and possibly his mother as well. And I, um…"

"You still love him, don't you?"

Jenna could hear her sister's displeasure in her words. "Well…well that I don't really know, thanks to you."

"Oh, don't even go there. We made the best decision considering the circumstances."

"For who? You or me?"

Marla Kay uncrossed her arms, walked back over, and gently placed both hands on her sister's shoulders. "For Rosemary."

Jenna closed her eyes and then quickly reopened them. "But, was it the right decision?"

Marla Kay frowned. "Jenna, I'm tired. My best friend died, and I wasn't allowed at the service tonight. Maybe not at the one tomorrow either. I'm sorry, but I just can't do this tonight."

"Fine." Jenna pulled away and headed toward her bedroom without another word.

Marla Kay watched with worry. She frowned as she turned off the light and headed to bed.

***

Forest sat at the kitchen table at eleven forty-five. Lilee had fallen asleep in his bed waiting on him to finish up with some paperwork. When he'd finished at ten thirty, he had found her asleep, smiled, and forced himself to walk away. He knew she must be really tired with all she had been through over the last several days. So, he had left her in bed alone and gone back to the kitchen to work some more.

He held a sheet of paper up closer to his eyes and studied the numbers and accounts of William and Christa Hart. All had added up right. Nothing seemed out of place or missing. Money was deposited, and money was spent. Lots of money was spent. But all in all, everything was accounted for. Forest set down the paper and reached for a handout on Christa's business, Elegant Grace Designs. This was much harder to read and follow. There were several accounts and ongoing purchases with money flowing both ways, in and out. He set the paper down and rubbed his eyes. He was tired as well.

"Coming to bed anytime soon?"

Startled at hearing her voice, he turned to face her. His body stiffened at the sight of Lilee Parker standing barefoot wearing only a T-shirt, his T-shirt. He smiled, stood up, and walked toward her. Carefully he lowered his mouth to hers and pushed her backward toward his bedroom. Suddenly he felt wide awake as her hands wrapped around his body, removing his shirt. They tumbled into bed together, and it was well after midnight before Forest finally got some sleep.

Chapter 31

Tuesday, October 16

"Good morning."

Lilee slowly awoke and found Forest within inches of her face, smiling. He leaned closer and kissed her nose. She giggled and wrapped her arms around him. He felt warm as his body touched hers. They kissed and kissed some more. Slowly his lips found her neck, and he continued kissing her tenderly as he moved lower and found her bare chest. Playfully he teased with his tongue, awakening her soul and her immediate needs.

Her legs parted and he entered her as his lips met hers. They touched and felt each other as their bodies connected so nicely once again. Their lovemaking was slow and gentle, filled with a desire that was both passionate and fulfilling. Afterward Forest rolled away but brought her body close to his. Her chin rested on his chest, and their eyes met. They needed no words as they studied each other.

She smiled, and he smiled back.

"I want to stay like this forever, but we can't," he said. "Someone has to break a major case and fast, or heads are going to roll."

She pouted as she rolled away and sat up, her blond hair falling over her bare back. He touched a golden curl and ran his hand down her pale skin to her lower back. She turned. "You better stop right there, or you won't get up."

His hand lingered a little longer before he finally jerked it away, jumped up, and walked to the bathroom naked. She watched his backside as he left and rounded the corner. She heard the water turn on for a shower and twisted her mouth, pondering her next move. She didn't have to think long because she heard him call for her. "Lilee! Get in here!"

She smiled and climbed out of bed, running into the bathroom and closing the door after her.

Forty minutes passed before Forest grabbed his keys and his tall coffee cup for the road. Lilee was seated at his breakfast table eating cereal and reading the day's paper. She announced, "Henry Wells has made the front page, along with Maggs and Ronny Jordan."

She frowned as she read. Forest sat his coffee back down and walked over toward her. "It won't stay on the front covers for long," he said. "Not after today's funeral."

She looked up and caught his frown. She knew he was going to be pressured for an arrest, and soon. She set the paper down, stood up, and cupped his face with her hands. She spoke tenderly. "Go and crack a case, detective, and I'll be waiting for you at six thirty tonight at my place."

"Your place?"

"Well, yes. I can't wear this," she said, pulling at his T-shirt, "can I?"

He lost his frown and smiled. "No, I guess not. I'll see you at six."

Coyly she asked, "Six?"

He wrapped his arms around her tighter. "I'm gonna work through lunch, so I'll see you at six."

"But we have to leave at six thirty," She playfully added.

He winked. "We will."

She watched as he pulled away and turned to leave, grabbing his coffee and keys once more. He opened the door and turned once more, and she blew him a kiss when their eyes met.

He grinned and said, "Tonight," and left, closing the door.

***

At eight a.m., Todd and Tim stepped off the hospital elevator on the second floor. Together they entered their mother's room and found her awake and alert. She smiled when she saw them.

She found her voice and forced out, "Boys, come here."

Todd stepped forward first and grabbed her hand. "Welcome back, Mom. You gave us quite a scare."

Tim came closer and placed his hand on her forehead. "We hired someone to watch over you as well. The mistake won't happen again."

She took a deep breath and tried to answer.

"Mom, take it easy. Pace yourself. We don't have to talk. Just seeing you and holding your hand is enough."

Tears formed and she blinked, pushing a tear down her cheek. Todd reached out and wiped it away. "Mom, the viewing was last night. It was beautiful. You would've been pleased at the large turnout and arrangement."

Tim added, "Everyone sends their love. They wanted you to know that."

She nodded. "And…and the funeral?"

"At two," Todd said and turned at the sound of a door opening behind them with a knock. Dr. Griffin entered. "Gentlemen, how's our patient doing?"

Todd squeezed his mom's hand and stepped away as Dr. Griffin neared with his instruments. Patiently, both boys remained quiet as the doctor listened to her heart and breathing. He leaned up and then studied a readout on a monitor before turning to face all of them. "Everything looks and sounds good. But she needs her rest, so don't stay too much longer."

He took another step toward Christa. "The service was nice last night. You were missed by all. Get your strength back, Christa. You have a lot of friends waiting on you."

She forced a reply. "Thank you."

He stood up and patted her on the hand. "Keep it short. I'll check on her again later."

They nodded and watched as he left.

Todd turned back toward their mother. "He's right. You should rest. We'll come back once more before we leave for the service."

She forced a smile and nod. Each gave her a kiss and then turned to leave. When Todd stepped out first, she called out, "Tim."

Both boys turned and then Tim stepped forward and leaned closer where she wouldn't strain her voice. "Talk, you and I."

Todd walked over and asked, "Tim, what's this about?"

Tim looked into his mother's moist blue eyes and answered, "OK."

He slowly turned to Todd. "Can you give us a minute?"

Todd narrowed his eyes and frowned. "Please, Todd. I'll explain in the lobby."

Reluctantly Todd turned away, but not before saying, "I'll be waiting."

Tim watched him leave, knowing his brother was unhappy. He would deal with that later, though. Apparently this was important to his mother, and he wasn't going to deny her the chance to speak because of hurt or insecure feelings from his brother.

He placed a hand on her cheek and softly said, "I'm listening, Mom. What's on your mind?"

"Rosemary."

Tim tensed at the word but forced his heart to listen without disrespect. "OK. What about Rosemary?"

"Talk to her mother."

"Why? Why do you want me to do that?"

She forced her voice, "Because…" and her voice broke.

"Mom, maybe we should talk about this later, when you've gotten some more rest."

She shook her head. "We need to heal our family." She swallowed, took a deep breath, and added, "It starts with…with Rosemary."

Getting all the words out, she felt tired and closed her eyes from exhaustion. Tim squeezed her hand and leaned down and kissed her forehead.

He waited for more, but she didn't open her eyes again as she was pulled back under to sleep.

Slowly he stood and walked away. He quietly closed the door, walked through the double doors, and found Todd waiting on him in the lobby.

Seeing him, Todd walked over and demanded, "What the hell was that all about?"

"She was worried about your grades."

Todd placed both hands on his hips and shook his head. "That's not funny, Tim. What did she say?"

Tim raked a hand over his forehead and rubbed his blue eyes. Todd continued with his finger pointing down the hallway. "Is this about that nurse, Marla Kay Abbott? It is, isn't it?"

"Yes."

Todd got angry. "Why did she want to talk to you about it and not me?"

Tim could see the hurt expression on his brother's face. It was unfair to him, and he felt guilty. "I'm sorry. She doesn't think you know. Just me. So let's keep it that way."

Todd paced and then angrily replied, "I don't want her there today. She better not be there."

Tim tried to reach out and console his brother, but Todd pulled away and stepped into an open elevator. The door closed before Tim had time to think of a reply. He turned back toward the double doors to the ICU and found himself all alone. Todd didn't understand any of this. He had been purposely kept in the dark. *Was now the time to tell him?* he wondered. Tim placed a hand on his blond hair and paced as he tried to figure out what to do. *Was Mom right? Should I go to the Abbott house?* Tim sat down and looked around the empty room, but no clear answers would come.

Chapter 32

When Forest arrived at the station, he was greeted by his partner, Trevor Watts. The place was alive with action, and he caught sight of Ronny Jordan's family sitting around a table in a conference room with the blinds open. A kid sitting beside a girl holding her hand turned and met his stare and suddenly bolted up, walked over to the window, and closed the blinds.

Forest pushed away the Wells case and concentrated on the Harts. He turned to Trevor. "I want to start with Elegant Grace Designs. I have some questions about their account."

Trevor picked up his coffee and motioned Forest to lead the way to the conference room that had been set up over the weekend to use on the Hart case. Staff workers greeted them as they entered the room and gave each a handout on the latest discoveries. Forest scanned the list, pulled out a chair, and sat down. Trevor took the seat across from him and picked up the file on Elegant Grace Designs.

"The business has lots of open and active accounts with many withdrawals and deposits."

Trevor replied, "Sounds legitimate."

"Yes, but there's one that caught my attention," added Forest.

Trevor looked over his copy and said, "OK. Which one?"

"Line five. The amount is the same each month."

Trevor slid his finger to the right and stopped at the number. "Twenty-five hundred dollars. Could be the rent."

"That's what I thought, but look at line nine."

Trevor repeated the action four lines down. "Thirty-five hundred dollars."

"Yeah. Neither of those amounts ever change. They're the same each month."

Trevor studied the list. Several of the same account numbers were repeated, but with different amounts. It appeared the ladies had about dozen or so open accounts with different suppliers for their various jobs. Trevor looked up and asked, "What else?"

Forest smiled. They knew each other so well. "Notice how all the accounts start with either a number or letter?"

"Yeah. The thirty-five hundred starts with a letter, and the twenty-five hundred starts with a number."

Forest nodded. "Now look at the many deposits. They each start with a number, and most of the withdrawals start with a letter."

Trevor looked over it some more. "Without a warrant this is all we get, but it appears that an individual is receiving that twenty-five hundred, and a company is receiving the thirty-five hundred, probably for rent."

"I made a call," Forest said. "The landlord receives anywhere from three to five thousand for rent of office space but wouldn't divulge their rent amount."

Trevor leaned back and thought for a moment. Soon he leaned forward. "What about their sons? Maybe an account was set up for spending money."

"There is, but it was established through the Harts' personal account. Each son gets fifteen hundred deposited on the first of each month."

Trevor smirked. "Not bad, since they have a full scholarship with living expenses."

"So the question remains, who is getting the twenty-five hundred?"

"Yeah, and are both ladies aware of it?" asked Trevor.

Forest called out, "Shannon, I need you to fill out a request for more bank details on Elegant Grace Designs."

"Yes, sir. I'm on it."

They analyzed phone records, bank accounts, clients, and Hart's patients over the next several hours. As he had indicated to Lilee, Forest ate a protein bar for lunch and kept working. Trevor went home to the missus, and they were to meet up again at one thirty for William Hart's funeral.

On the drive to the church, Forest hooked up his headset and called Lilee.

"Hello?"

"Hi, Lilee."

She smiled. "How's it going?"

"Slow, but I think I might be on to something."

"Oh? Anything you need to tell your lead prosecutor?"

"Sorry. Not yet."

She frowned. Lilee was enjoying her day off, but she couldn't deny how much she loved her job. "Still gonna be able to finish up on time?"

Forest tensed a moment. Going out on a date was the last thing he needed to do. He was getting heat from the captain. Suddenly he remember Diane and how he had blown his chances by standing her up three straight times. His thoughts went to earlier that morning with Lilee wrapped up in his arms and her wearing his T-shirt when he left. He relaxed. No way was he going to blow Lilee off. Work will always be there. "Absolutely. Six o'clock."

"Well then, I better let you go so you can get back to work."

"I'll see you tonight. Enjoy your day."

"Thanks. Bye now."

He ended the call just as he pulled into the large parking lot adjacent to St. Mary Cathedral. The Catholic Church was the largest in Atlanta, and the Hart family had been lifelong members. The parking lot, built to hold about five hundred, was nearing full capacity. Men had been hired to help with parking, and Forest followed their directions and pulled into an empty slot beside a white SUV. Forest got out and looked at the many vehicles. He couldn't help noticing that most of the cars were valued at over forty grand. Others had parked beside him and were exiting their cars at the same time. Nodding, he followed the others along the walkway to the entrance of the church.

Crossing the street, Forest found Trevor talking to an officer. Trevor was always easy to spot with his large frame and height. He was also one of only a few African Americans in attendance. He spotted Forest and nodded.

"Looks like we're gonna have a full house, Forest."

Forest watched as people continued to pull into the parking lot. Suddenly he caught sight of Marla Kay Abbott crossing the street with her sister. Both ladies were impeccably dressed. Jenna wore a navy suit with a white silk button-down blouse and Marla Kay had her long, dark hair pulled back into a fashionable knot. Her black dress was fitted, and her legs looked amazing as she climbed the stairs in her two-inch black heels. She had noticed the detectives staring but turned away quickly and looked forward, avoiding further eye contact.

"This could get interesting."

The music started and Forest responded, "No doubt," as he climbed the stairs and entered with Trevor right behind him. Quickly they found two empty seats in the back and took a seat. Forest searched for Marla Kay and Jenna and finally found them seated on the other side a few rows up. Soon the music stopped, and a man wearing a white robe stood from a high-back chair and walked to the podium.

As the priest talked, Forest looked around and noticed some familiar faces from the night before. The Raineses were seated a few rows ahead of them. Dr. Raines had his arm protectively around his wife, and on each side of the couple sat a teenage girl. Forest could identify Andrea's golden red hair anywhere. She truly was stunning.

Forest turned his attention back toward the front, where his eyes settled on the massive display of white roses lying across the closed casket. He tried to spot Todd and Tim, but too many people sat between them. Forest settled back and began to concentrate on the words spoken for the next half hour.

At three o'clock, Forest followed Trevor over to the cemetery. The service had been longer than either had anticipated, so the decision to leave early to get ahead of the crowd was agreed upon quickly. They had eased from their seats and left without a scene. That was one reason why they had chosen to sit in the back.

Forest pulled his black Mustang along the shoulder of the narrow road behind Trevor's black sedan. Parking at the entrance would make it easier to get out than if they parked closer to the gravesite, which had already been set up with chairs and tents. Rain was expected, and the funeral home had prepared nicely.

"Let's wait here," Trevor suggested. "I don't like graveyards, and I sure don't like graveyards that have dirt removed waiting on a casket."

Forest smirked. "OK. Why don't you like graveyards, besides the obvious reasons?"

Trevor stuck his hands in his dress pants pockets and looked around. "We lived across from one growing up. My brothers and sisters would always play pranks on me. Of course, it wasn't as nice as this one."

"Oh."

"No. It was an old cemetery, dated back to the early 1800s. You could even see some of the tombs opening up and splitting away."

Forest noticed him shivering as he continued. "Gives me goose bumps just thinking about it."

"This in Alabama?"

"Yeah. South Alabama. Lots of slaves buried there too."

Forest decided to change the subject. "What did you think of Marla Kay and Jenna showing up? I'm sorta surprised."

"Yeah. I'm sure it wasn't easy. She knows about the rumors."

"So if she shows up, is that her way of disproving them, sending a message to everyone that she wasn't his mistress?" asked Forest.

"Maybe we should rattle her cage and ask her if she has twenty-five hundred appearing in her bank account each month."

"Yeah, maybe."

"If so, why? Do you think Christa is paying her to stay away from her husband?

Forest thought back to Marla Kay's home. It was a nice home, but at the same time, Marla Kay had a good-paying job to go with it. He remembered the open garage and her yellow sports car parked inside. It was flashy and cost at least thirty to forty grand, maybe more. He heard Trevor say, "Did you see her dress? It had to be designer, along with the shoes."

Forest heard his words, and an image of Marla Kay climbing the stairs filled his mind. Her legs were toned, probably just from walking all day and standing on her feet for hours at a time. He tried to remember any gym equipment in her garage. She had closed it before she came and greeted them. Why? And why did that bother him so much?

"Her sister looked nice too. She's still in school, so she doesn't have a job, which means Marla Kay takes care of her too."

Forest looked up at Trevor. "Jenna's car wasn't in the garage that day."

Trevor thought back to the day of their visit. "So if Jenna wasn't there, who was Marla Kay talking to?"

"Maybe Jenna doesn't have a car, or maybe it was in the shop."

"Yeah, I guess. Or Marla Kay had a friend who rode home with her, a friend whose car she didn't want her neighbors to see," suggested Trevor.

"Well, we will never know," Forest said and paused as he saw a light flash up ahead on a patrol car followed by a hearse. "Let's get in place."

Chapter 33

A black Lincoln Navigator was the eighth car behind the hearse. Inside were Derrick and Andrea Raines with both their daughters sitting in the backseat wearing headphones. Three cars behind them, Marla Kay's yellow sports car followed with Jenna sitting quietly in the passenger's seat. Everyone was in deep thought, and no one had spoken a word over the last twenty minutes on the way to the cemetery.

By the time everyone had gathered around the casket and priest, it was three forty-five. Tim and Todd Hart sat on the front row surrounded by close friends. The Raineses were a part of that exclusive group. The priest only spoke five minutes, and then Tim and Todd stepped forward and each placed a rose on the casket. All watched as it slowly lowered into the ground. Sobs could be heard as well as the crank that continued to lower William Hart to his final resting spot.

A few people hugged the twins, and some just shook hands. Forest was carefully watching the young men, observing their behavior to make sure he hadn't missed anything. They genuinely looked heartbroken, just like any grieving sons should look at the sudden loss of their father. Suddenly Todd's head jerked to the side as if he saw a ghost. Forest followed his stare and found Marla Kay and Jenna talking to some other women, probably nurses. Forest watched as his face became angry and then he turned toward his brother and pulled him away from another couple.

"Excuse me, Dr. and Mrs. Thomas," Tim said. He turned to his brother and whispered, "Todd, that was rude. What?" and then he saw them as well. "Oh."

"Yeah. What the hell are they doing here?"

Tim tried to calm his brother. "Blame me. I gave them permission."

Todd looked at his brother as if he'd been slapped. "Why? Why in God's name would you allow Dad's whore to show up here?"

Tim glanced around to make sure no one had heard his brother. "Todd, enough. Mom said…"

Todd yanked his arm away. "Mom said! Is this what ya'll were talking about today?"

Tim leaned close to his brother. "Todd, pull it together! The last thing we need is a scene that would bring shame to Mother."

Todd turned away from his brother and walked up to the priest. He quickly thanked him and then walked straight to the limousine they rode in and climbed in without another word.

Tim did his best to shake some more hands but stopped cold when his eyes met Jenna's. She broke away from her sister and walked his way.

Forest continued to watch the exchange. Something was there between Tim and Jenna. He could clearly see it in both of their body language. At first he saw their bodies tense and then, after a few more exchanges, relax in a way that seemed comfortable.

Marla Kay turned away from her friends, walked forward, and placed a hand on Jenna's arm. Slowly the two ladies walked off, but it was clear that Marla Kay was pulling her sister away. *Interesting*, thought Forest.

As Marla Kay walked away, she continued to hold on to Jenna. He watched as she passed the Raineses, who still stood close by. Marla Kay slowed her steps and looked at Dr. Raines. He saw her but never acknowledged her and continued talking to another doctor and his wife. Andrea never saw Marla Kay or the look Marla Kay gave her husband. Forest saw it. *The plot thickens*, he thought.

Forest felt his phone vibrate. He pulled it out and answered, "Forest."

"Shannon. Look, we got the approval. We're getting the bank records."

"So fast. Wow. OK. I'm on my way."

Forest pocketed his phone and motioned toward Trevor. When they met up at their vehicles, Forest shared the news. Both eagerly climbed into their vehicles and drove away. Forest looked at the time: four fifteen. It would take another fifteen minutes just to get to the office. *Damn*, he thought. He had a sickening feeling he was going to be late.

***

A yellow sports car came to a quick halt in Marla Kay's driveway. Jenna and Marla Kay had been fighting since they left the cemetery.

"Look, Jenna. I've had a long day, and now, I've got to get to work. The last thing I need or want is to be fighting with you."

Jenna bowed her head. She felt guilty. She knew how much William Hart meant to her sister, and it must have been unbearable for her to see him buried. "I'm sorry, Marla Kay. You're right. Probably about everything. It's just…well, it's hard to just turn off feelings sometimes."

Marla Kay grabbed her hand. "It's been over three years now. You're about to graduate. You have a bright future ahead of you." She squeezed her hand and added, "Without him."

Jenna didn't pull her hand away. "I know. You're right. I'm gonna go now, so you can get to work."

"I won't be home until around one thirty. We all shifted our schedules around to accommodate…" Her voice trailed off.

Jenna opened her car door just as a light rain began to fall. Feeling the strong wind, she leaned back in. "Better get to work before the bottom falls out of the sky."

Marla Kay nodded, and Jenna shut the passenger door and ran toward the front door. Marla Kay reversed down the driveway and then pulled away, never noticing the car parked down the street, or its driver watching their every move.

Adam Kolar, age thirty-three, sat in a dark car. He had waited for years to strike back. He had plotted his revenge well over the last twelve months, and tonight was the night to finish it once and for all. He watched as Jenna Abbott went inside the house and closed the door. He waited. As expected, a young lady emerged, the regular babysitter, and ran down the driveway and down the street where she lived three houses down.

Cutting off the engine, Adam got out and ran across the lawn to the overhanging porch. Hidden behind the door, he looked back at the street looking for any witnesses that had possibly seen him. No one. He reached into his pocket and retrieved a key that he had stolen eight months earlier from the babysitter. No one was the wiser, and the Abbotts, assuming she had simply lost it, had not thought to change the locks.

Adam turned around and reached for the doorknob, taking a chance. He wasn't really surprised to find the house unlocked. He made one quick glance behind him and then quickly entered the home without a sound. Seeing no one, he darted into the study and waited.

On the other side of the home, Jenna was looking in on Rosemary. She found her playing with her dolls. Jenna walked over and sat beside the little dark-haired girl and picked up one of her dolls. Together they played, dressing each doll and then giving each a bottle and placing them in a pretend baby bed made of pillows and blankets. Rosemary lay down on the pillow alongside her doll, and Jenna ran a hand through her beautiful hair.

"Are you tired, Rosemary?"

She shot up. "No. Rosemary not tired."

Jenna smiled. She loved Rosemary's stubbornness. At age three, she was a force to be reckoned with. She had a very independent attitude. Jenna studied her outfit. Her socks didn't match, and she had chosen to wear jeans under her dress. She loved to dress herself, and Marla Kay and Jenna thought it was healthy to let her choose each day what she wore. Besides, did it really matter? On the days that it did matter, they asked her nicely to let them select an outfit, and she always complied without a fight. Yes. Rosemary was just as adorable as she was beautiful.

Rosemary picked up her doll and looked toward the door behind Jenna. Curious, Jenna turned around but saw nothing in the empty hallway. Rosemary put her doll down and jumped into Jenna's lap. Immediately Jenna became frightened.

"Rosemary, sweetie. What's wrong? What did you see?"

"Him."

Startled, Jenna looked back at the door and froze at the sight of a strange man standing in her doorway pointing a gun at her. Jenna opened her mouth to scream, but he took one giant step toward her and placed the gun at Rosemary's head.

"I wouldn't do that, if I were you."

Jenna couldn't breathe. She was suffocating. Who was this man? What did he want? She searched his face for clues and then recognition came to her. Adam noticed the change in her eyes as they widened with the memory of who he was. He smiled. "Yeah, Jenna. I'm back."

Chapter 34

At 4:35, Shannon Miller, a team member working the Hart case, walked into the conference room where Forest and Trevor sat and handed them each a file. "More information on those bank accounts."

"Good work, Shannon," Forest said. "Anything else come up while we were gone?"

"No, not really, but we have tracked down most of Dr. Hart's patients. So far, nothing looks too suspicious."

"OK, thanks," replied Forest as he took the file and began reading. Moments passed as both men cross referenced the accounts with their given names.

"Thirty-five hundred is rent, but there is no name to the account for twenty-five hundred," Forest said as he looked at Trevor.

Trevor asked, "Shannon, why are these accounts not complete?"

"I'm sorry. They should be. We were granted full permission." The petite brunette walked around the table and looked at the open file. "What's missing?"

Trevor pointed at a blank space beside an account number. "The one with a withdrawal of twenty-five hundred each month."

Quickly Shannon looked at her watch. "I'll call the bank. They close at five."

Forest continued to study the other names. All looked legitimate. There was a clear pattern on small deposits from personal accounts and then larger deposits over the next several months by the same account. The only thing on the bank spreadsheet that seemed odd was the missing name for the account with the twenty-five hundred dollar withdrawal.

"Detectives, I've got Mr. Morris from the bank on line five."

Forest picked up the phone and pressed the number five and then the speaker button.

"Good afternoon, Mr. Morris. This is Detective Styles with Atlanta PD. We received the bank records earlier on the Elegant Grace Designs account."

"Yes, of course. How may I assist you?"

"We are missing a name on one of the accounts. Can you get us that name, please?"

"I don't see why not. Not real sure why it didn't print. Just hold on a moment and let me pull up the account."

Forest waited patiently as he continued to scroll through the many accounts.

"OK. I'm in the account now. Which account number is in question?"

"Number eight, four, five, six, zero, five, one, one."

"OK. Give me just one more moment." Thirty seconds passed before Mr. Morris said, "Um, that's interesting. Look, I need to check with someone on this. Can I ring you back?"

Forest took a deep breath before answering. "Yes, please."

Forest had just finished giving their phone number when Mr. Morris quickly said, "OK. Give me about five minutes, or definitely by five o'clock, I will ring with an answer."

"Thank you. We'll be waiting to hear back from you."

***

The gates to the Hart estate stood open and several cars were parked around the circular drive as well as down their street. Over fifty guests had been invited back to the home for food and drinks. Tim was making small talk with a doctor as he carefully watched his brother. Todd had relaxed some in the limousine on the ride back home. Tim had done his best to calm his brother. "Just a few more hours, Todd, and then we can talk more, but you have got to stay strong. Think of mother and what she would expect from us." That had done the trick for now, but Tim wondered how long it would last.

The Raineses walked over to Tim. "Everything looks wonderful, Tim. Christa would be so proud that you were able to pull this off without her."

"Yes, she would. Of course, I wouldn't have known who to call if it weren't for you."

Andrea lovingly hugged Tim. She had known him since they were born. They had spent countless family barbecues together while the kids swam in the backyard pools of each other's homes over the last twenty years. She and Christa had also gone on trips with their kids since their husbands had been so busy with their jobs. The beach was everyone's favorite vacation. Lots of memories had been shared.

She smiled at the fine young men they had become. Christa would be so proud of how they had managed to hold it together. It wasn't easy for the boys. The press was everywhere. As advised by their lawyers, they had not spoken to the media and allowed their lawyers to do all the talking, just like their parents would have wanted.

"Dr. and Mrs. Raines."

Andrea turned and saw Todd. She walked forward, gave him a hug too, and placed her hand on top of his head to smooth out a dark curl that had flipped. "We are just a phone call away. Please don't hesitate day or night to call."

He nodded. "Thank you. Did you see Mom today?"

"Briefly."

"She was talking some today, but we tried to encourage her to rest." Todd looked at Tim as he said it.

"Well, getting your mom to rest and not talk is a challenge. I'm gonna see her again in the morning. I'll be careful, though, not to tire her out."

Tim said, "Of course you will. Your visits are important to her, even if it's just a few minutes at a time."

"When do you have to return to Auburn?" asked Derrick.

"We are planning on driving down tomorrow night. We'll return on Friday."

"Good. I know it's hard. But we all know your mother will worry if she knows you two are getting behind with your studies."

Todd answered. "Yeah, that's why we're going. Our professors have been great, though, very understanding."

Another couple approached the boys and Derrick and Andrea excused themselves.

"I'll find the girls and meet you out front," Andrea offered as she maneuvered around more guests. Five minutes later they pulled out of the Hart estate. On the drive home, Derrick thought of nothing else but his family. Andrea and the girls sitting in the back seat were his family. They were his life. Over the last few days, the event with the Harts had taught him that life was short, too short. Any given day, it could all be gone.

Four years, he thought. *Four years of wasted energy filled with doubt and betrayal. Well, no more.* He didn't love Marla Kay. Her only purpose had been to alleviate his hurt over his wife's betrayal. He glanced over at Andrea and grabbed her hand.

Fifteen minutes later, Derrick pulled their Lincoln into the garage and pressed the button. As the garage door closed, both girls jumped out and ran into the house. Andrea reached for the door handle, and Derrick grabbed her shoulder. Quickly he pulled her into him and held her tight. He whispered in her ear, "Don't...don't ever die on me, Andrea."

Andrea put both arms around him and hugged him back. Moments passed as they continued to hold on to one another. Slowly Andrea released her hold and found Derrick's face with both hands. Cradling his face, she spoke tenderly. "I won't go anywhere, Derrick." Her eyes met his and then she leaned forward and their lips touched.

***

At 4:55 p.m., on the second floor of the Atlanta Police Department, Shannon set a file down and answered the phone. "Yes. Just a moment."

"It's Morris, line two."

Forest sighed, "Finally," picked up the phone, and pressed two and the speaker button once more. "Yes, Mr. Morris. This is Detective Styles. What did you discover?"

"Sorry for the wait, Detective Styles, but I had some difficulty."

Forest had lost his patience. "How's that?"

"Well, the account is in a minor's name; therefore, the account name was left blank."

Thoughts of Tim and Todd flashed in Forest's mind, but he quickly pushed the idea away because they were over the age of eighteen. He tuned back in just as Morris finally divulged the name: "Rosemary Hart."

Trevor looked at Forest and shook his head. He had no clue who that was either. Forest thought a moment and then asked, "Well, is there a guardian named for Rosemary Hart?"

Forest heard paper rattling and Morris said, "Yes, I have that." After another pause, he said, "Marla Kay Abbott."

Trevor nodded and smiled. Forest grinned and replied, "Thank you, Mr. Morris. I will need you to fax that information over to our office. Shannon will be able to assist you."

Forest watched as Shannon picked up the phone and began talking. He pushed a button to end the call on speaker phone.

Trevor stood. "I say we head on over to the Abbott home, surprise the sisters, and find out just who Rosemary Hart is, the minor in question."

Forest stood and grabbed his jacket. When he saw a red folder on the table, a memory hit him. "That was it."

Trevor pulled his own jacket on, asked, "What?" and stared at Forest, waiting for him to elaborate.

"I thought I saw something at Marla Kay's house the other day but couldn't remember what I saw that was odd. Now I remember. It was a red tricycle in the garage."

"That is why Marla Kay closed the garage door and kept us in the front study, to hide a child."

Forest grinned. "If we knew Marla Kay had a child, we would've asked more questions."

Trevor said, "Time to go, partner. I think we're about to bust this case wide open!"

Trevor drove the black four-door sedan as Forest made some calls from the passenger's seat. It had taken twenty minutes to go six miles with five o'clock traffic and the heavy rain and wind that had moved in. Trevor pulled into the Abbott driveway and immediately noticed the garage door was closed and all lights were off.

"Doesn't look like anyone is home."

"Don't count on it," Forest said. "We made that mistake once already."

"Yeah, but no one is gonna be in the backyard with this storm."

Both men exited the vehicle, ran toward the porch, and stood close to the door, out of the blowing rain and wind. Forest rang the doorbell, and they waited.

Jenna heard the doorbell and tried to scream, but she couldn't. She was tied up to a chair in the kitchen, and her mouth was taped shut. She shook her head as tears spilled over her cheeks. She was so afraid, but more afraid for Rosemary. She hadn't seen her since he had taken her away.

Rosemary was screaming and fighting in his arms. With such calm, the man had poured some liquid onto a cloth and held it to her little face, silencing her cries as her body went limp in his arms. Jenna closed her eyes as the doorbell sounded again. She rocked back and forth trying to make the chair fall to make a noise. Finally she got enough rhythm going and flipped over, landing hard on her side. She patiently waited, but no one came and the doorbell never rang again.

Forest and Trevor ran back and jumped in their car. Forest wiped the raindrops from his face and said, "Let's call the hospital. Maybe Marla Kay went in to work."

"Maybe, but where would Jenna and Rosemary be in this storm?"

Forest shrugged and dialed the office. "Hi, Shannon. Can you find out if Marla Kay Abbott is working right now at General?"

Forest held the phone to his ear as he continued to stare at the dark house in front of them. "Where would they be in this storm? It wouldn't be a time to take a child out, especially after attending a funeral service."

Trevor offered, "Maybe they had a couple of glasses of wine and are sleeping it off."

Forest looked at his watch: five thirty. "I don't know. Don't think it's been enough time to get drunk and pass out."

Shannon came back on the line. "Yes. Marla Kay Abbott is working at the hospital until one tonight."

"Thank you, Shannon."

Forest hung up the phone. "Let's get to the hospital."

Forest continued to watch the dark house as they backed out of the driveway and wondered if Jenna was really not at home.

Several minutes went by as Trevor maneuvered in five o'clock traffic. When Trevor pulled into another lane and took a right turn, Forest asked, "Hey, where you going? General is to the left, old man."

Trevor laughed. "Yes, but your car is only two blocks away."

"So, I can get it afterward."

"You could if you were going to the hospital."

Forest lost his look of confusion. "My date can wait."

Trevor turned on his turn signal and pulled into a near-empty parking lot beside Forest's Mustang. He cut the engine and turned toward his partner.

"Forest, you are thirty-two years old. If you keep going down the same stupid path, you will never have a family."

"Trevor, I…"

He held his hand up. "I've been doing this job for twenty-six years. You don't think I can handle one Marla Kay Abbott by myself?"

"Yes, but what if…"

Trevor spoke loudly with an air of authority. "No. I got this. If it leads to her arrest, I will kindly inform you, but until then, I've got this."

Forest looked his partner in the eye. *Is he right? Should I go and take Lilee to dinner? It's just a dinner. She would understand. Besides, look at what kind of job she has. It's just as demanding as mine. A dinner with friends; that's all it was.*

Trevor interrupted his thoughts. "I would change first. I believe you have a fresh shirt and pants in your office."

Forest looked at the door handle. Trevor yelled, "Go! Now!"

Forest grabbed the handle, opened the door, and took one last look at Trevor and smiled before he closed the door and ran up the many stairs to their office building.

Chapter 35

At five o'clock Lilee stepped out of her shower, dried off, and wrapped up in her warm, pink fuzzy housecoat. She carefully brushed out her hair and then applied her facial cream. Next she pulled out her stool, sat down, and began drying her hair. Ten minutes passed as she styled her hair using a brush with the blow dryer. Setting the brush down, she heard a loud noise and quickly turned off the dryer. She turned around, but she was all alone in her large master bath with the double doors closed. She stilled as she listened. Nothing.

She shrugged her shoulders and faced the mirror once more. Her blond hair looked shiny and radiant, and she couldn't help herself as she shook her head and watched as the golden strands bounced over her shoulders. Next she opened her makeup drawer and began to apply with less in mind. Forest had seen her without makeup several times, and she was really not a big fan of heavy eye shadow. She found her eyeliner and applied a light brown shade. She applied her mascara last and shut the drawer. Standing, she heard another noise and froze.

That's not my imagination. She looked around for her phone but suddenly remembered it was on the nightstand in her bedroom. *Shit!* She ran toward her double doors and, instead of going for her phone, locked them. Next she ran toward her large closet to look for anything she could use as a weapon to protect herself. She closed her eyes as she realized she had cleaned out her closet and there was nothing in there but clothing and hangers. She imagined unwrapping a hanger and using the tip as a knife if needed, but she shook her head realizing it wouldn't work.

Then she saw it, lying on the top right corner on her shelf: the tip of a baseball bat. It was Landon's. She had missed it earlier when she had packed his things. She walked over and stood on her tippy toes but couldn't reach it. Hurriedly she ran back into the bathroom, checked the locks, and grabbed the stool. Setting it down in her closet, she climbed it, grabbing the bat. She jumped back down and held it tightly in her hands and waited.

Time went by as Lilee stood in her closet staring at the mirror ahead that gave her a view of the locked double doors. She hadn't heard anything for the last five minutes. More time passed, and she began to feel foolish. *What exactly did I hear?* She shook her head and gripped the baseball bat tighter. *No. It was a noise. It's not my imagination.* A few minutes later, she sat down on the stool.

She saw a shadow fall across her bathroom floor and tensed. Looking around, she found its source. A tree limb blowing outside suddenly scraped across her window. The wind had picked up, and she could hear it howling outside her home. The sound of rain soon followed, creating a patter along her metal roof. She continued to sit and listen.

A storm was blowing through, just as they had predicted. She remembered it wasn't to last long, but temperatures were expected to drop significantly when it was over. Listening to the rain she began to calm down as her nerves settled. The noise could have been anything. She had plants hanging on her back porch. Maybe one of them had been caught by a gust of wind and fallen. Or maybe she had left something on the back porch from earlier. The back porch was right off the master suite. She searched her memory to find what items she had taken outside that day. *Did I bring in my drinking glass? What about the white Tupperware bowl that held my cut up fruit?*

Lilee looked back out the window and noticed it was getting darker. Forest would be here soon. Slowly she set the bat down, grabbed her black cashmere sweaterdress, and laid it on the stool. She removed her robe, opened a drawer, and found a matching pair of black panties and bra. Quickly she put them on and then took the dress off the hanger and carefully pulled it on without smearing her makeup or messing up her hair. Next she found a black and silver belt and wrapped it around her hips. She faced the mirror and looked over her appearance. She began to relax. Lots of time had passed since she'd been hiding out in the closet holding a baseball bat.

Walking forward, she picked up her watch and saw that it was five forty five. She put the watch on and then chose a matching black and silver earring and necklace set. Last, she walked back into her closet and looked at her shoe options. Deciding it was going to be cold, she grabbed her long Italian black leather boots. Sitting on the stool, she rummaged in her drawers until she found her black tights. Carefully she pulled them on and then stepped into her boots and pulled up the tight leather. Standing, she looked in the mirror and smiled.

A doorbell sounded, and she glanced at her watch: 5:53. "You're seven minutes early, Forest. Nice." She walked to her double doors and, without giving it much thought, unlocked them and opened them, revealing an empty bedroom. She shook her head and smiled and then walked through her bedroom and down the short hallway to the front door to greet Forest.

Outside was darker than normal due to the storm, so she flipped on the light, peeked through the peephole, and found not Forest but Andy, Andy Kane.

"Great," she mumbled as she opened the door. "Andy, what are you doing here?"

"I'm glad I caught you, Lilee. We need to talk."

"I'm sorry, Andy, but now is not the time."

"It's important. It's about the Wells case, and I…"

She cut him off and held up her hand. "Andy, make an appointment with my office tomorrow and we'll discuss it then." She began to push the door closed, but Andy stuck out his foot.

"Lilee, please. This is important!"

Flabbergasted, Lilee sighed and then opened the door wider. "OK. You can come in, but you have five minutes and not a minute over."

She walked down her foyer and into the family room adjacent to the kitchen and turned. "OK. You can start talking now."

Lilee waited for him to speak and then noticed how frazzled he looked. His shirt was untucked, and his tie hung loosely around his neck—very out of character for the hot-shot public defender Andy Kane. She crossed her arms and narrowed her eyes as she tapped the toe of her leather boot.

Andy ran a hand through his blond hair and took a seat. Lilee slowly uncrossed her arms and walked over and took a seat across from him. "Andy, if this is so important, you should start talking because now you only have four minutes."

"Lilee, something's off with the Wells case, and…and I can't quite put my finger on it."

"Andy, it's gonna be a tough case to defend. There's clear motive involved with Kenny Wells and his grandfather, Henry Wells. The best you can hope for is a reduced sentence based on sympathy."

"No. I mean, yes. Look, I went over the case with Kenny, and yes, he was at your house and got arrested, but he is denying any involvement with the incident at the hotel where the officer and waiter were attacked."

Lilee tried not to roll her eyes. "Of course he would deny that. Assaulting an officer brings on another harsh offense. And the…"

272

He cut her off. "There's something else."

"Oh? Well, enlighten me."

"I talked to Johnny Rae Jordan this morning. You remember him? The brother of Ronny Jordan."

"No, not really, but OK." She looked at her watch: six o'clock. She wanted him to finish up and leave before Forest arrived. The last thing she needed or wanted was Andy Kane aware of a relationship between her and the detective. It could get complicated if he was pitted against her in the Hart case. She added, "Go on."

"Johnny Rae was in the house when he heard the multiple gun shots fired from an automatic. He said the first thing he thought was, 'They found him. It's too late.'"

"They found him?"

"Exactly. Now do you really think a sixty-eight-year-old dying man would be carrying around an automatic machine gun?"

"No. But wait, are you saying that Henry Wells didn't kill Ronny Jordan even though there was an eye witness placing him at the scene?" She looked at her watch again.

"Look, Lilee, I want to get back to Kenny Wells. He said he wasn't at your hotel." He reached out and grabbed her hand. "And I believe him, Lilee, which means, if he didn't knock out the officer, and he's telling the truth, who else is after you?"

A cold shiver ran down Lilee's back and she jerked her hand away. "Go back to Johnny Rae. Who are 'they'?"

Andy raked his hand over his head. "I'm not a hundred percent sure, but he said something about a botched drug run."

Lilee shook her head as she tried to process it all.

Andy continued. "Lilee, I don't think the attempt on Maggs and the hotel incident are related to any of the Wells family."

Lilee stood up. She was mad. "Andy, enough! You go and build your case, and our department will build ours." She walked toward the foyer, swung the front door open, and added, "And we will see you in court."

Andy had followed her over to the front door. "Lilee, this isn't about winning a case. I'm genuinely worried about…"

He stopped talking and all color drained from his face as a man appeared from Lilee's bedroom holding a gun. Startled, Lilee turned just as she heard a shot fired, hitting Andy Kane in the chest. Lilee saw Andy fall to the floor out of the corner of her eye as the man ran toward her pointing his gun. She took a step toward the open front door but stopped as her head burst with a sharp pain. She fell to the floor, and darkness filled her mind.

***

Todd and Tim were sitting in the family room surrounded by darkness. All the guests had left twenty minutes earlier, just before they lost power from the storm. There had been a large boom, and then the lights went out.

"Great. Just what we need to happen to top off a shitty day!"

Tim turned to Todd. "Yeah."

Holding a flashlight, Todd continued to press the button, on and off, on and off. Tim said, "Dude, enough. Save the batteries."

Todd laughed. "We used to do this as we told ghost stories, remember?"

Tim didn't think it was funny. They were, after all, in the home where their father was murdered. Now the damn power had been cut. Todd got up, struck a match, and lit four candles that decorated the mantle. "I don't think these are actually supposed to be lit, but I think Mom will understand under the circumstances."

Tim watched him. Finally he said, "Todd, I'm sorry about today. I should have told her no. Mom would've never known."

Todd surprised Tim when he replied, "Oh, yeah she would. Besides, what's done is done. I just don't understand why Mom would allow Dad's whore to show up at his funeral?"

Tim tensed. Todd only knew half of the story. Earlier he had explained to Todd how their mom had wanted Marla Kay there to end the rumors. If she wasn't there, then the rumors become true, and that would be more for her to deal with on top of her recovery. Should he tell him the rest of the story now? Would it help or just make things worse?

Tim rubbed his eyes. He was tired. Hell, both of them were. They had gotten little sleep over the last four days. He decided against it. Tomorrow they would both be able to think clearer after a nice, long sleep. "Since the power's out, I think I'm gonna call it a night."

"It's not even seven."

"Yeah, well, I think I only got three hours of sleep last night."

"Sure. Well, OK. I'm gonna stay up a little longer."

Tim walked over and grabbed a candle to use for light. "Just don't forget to blow all the candles out before you go up."

"I won't. Goodnight, Tim."

Tim paused and turned. "Goodnight, Todd."

275

Tim left the family room and made his way to the grand staircase in the foyer. Slowly he climbed the stairs as he placed his free hand behind the flame to keep it from blowing out. The house felt eerie with shadows bouncing along the walls as the flame flickered. When he reached the top of the stairs, he felt goose bumps at the thought of his parents' room at the end of the hall. He turned in the opposite direction quickly and the flame almost went out. "Shit," he mumbled.

Tim found his bedroom, which was next to Todd's. The house was designed for privacy, and both he and his brother had had that growing up with their rooms on the opposite side of the house from their parents' on the second floor. Tim looked at the large game room to the immediate right of Todd's bedroom and remembered the flashlight kept in the top drawer.

Bypassing his room, he entered the large room and opened the drawer. Finding the flashlight, he pulled it out and turned it on. Nothing. He smirked. Todd had run down the batteries and never replaced them. Thankful his mom was well organized, he opened another drawer and found several different battery packs with different size batteries. He opened the correct pack, and a minute later, the flashlight was working. Tim sat the candle down and blew out the flame.

Using the new light, Tim made his way toward his bedroom but stopped when he saw the model skeleton in the corner of the game room. He took a deep breath. He and his brother were the only kids they knew who had studied and memorized the skeletal system by the time they were ten years old. He shook his head and continued on.

Suddenly his heart stopped at the vibration in his shirt pocket. It was his phone. He was getting a call. He pulled it out and read "Unknown caller" as the ID. He thought about whether he should answer it. Probably just more family friends calling to check up on him. He was about to discard his phone when he thought it could be the hospital calling. Quickly he pressed a button.

"Tim Hart."

"It's me, Jenna."

Tim could barely hear her. She sounded far and away. "Jenna. We don't have a good connection."

He secretly hoped she would end the call, but she did not. "Tim, I need you to come over."

"What? No, Jenna. That wouldn't be a good idea."

He thought he heard a whisper in the background as she continued. "Please, Tim, I need you. It's important."

"Is Marla Kay there? Is that who I hear?"

"What? No. Just me and Rosemary. Look, please, please, Tim, come over. I've got to talk to you."

Tim tilted his head back and let the phone drop to his shoulder. He couldn't do this, not tonight. He held the phone back up to his ear and repeated again, "I can't. It's a bad idea."

He heard the hurt in her voice as she pleaded once more. She was crying. *Damn,* he thought. Jenna was crying and begging for him to come over. She had never done that. It was he who had been the heartbroken one, begging for her to give them another try. He couldn't tell her no. He couldn't. He remembered his mother's words about making it all right. Finally he said the words she wanted to hear. "Fine. I'll come over. It should take about a half hour."

"I'll be waiting, and Tim?"

"Yes?"

"Be careful. It's…"

Tim listened for more, but the line had gone dead. He shrugged it off. It was raining and he was about to get behind the wheel. He knew what she was trying to say. He pocketed his phone, went into his bedroom, and quickly changed into an Auburn sweatshirt and jeans. Next he put his tennis shoes on and grabbed his keys and wallet. As he left the bedroom and made his way down the hall and down the stairs, he thought about what to tell his brother. As his feet hit the last step he thought, *Nothing. I'll tell him nothing.* Five minutes later, Tim was driving out of the neighborhood.

Chapter 36

At 6:22, Forest arrived at Lilee's home. He quickly shut off his engine and climbed out. The heavy rain had stopped, and now only a light mist fell. Forest ran to the front door. He was finally dry and wanted to keep it that way. The front porch light was on, and another light shone down the hallway leading to the kitchen. Forest rang the doorbell and waited. A minute went by, and he hit the button again. Still no response. He touched the doorknob and turned it, but it was locked. Forest pressed his face against the glass and peered inside. He couldn't see anything but the faint light coming from the kitchen. Forest took a step back and walked across the wet grass toward her master bedroom window. Through the small crack in the blinds, he could see that the small lamp by her bed was on.

He walked back toward the front door, rang the bell again, and waited another minute. He looked to his right at the garage but had no way of knowing if her car was in there or not. *Did she go on without me?* He glanced at his watch. It was now nearing six thirty. *Damn. I'm late, and I didn't call. Why didn't I call? Shit, because I was giving orders on the phone to Shannon.*

Forest ran back to his car and climbed in. He picked up his phone off the center console and quickly dialed her number. No answer. He convinced himself she was driving and wouldn't answer her phone. He ended the call, fired up his engine, and took off in the direction of Mario's, the restaurant where they were to meet with Charli and Mark.

***

Trevor stepped off the elevator of the third floor in search of Marla Kay Abbott. He looked around and found a few people sitting in the small waiting area. A sign posted displayed an arrow pointing the way to the nurses' station. He proceeded down the hall and saw an older lady dressed in pink shrubs beside a food cart, delivering dinner to the patients. Trevor smiled as he passed the lady. He couldn't help but look at the food she was holding. He must have made a face because she smiled as she walked away and knocked on a patient's door.

Turning, he passed about eight patient rooms, all with their doors closed. A tall, dark-haired nurse standing at the nurses' station saw him approach. She set a chart down and asked, "May I help you, sir?"

"Yes. I'm Detective Trevor Watts, and I'm here to see Ms. Marla Kay Abbott. Is she available?"

The lady lifted her head as he stepped closer. She was five nine, and she felt like a mouse compared to this large man. "Um, is she expecting you?"

"No, ma'am."

"I see. Let me go find her and see if she's available."

Trevor nodded politely and waited as the nurse with the name tag that read "Brenda West" walked away.

Five minutes passed before Nurse West rounded the corner, alone. "I'm sorry to keep you waiting. Ms. Abbott is finishing up with a patient. She needs another ten minutes. Perhaps you could wait for her in the waiting room."

She showed no emotion as she gestured back down the hall toward the elevator. She was hard to read. *Is she a friend or just a co-worker?* he wondered. "Thank you. I'll be waiting." Trevor turned and walked down the long hall and once again passed the food cart as the lady grabbed another tray. She politely smiled again and then read over her notes on her clipboard before turning away with the food to deliver to the patient in 304.

The small waiting room held only four chairs and one couch with a small table filled with magazines and "get help" pamphlets. With his large frame, Trevor took the couch and picked up a magazine on hunting and fishing. When he completed his third article, he heard Marla Kay's voice and looked up.

"Detective."

He set the magazine down and stood. "Ms. Abbott, I'm sorry to bother you at work, but I have a few more questions."

Marla Kay didn't waste any time showing her dissatisfaction. "Detective, I'm really busy now. Can we do this tomorrow?"

Trevor stepped forward. "It's in your best interest to answer a few questions now."

She took a step back and looked up. "Do I need a lawyer?"

Great, he thought. He tried to downplay the situation. "Well, Ms. Abbott, I hope not. Please, just a few questions and I will leave you to work."

She sighed loudly, moved past him, and took a seat on the couch. "Five minutes, detective. That's all I can give you."

Trevor nodded and took his seat beside her. "Who's Rosemary Hart?"

Color drained from Marla Kay's face and she bowed her head and touched her forehead. She was shaking her head. He continued. "It's really a simple question. No need to make this more complicated than what it is."

She looked back up with cold eyes. "Rosemary has nothing to do with any of this."

"Oh. So the fact she receives twenty-five hundred dollars a month should just be swept under the rug, and we should continue looking elsewhere in our investigation into the death of William Hart?"

She looked around the small waiting room. The older woman who'd been sitting in one of the four chairs had left. They were all alone.

"Detective, Rosemary is a precious three-year-old little girl." Tears began to form in her eyes as she continued. "She really doesn't need to be splashed around in the media and…"

He interrupted, "You mean you don't need to be displayed as the mistress with the love child."

She narrowed her eyes and stood. "We're done. I have done nothing wrong!"

She took a step and Trevor grabbed her arm. She jerked away and squared her shoulders, facing him. "Arrest me!" Trevor didn't respond. "I thought so. The next time we answer questions, I'll have my lawyer present." She quickly spun around and stepped away.

"Ms. Abbott." Trevor's voice beamed loudly in the small room.

She stopped but didn't turn.

"Bring your lawyer to the station at nine a.m. If you fail to show, I'll issue a warrant."

She stood dead still listening to his words. Once again she straightened her back and walked down the hall without ever looking back.

As she walked, she felt his eyes burning a hole in the back of her head. When she was out of sight, she darted into an empty patient's room. She quickly walked toward the tall windows and pulled out her cell phone.

The line continued to ring on the other end. Finally his voice answered, but it was his voice mail. "Damn. Where are you, Derrick?" She quickly left a message and then ended the call. Next she pressed another number on her speed dial and waited for Jenna to pick up. Five rings soon turned into another voice mail. She leaned her head back and ran a hand through her long, dark hair. After the tone, she left a message. "Jenna, I need you to keep Rosemary at home and out of sight until I get home. The detective came back. They know about the money and her. Just…just keep her inside and don't answer the door to anyone."

She quickly ended the call, put her phone into her pocket, and left the room.

***

The room was dark. Lilee tried to reach up to feel her head, but her arm wouldn't cooperate. She closed her eyes as pain ripped through her head and willed her mind to remember what had happened to her. Moments passed before she tried to move her arm again. Nothing. She opened her eyes once more and concentrated, but it was so hard. The pain was so great. She felt a tug at her consciousness as it willed her back to sleep. She didn't fight it and closed her eyes, hoping the pain would just go away.

"Hey, blondie!"

She heard a voice and cracked her eyelids but found only darkness. Soon a bright light flipped on and the shock traveled through her brain at lightning speed. She closed her eyes and cried out from the pain, but the voice continued.

"It's showtime! So wake up, sleepy head. Time to go to work!"

Who is making all that noise? And why is the light so bright? Please. Please, someone, turn it off! she thought. The voice continued, and she felt a jolt as her body was lifted into the air and suddenly stopped. Someone set their hands on her shoulders to steady her. Slowly she took a deep breath and opened her eyes.

She screamed.

Chapter 37

Forest was five miles down the road from Lilee's home when he felt a sickening feeling in his gut. Their morning as well as last night had been too perfect to believe that Lilee would leave without a note or a call. His heart was trying to convince him that everything was OK, but his mind was making him think like a cop. Suddenly he pulled his Mustang off the highway, looked both ways, and did a three sixty. *No*, he thought. *Lilee would not have left me. What we have is real, and I wasn't that late*. He shifted quickly through four gears and traveled back to her home at high speed.

Seeing the lights from the neighborhood entrance up ahead, he down-shifted and then skidded on the wet road as he turned sharply into Spring Lake. Another three minutes passed as he flew down the country road estate hoping no livestock was out roaming around in the dark. He braked and then downshifted and turned into Lilee's driveway. Everything was the same as before. No additional lights were on, and none had been extinguished. Cutting the engine, he pulled out his phone and pressed a button on speed dial.

"Detective Forest Styles. I'm requesting backup at 34 North Spring Lake."

"Sir, what's your situation?"

Forest slammed the door and walked toward the house. "Lilee Parker is not answering her door. She should be home. Send backup." He quickly ended the call and climbed the few steps once again. He reached out and turned the doorknob. Still locked. He rang the doorbell, pressed his face up against the glass, and searched the long hallway for any movement. He looked to the left toward Lilee's room but found only darkness. He closed his eyes and tried to think. When he opened them back up, he noticed something on the floor to his right out of the corner of his eye. He squatted down and pressed his face harder against the glass in an attempt to see more. He could barely see in the darkness, but it looked like dark liquid on the tile.

Forest stood and rammed his shoulder into the door. Realizing that wasn't going to help, he turned around in search of an object he could propel through the glass. There on the corner of the porch sat a large potted plant. Acting on sheer gut instinct, he picked up the large pot, hoisted it over his shoulder, and threw it into the glass window with all his strength. Stepping forward, he reached in and hit the switch on the wall, illuminating the foyer. Forest looked down and felt sick at the sight of a man lying on his back bleeding from his chest, soaking his shirt and the floor with dark red blood. He removed his gun and flipped the safety switch.

Forest reached inside, careful not to get cut, and unlocked the door. He then pulled his hand back and opened the door and entered, yelling, "Lilee! Lilee!"

He knelt and felt the man's neck for a pulse. He had one, but barely. He stood and dialed the same number as before. "Detective Forest Styles requesting an ambulance at 34 North Spring Lake. Man down with GW to the chest."

"Yes, sir. Backup should be there within two minutes. Proceed with caution."

He ended his call and yelled again, "Lilee! Lilee! Answer me! It's Forest!"

Nothing but silence.

Forest eased forward to the master bedroom, found the light switch, and turned it on. He quickly scanned the room and then the closet—no sign of Lilee. He turned and made his way back down the hallway carefully and then over to the door leading to the garage. Checking around him, he slowly opened the door and took a stance, holding his gun forward. Just enough hall light revealed two cars: Lilee's silver Mercedes, parked in its usual spot, and an SUV he had never seen before. He closed the door and mumbled.

He heard a siren and made his way toward the kitchen and living room. Nothing. No sign of Lilee or a gunman. Hearing a door slam, Forest yelled out, "Detective Styles. Proceed with caution." He continued back toward the hallway and came face-to-face with Officer Carter. "What the hell happened in here?" the officer asked. "Aw, shit! It's Andy Kane." The officer kneeled and felt a pulse. "He's still alive."

Forest nodded. "I need to finish searching and securing the home. Stay alert."

Carefully Forest continued, checking every room and securing the house, but still no Lilee. Forest heard an ambulance and made his way back to the front door. He lowered his gun and announced, "Home secure. We got one GW to the chest with light pulse."

Forest stepped aside as the paramedics rushed in and took over. Officer Carter stood and looked around. "Where's Ms. Parker?"

"I don't know." Forest frowned as he picked his phone back up and dialed Maggs.

Maggs answered on the third ring.

"Daniel, it's Forest. We got a situation."

The paramedics continued to work, and soon they had Andy Kane loaded into the back of the ambulance and pulled away.

"Maggs, contact everyone on your staff. We've missed something."

"I don't understand. Henry Wells is dead. This can't be happening."

Forest paced back and forth and replied, "I'm gonna head over to Mario's. Lilee and I were supposed to meet Charli Pepper there for dinner. Maybe…maybe Lilee is already there."

"I'll call Charli and tell her to wait until you get there."

Forest added, "And if she hears from or sees Lilee, tell her to stay put. I'm on my way."

"But Forest, why…why was Andy Kane at her house?"

He stood in the foyer and looked at the blood left behind. "I don't know, Daniel. I just don't know."

Forest ended his call, gave Officer Carter instructions, and ran to his vehicle, climbed in, and sped away.

I-75 wasn't that crowded on a weeknight around seven. Most cars got out of his way as he continued traveling at high speed. He tried to concentrate as he shifted down a gear and took the exit that would take him downtown to Mario's. He eased through three green lights and pulled into the valet parking area outside Mario's. Tossing the keys to an attendant, he flashed his badge and commanded, "Hold my car. I need five minutes inside."

The attendant nodded and then looked back at his partner with a strange look.

Forest climbed the stairs two at a time, pulled the thick glass and wrought iron doors open, and stepped inside. Immediately he saw Charli and Mark sitting at the bar—without Lilee. His throat caught as he moved through the crowd and approached the couple, who were chatting without a care in the world.

Charli noticed him and then frowned when she saw his worried expression. His untucked shirt was rumpled with a dark stain. She looked behind him but found no Lilee. Before she could ask questions, he asked, "Did Maggs not call you?"

Charli opened her mouth to speak, but no words formed. Mark quickly said, "I made her leave her phone at home, beside mine. Why? What's wrong?"

Charli finally found her voice and asked, "Where's Lilee?"

Forest shook his head and placed his hands on his hips. "I don't know, but we need to get out of here. Something's gone wrong."

Mark nudged Charli off the chair. "I'll take care of the bill and meet you two out front. Charli nodded and followed Forest through the crowd and out the door. As soon as they were outside, Charli blasted away. "Forest, tell me now. Where's Lilee, and what's wrong?"

"I went to her house, and she wasn't there. Instead, I found Andy Kane shot in the chest."

Mark walked out and heard the last part. "Is he alive?" he asked.

Forest looked at him and then back to Charli. "He was twenty minutes ago, but barely."

Mark wrapped an arm around Charli as she swayed back and forth. An attendant walked up to them, and Mark handed him his ticket. Forest glanced over and saw his Mustang in the same place and the young man waiting on some new instructions. "I want you to take Charli home. There will be an officer there waiting."

"But Forest, we've got to find Lilee!"

"I'm going to do my best, Charli. Mark, take her home. It's safer."

Charli looked as if she was going to be sick. Forest tried to comforter her by saying, "I will call you when I know something, promise!" Then he turned and sprinted toward his car.

***

The man dressed in black wearing a ball cap stepped forward and shoved a cloth in Lilee's mouth, ending her screams. Her head was pounding, and she felt as if she was going to be sick. *No*, she told herself. *Not now. You'll choke to death!* Lilee tried to calm herself and steady her breathing. She blinked her eyes trying to clear her head and adjust to the bright light. This man hadn't killed her. Instead she was tied to a chair in what appeared to be someone's kitchen. *Whose?* she wondered. *Where am I, and who is this man?*

Suddenly a memory of Andy Kane getting shot flashed before her eyes. *Oh, no. Not Andy. Oh my God! He's dead at my house.* She started to panic and couldn't breathe. A sharp pain radiated through her skull, and her stomach twisted. She was going to be sick. The man tilted his head to the side and narrowed his eyes. Just before Lilee choked to death on her own vomit, he stepped forward and removed the rag just in time for her to lurch forward, throwing up on herself and coughing madly.

"Oh, for crying out loud! Really?"

Lilee stopped coughing and was about to scream before he held out his hand with the rag and said, "Scream and this goes back in!"

Lilee closed her mouth and eyes and bowed her head. She heard him walk away and then more noise as he poured a glass of water from the tap. At the sound of his footsteps, she looked up and opened her eyes once again. She spoke softly. "Please untie me."

He laughed. A laugh from a dark, twisted soul. He placed the glass to her mouth and tilted it. She was chattering and could hear her teeth rattling against the glass. Water ran down her neck and onto her clothing, but it was refreshing since she was covered in her own vomit.

He pulled the glass away and then set it on the table. Lilee swayed to the side as the man watched her. The pain in her head was so great.

"I think you might have a slight concussion. That wasn't my plan. For a while, I thought you weren't gonna wake up, and that would've been bad, really bad."

She tried to study him and place whether she knew him, but it was so hard and her brain refused to cooperate. He looked at his watch and then turned once more and grabbed a dish towel and wet it. He walked back over and began wiping Lilee's face, neck, and chest. When he lingered a little too long over her breasts, she whimpered, "Don't."

He smirked. "No. That's not what I have in mind with you, Lilee."

She watched as he dropped the towel on the floor, put his boot on it, and began to wipe up her vomit. She had to tear her eyes away so she wouldn't get sick all over again. When he backed away, she looked at him and met his eyes. Timidly she asked, "Why…why am I here?"

"Because you're the best."

"Wh…What?"

"A crime has been committed. A serious crime, and you're gonna see to it that the case is brought to trial."

She heard his words and her first thoughts were, *Yeah, you killed Andy Kane in my home!* But she forced herself not to speak but to listen. She wanted to get out of here alive, not send him over the edge and take a bullet in her chest. So she closed her eyes and nodded as she took a deep breath.

He looked at his watch once more and continued. "We don't have much time. I'm gonna move you now." As he neared her, he spoke sharply. "Don't scream and fight me. I'll kill you if you do."

She nodded.

He stepped closer and then bent down and picked her up, along with the chair he'd tied her to, and carried her down a small hallway and set her down with the chair back against the garage door. He flipped off a light switch in the hall and then commanded, "I'm not gonna gag you again." He lifted his gun and placed it to her heart. "If you talk before I give you permission, I won't hesitate to kill you. I can always find Wes Schultz, or perhaps your partner, Charli Pepper, to finish the job."

Lilee's eyes widened and she shook her head without making a sound.

"Good. No one will see you back here, or at least for your sake, you better hope not."

She took a deep breath through her nose and exhaled through her mouth. *What the hell does he have planned?* she thought as she tried to steady her breathing. The last thing she wanted was for him to get Charli. *I can do this*, she thought. *Yes, I can*, and she closed her eyes and waited for what was to come.

Chapter 38

The power was still out at the Hart estate when Todd went into the kitchen and grabbed a beer. He was two years shy of the legal drinking age, but that had never been a problem when he wanted a beer. Todd didn't drink much—well, at least not as much as his brother. If he did drink, it was usually on weekends when it was time to cut loose and have some fun. The weeks were long, filled with studying and a rigorous class load.

He popped the top and tossed it into the full waste bin. Since it had started raining, no one had taken the trash out. He looked around. The place was always so tidy and clean, he struggled to remember the bin ever getting this full. His mom had always been the one to empty it, which was odd because most boys took out the trash as part of their daily chores, but not them. His mom had always insisted schoolwork and studying were more important.

Finally he stepped away from the bin and pushed thoughts of his mother out of his head. He wanted something else to occupy his time. He needed a release from all the pain. Todd left the kitchen and walked into the large family room. The power was out, but he decided to pick out a movie anyway for when it did come back on. Raising the flashlight he had found earlier in the kitchen, he shined the light on the wall that held rows of cabinets. The cabinets on the far right held the movies. He opened the double doors to reveal three shelves of DVDs and smiled, noticing they were all still alphabetized. He had surprised the family one Saturday about two years earlier. For whatever reason, everyone had stuck to the system.

Todd found one of his favorite action-packed thrillers staring Matt Damon. He was a big fan of the *Bourne* series. He set the small case down on top of the DVD player and then walked over to the matching set of cabinets displaying several photo albums in all shapes and sizes. His mom had discovered scrapbooking five years earlier and had redone all their pictures according to vacations and special events. He remembered one day how she had proudly showed them to him. He held up the light and slowly ran it across the albums. At the far right at the end, he saw something pushed back further, almost hidden. Curious, he pulled it out and walked over to the couch and sat down with it.

The album was thin and ordinary. No design and no cut-out opening for a photo on the front. His curiosity peeked, he opened it. There were a few old newspaper clippings in the front, and when he picked them up he saw the first picture of Rosemary. *Who is she?* he thought. He began to flip each page and watched how the little girl went from a small infant in the arms of his mother to a little toddler running around in the backyard with his mother laughing behind her. He didn't understand. *Is this a sibling I never knew, that maybe died? No. No, impossible! Mom looks, well, like she does now,* he thought.

He flipped another page and saw Marla Kay holding the same toddler. *What the hell? No. That can't be!* He slammed the photo album shut and tossed it onto the coffee table. A porcelain ball fell off a stand and began rolling across the wooden table. Startled, Todd reached out and grabbed it just in time. Carefully he picked up its stand and set it back on top. Looking at it, he thought, *How is this decorative?* He shook his head. "Damn it, Mother, why would you have photos of Marla Kay with a child? What the hell is going on!"

Angrily he grabbed the album once more, opened it up again, and saw the newspaper clippings. There were three. The first one was a story about an automobile accident that had taken the life of a young mother. He glanced over the picture and title and then looked at the next one. This one was an obituary with a picture of a beautiful young woman. Todd read the name: Kimberly Lewis Kolar, age twenty-seven, Atlanta, Georgia. She was pretty. He set it down and picked up the last clipping. It was another article, but it was about the same crash, just one year later, the anniversary of the same crash from the first clipping. Todd set it down, picked the first one back up, and sat back down and began to read the article with his flashlight.

The story was tragic. A two-car collision on a dark, wet country road had sent one teenager to the hospital, a minor, and one Kimberly Kolar was pronounced dead at the scene. A third passenger, also a minor, was unharmed. Cause of the accident was unknown, as police reported that a drug and alcohol test had been negative.

Todd picked up the obituary next and read it. *Kimberly Lewis Kolar was a second-grade teacher who will be greatly missed by her staff and students.* He paused and set the clipping down for a moment. More sadness filled his heart. It had been a long, tiring day. Soon he picked it back up and learned that Kimberly was survived by her husband of four years and a two-week-old baby girl. "Oh my God!" he said aloud. His voice felt loud in the large, dark home. Suddenly he felt a chill down his spine and remembered he wasn't alone. Tim was upstairs, sleeping.

He picked up the last article again and read. It restated most of what he had learned from the other two clippings, but this one stated the cause of the accident: brake failure on the car driven by Kimberly Kolar. An investigation was conducted to determine whether the teenagers in the other car had run a red light, but it was finally ruled that Kimberly had caused the accident.

Quickly he picked up the album and began flipping through the pages once more. *Is this the little girl who lost her mother? Is that possible?* He set the album back down and picked up the first article to read the date: October 13, 2009. Three years earlier. *The little girl would be three*, he thought. Frustrated, he stood up, closing the album, and went in search of his brother. Just as he rounded the corner to the foyer, the lights came back on. "Thank you, God!"

Todd ran up the spiral staircase, forgetting all about his movie. When he got to the top, he couldn't help but stare down the long hallway leading to his parents' master suite. He paused for a moment to catch his bearings and then ran in the opposite direction and down another hallway to Tim's room. When Todd reached the doorway, he flipped the light switch and found Tim's room empty. "Tim!" he yelled and then ran to his room and found it empty as well. Next he climbed the stairs and entered the game room—also empty. "Tim! Where are you, dude?"

Todd jogged down the hallway and then stopped when he saw his parents' door. *Is he in there? Oh, God. Surely not*, he thought. The power flickered off and then back on. "What the hell? Tim! Where are you? This isn't funny!"

The lights flickered two more times as Todd stood, frozen, and then his greatest fear happened. The lights went back out.

Todd fumbled for his flashlight but dropped it. He heard the case pop off and the batteries spill out as it hit the floor. "Shit!"

Spooked, Todd held onto the banister and flew down the stairs toward the faint light from the candles that were still lit. Standing in the large family room, he took a deep breath and then reached into his pocket and felt his phone. He pressed one on his speed dial and soon heard Tim's phone ringing against his ear. He mumbled, "Answer, Tim. Answer the damn ph…"

"Hello?"

Todd sighed loudly. "Where are you?"

"I'm driving down the road now."

"What? When did you leave?"

"A while ago. Look, I'll explain when I get back."

"No. Explain now!"

"Easy, Todd. I'll be back in an hour, and we…"

"Damn it, Tim! Don't tell me to take it easy. There's too much stuff going on that I have no idea what's it about."

Tim could hear the hurt and frustration in his brother's voice. "Tell me what happened."

"I…I was bored, so I was looking at the photo albums."

Tim frowned. He had left his brother home alone after they'd just buried their father. He felt bad. They were a close family, and his brother needed him. Tim slowed his car and was going to find a place to pull over and turn around when he heard his brother continue.

"I found this other album, and it's full of photos of Mom, Marla Kay, and some little girl."

Tim tightened his grip on the steering wheel and didn't respond.

Todd heard the silence and immediately knew what it meant. "Damn it, Tim. You know about this, don't you?"

"Look, I can explain, Todd. It's not what you're thinking."

"Oh, how do you know what I'm thinking? There's newspaper clippings as well, something about a crash where a young mother was killed."

Tim didn't respond.

"Tim? Tell me what all this means, damn it!"

"OK. Take it easy. I will."

"Take it easy? Seriously? You know about all this. I…I have no clue what's going on."

Tim felt terrible. This was not the way he'd wanted his brother to find out, and of all nights. "Todd, I'm sorry. I was wrong to keep this from you. When I get home, I promise to tell you everything."

"When you get home? What's wrong with now?"

Tim made a decision to keep moving. He was almost to the Abbott home. "Look Todd, I'm driving now to see a friend. I won't be long."

"Oh, well does *she* have a name?" Todd asked sarcastically.

Tim knew he was angry and didn't want to continue the conversation because he knew it would end badly. "Todd, I'm hanging up now. I'll be home in about an hour. Bye."

The line went dead, and Todd threw his phone at the plush sofa. Angrily he paced back and forth. Finally he picked his phone back up, opened a drawer, and took out a set of keys to his mother's car. Beside the keys lay another flashlight. He took it also, turned it on, and quickly blew out all the candles, and walked to the front door. *If Tim isn't gonna give me answers, then Marla Kay will*, he thought. Just as he touched the door-knob, he froze as the date from the article clicked in his mind. He ran back into the family room and picked up the album.

Finding the article of the crash, he looked at the date: October 13. The crash had happened the night before, on the twelfth—the same date his father was killed and his mother attacked. "This can't be happening!" He set the article back down and raked his hands through his dark hair. *This is bad*, he thought. *And Tim, where is he going?*

Standing up he looked around the room but couldn't find what he was looking for. *Now, where is that card the detective gave me?* Giving up because he honestly had no clue, he dug his phone back out of his shirt pocket and dialed the operator.

Before the voice finished with a greeting, he blurted out, "Atlanta PD. Forward me. Hurry."

***

Headlights flashed across the kitchen wall of the Abbott home. Someone had pulled up, and Lilee could only wait with dread to see what happened next. The doorbell rang and she heard a door open. Then something crashed to the floor. A few minutes later, a tall young man entered the room followed by her kidnapper with a young woman, his gun placed against her temple. Lilee wanted to scream out but didn't. The man was unstable, and she had no doubt he would shoot her.

"Sit down, Tim!" The young man quickly sat in the chair the man pointed to. Carefully the kidnapper stepped away from the young lady and shoved her into another chair on the other side of the table. Lilee focused on the young couple but had no clue who they were. The woman with long, dark hair was shaking uncontrollably as she clutched her shoulders for some kind of support. She wore fitted black lounge pants and a long, thin, gray T-shirt with no shoes or socks. *Is this her house?* Lilee thought. *Was she already here earlier, hidden away?*

Lilee turned her attention back to the fit young man with blond hair. He couldn't be much over twenty. He wore sneakers, jeans, and a university sweatshirt. He must have been the one who just arrived. A clearer picture began to form. She was in the young lady's home, and the man with the gun had somehow manipulated Tim into showing up. The deranged man pulled a tape recorder out of his jacket, set it on the table, and began talking.

"Today is Tuesday, October 16, 2012. My name is Adam Kolar, age thirty-four."

"Oh, mister, please," said Tim in an anguished voice.

Adam hit the stop button and pointed the gun at the woman. "You interrupt again, I will kill her. Do we understand?"

299

Tim nodded.

Adam rewound the recorder and pressed the record button once more. "Today is Tuesday, October 16, 2012. My name is Adam Kolar, age thirty-four. I'm here today with Tim Hart, age…" and Adam gestured for him to answer.

Timidly Tim spoke. "Nineteen."

Lilee narrowed her eyes and concentrated on the man's face. *Is that one of the Hart twins I read about in the paper? What is going on?* she wondered.

"And Jenna Abbott, age…" Adam nodded to Jenna, who, in a shaky voice, responded, "Twenty-one."

"Three years ago, my wife, Kimberly Lewis Kolar, age twenty-seven, was tragically killed in an automobile accident, which involved the present two teenagers, Tim Hart and Jenna Abbott."

Lilee saw Tim bow his head, and Jenna began to weep. At that moment, Lilee knew that Adam Kolar had killed William Hart and his housekeeper.

"My beautiful, gifted, talented wife left behind a beautiful baby girl, Abigail Kristina, who has now had three birthdays without her mother."

Adam pressed the stop button. "Each of you will have a chance to speak, and when you do, I caution your tone. And no crying will be heard, or else…" he waved the gun around "…you won't take the stand to testify tonight."

Oh my God. He's creating a trial, and he expects me to weigh in! thought Lilee. She closed her eyes and swallowed. *He's not done. He's gonna kill them*, she thought. She forced herself to remain calm. If she cried out, she was sure to die as well. Slowly she opened her eyes to face the tragedy that had found all three of them again, after three years.

Neither spoke. Both looked defeated and guilty as the man in front of them continued after pressing the record button again. "Jenna Abbott, a young tramp who at the age of seventeen got herself pregnant by Tim, who at the time was fifteen, and who happened to be the son of a wealthy family."

Lilee noticed Tim ball his hands into a fist, but he refused to look at either Jenna or Adam.

"Instead of marriage and bringing her baby daughter up into a family with a mother and father, she pawns off her daughter on her sister and continues her wild ways."

Adam made a face at Jenna as if the very sight of her made him ill. He turned to Tim next. "Tim Hart doesn't marry the tramp because it would bring shame and embarrassment to the great and almighty Hart Family. Instead he doesn't own up and become a man and chooses the easy way out and allows his parents to pay for his mistake. Now, I know what you might be thinking: Fifteen is too young for marriage, but to deny his daughter a relationship with her own father is unforgivable and shallow."

Tim looked up with fire in his eyes, and Adam stopped talking and raised the gun. Lilee could see the anger building in Tim, and she thought he was going to explode at any moment—ending it all in the worst way. Adam stepped closer with his gun still aimed and finally Tim backed down and turned away to face the wall in the opposite direction.

Adam continued. "Jenna, who isn't tied down with a child, continues her carefree life and once again meets up with Tim Hart for a little romp up on Lookout Road on a dark October night. That is the road you were traveling down late one Friday night. Correct, Jenna?"

She nodded.

"Jenna, I need you to answer verbally for the court."

She looked at Tim with such sadness and softly said, "Yes."

Adam turned to Tim. "And did she give you what you wanted again Tim, or did she tease you into giving her more money?"

Tim met his stare. "I've always loved Jenna. I've never stopped."

Adam laughed and genuinely looked perplexed. "And did you know about these feelings, Jenna?"

She studied Tim and their eyes met. "You still love me?"

Adam slammed his fist on the table and Jenna jumped. "Um…um…I'm sorry. What was the question?"

"Doesn't matter. So he loves you and always has, but not enough to marry you and give you the prestigious Hart name, right Tim?"

Tim didn't respond, so Adam continued. "Have you asked Jenna Abbott to marry you, Tim?"

"No."

Adam's tone was cold. "And do you ever plan on marrying this little tramp?"

Tim looked away from Jenna, and his face turned a shade pink.

Adam laughed. "Thought not. But I'm sure she will be forever your little whore as you lead a different life surrounded by money and power. She would never live up to the standards of a doctor's wife, now would she, Tim?"

Tim suddenly looked up at Adam and then toward Jenna, who looked hurt and humiliated. With all the confidence Tim could muster, he asked loudly, "Jenna Marie Abbott, will you marry me?"

A shot was fired.

Chapter 39

An officer walked into the conference room that had been assigned for the Hart case and immediately saw Detective Watts looking over a file and making notes.

"Detective, I've got a call on line three from Todd Hart. He claims it's urgent."

Trevor rolled his chair sideways, leaned over the table, and picked up the phone.

"Detective Watts speaking."

Immediately he heard fear and panic. "It's Todd Hart. I know who killed my father, and I think my brother's in danger!"

"OK, Mr. Hart. Calm down and give me a name."

"I…I don't have a name."

Trevor sat back in his chair and set his pen down. Calmly he said, "OK. Maybe you should start from the beginning."

"I found a photo album tonight, and it had newspaper clippings of an accident and photos of a little girl."

Trevor immediately thought, *Rosemary Hart,* but he didn't interrupt.

"Three years ago, on the night my father was killed, there was a car accident that killed a woman. She...she left behind a small child."

Trevor snapped his fingers to get Shannon's attention and hit a button on the phone for speaker. "What was the name of the woman in the article?"

"Kimberly Lewis Kolar. I found three clippings, and Tim is missing."

Trevor saw his team go to work and then frowned. "Missing?"

"I mean, he left the house without telling me. When I tried to find him, I couldn't. I called his mobile, and he explained he had to see someone."

"He didn't give a name?"

"No. I told him about the articles, and he said he would explain everything when he returned. It's not like him to leave without telling me. It's almost like he was sneaking out."

"When did you talk to him last?"

"About ten minutes ago," responded Todd.

"Any idea who this friend is?"

After a long pause, Todd finally answered. "I think it could be Marla Kay. Marla Kay Abbott. She's a nurse that worked for my father. She was in the pictures holding the little girl. Or it could be..."

"Who?"

"Jenna, her sister. Tim and her were once real close."

"When was this?" asked Trevor.

"Off and on for a couple of years, since they were teenagers."

Trevor inquired, "Where are you now?"

"I'm home."

"Good. Stay there. I'm sending an officer over. Don't leave."

"OK. But what about Tim?"

"Ms. Abbott is working, so we'll go to her home."

"How do you know that about Marla Kay?"

Trevor smiled. "We always find out everything. It's our job."

***

Forest's phone rang and he quickly hit a button. His headset was hooked up as he drove toward the station where he was to meet his partner, Trevor.

"Forest," he answered in a serious tone.

"It's Trevor. We got a call from Todd Hart. He's all upset because he fears for his brother's life. He's claiming he knows why his dad's dead."

"I'm turning into the parking lot now. Hold that thought. I'm coming up."

Forest pulled off his headset, quickly exited his car, and ran up the stairs to the Atlanta Police Department. Opening the door, he immediately saw Trevor, who handed him a printout. Forest took what appeared to be a newspaper article and glanced at the headline as Trevor continued.

"He claims his dad's death was because of some car accident over three years ago. He even found newspaper clippings and pictures of a little girl tucked away in some album. And get this: the two minors in the car accident were Tim Hart and Jenna Abbott—Marla Kay Abbott's sister."

Forest tried to concentrate on all that Trevor was saying, but he couldn't get Lilee and the idea that she was in serious danger out of his mind. Trevor picked up on it when he didn't answer and added, "No word on Lilee Parker, but there's something troubling about the Wells case."

"What?" Forest demanded.

"It definitely looks like a suicide with Henry Wells, but it was a single shot to the head, a .22. We found no gun, but Mr. Wells does have a .22 registered in his name."

Forest interrupted, "It wasn't the automatic used on Ronny Jordan."

"Exactly. But there's a lot more. Andy Kane's assistant phoned. She claims Andy thought Lilee was in danger, that it wasn't Kenny Wells that was after her."

"Wait, this doesn't make sense. Kenny Wells was arrested at her home," commented Forest.

"The assistant claims Kenny only admitted to killing the cat. He said he wasn't at the hotel. It wasn't him."

Color drained from Forest's face and he spoke softly. "Lilee."

Trevor reached out and grabbed his arm. "I know. I looked into the police statements taken from Johnny Rae Jordan this morning. He's the brother. Well, he claims Ronny said he was in a hurry to leave because a drug deal had gone south and they were coming for him."

"Henry Wells was identified at the scene."

"He was, by a young woman named Marilynn Sutton. But we haven't found any automatic."

"So Henry Wells just happened to be outside when the druggies made their hit? This…this is unbelievable!"

"I think so," Trevor agreed. "Look, one more thing: I think the attempt on Maggs' life is connected to Lilee."

"What about the connection made earlier on the truck owner and Henry Wells?"

An officer ran toward them and interrupted. "Detectives, we got something."

Trevor and Forest looked up to find an officer holding a printout. Trevor nodded for him to speak.

The Officer stated loudly, "Police Officer John Norman was at the scene of the accident involving Kimberly Kolar and the minors, Hart and Abbott. He was the one who filed the report three years ago."

Trevor replied, "Wait a minute! The officer gunned down the day after Hart's murder?"

The officer nodded. "His notes state the cause of accident was brake failure by Kimberly Kolar, the deceased. We dug some more, and here's the disturbing part: the husband of the deceased, Adam Kolar, was not satisfied. Mr. Kolar hounded the district attorney's office, but his claim that the teenagers were at fault was denied and the case was closed."

Forest exclaimed, "Maggs and Lilee!"

The officer nodded. "Yeah. They were the ones who rejected the case."

It was all slowly coming together now. Adam Kolar was the one at the hotel. Adam Kolar had killed Hart and Norman and attempted the hit on Maggs. Forest felt sick. *Lilee. Where is she?* he wondered.

Forest placed both hands on his forehead and rubbed. He mumbled, "We're losing time."

"Maybe, maybe not. Todd Hart said Tim was going to visit a friend but didn't know who it was."

"Jenna. He's on his way to see Jenna."

Trevor nodded. "Could be. Come on! It could be a setup, and Lilee just might be there."

Forest shot his partner a look of doubt and then yelled, "Find anyone else associated with that car crash and put a man on 'em. Anyone hears anything, I want to know."

"Let's go, team," commanded Trevor. "Address: 1685 Holly Hills Road. Radios on channel three. Let's keep it quiet once in neighborhood."

Forest nodded. He hoped and prayed they weren't too late as he left the station, followed by their team of eight men.

***

The loud shot brought a throbbing pain back to Lilee's head, and she squinted her eyes. She didn't want to see more bloodshed. Hearing a loud cry, she opened her eyes to find Tim crouched on the floor and Jenna hugging her knees crying harder. There was no blood.

Adam still stood pointing the gun at Tim, but he hadn't shot anyone. *Thank God!* she thought. A memory of Andy Kane flashed through her mind. He was dead, killed in her living room. *This man is so unstable. Oh, God, I don't won't to be next,* she thought. *Help me, please!* she prayed silently.

"Get up, now!"

Tim was clearly rattled as he found his chair. Lilee looked past Tim and found a hole in the bar behind him. Adam had shot right beside him to scare him, not kill him. *Maybe there's a chance to get out of this alive after all,* she thought.

"We're not done with the story yet, Tim. Your time is coming, though. Count on it."

She was wrong. He was planning to kill him.

Chapter 40

It took a few minutes for Adam to rewind his tape recorder and stop the tape just before the "Marry me, Jenna" part. Satisfied, he set the device down again and hit record.

"The accident reports filed by Officer John Norman claim both minors were out of the crashed vehicle belonging to Jenna Abbott when he arrived. Kimberly Kolar, the driver of the second vehicle, was crushed behind the wheel, pronounced dead at the scene."

Tim looked at Jenna, who appeared white as a ghost. His eyes urged her to stay strong and silent.

Adam continued. "Jenna Abbott stated she was driving, not Tim Hart. Jenna, is this true?"

She looked at Tim. Bad move. It clearly showed her guilt. Adam commented, "Thought so. Tim Hart was driving, wasn't he?" He lifted a gun to her head and then yelled, "Tell the truth or I'll kill you now!"

Tearfully she nodded. "Yes. It was my car, and I was older, and…"

Adam laughed. "Don't make excuses for him."

He looked over at Tim. "Tell me why you lied. Or she's dead. Five, four, three, two…"

"I was scared, OK? I'm sorry."

"Were you drinking?"

"No. We both were tested."

Adam studied Tim and realized he was telling the truth. He never did know for sure if this was a cover-up or not. He pondered his next question over the next minute.

"OK. Why did you crash into my wife?

"It was an accident. She didn't stop at the red light."

Anger began to build within Adam. "My wife would never run a stop light. She…she was the most careful driver. You did! Tell the truth. You ran the stop light!"

Tim felt torn. He didn't know what answer to give. Either way he saw his life flash before him. He was going to die. He looked at Jenna. He couldn't admit they had run a stop light. She would die as well because of her knowledge of the cover-up. So, he did what he thought was best. He lied. "I did not run the red light. I came down from the hill just as the light turned from red to green, never brake checking. I…I should have slowed, but I didn't. The light turned green, and I drove through, except…she was in the way. I just remember a loud crash, and I temporary blacked out."

"Silence!" shouted Adam Kolar. He turned and faced Jenna. "Is that how it happened? My wife ran a red light?"

She looked at Tim and spoke softly. "Your wife's brakes were messed up. Even the mechanic said so in the investigation. It was her…"

"Silence!" Adam reached into his pocket and retrieved a folded paper. He tossed it to Jenna and demanded, "Read it aloud."

Timidly Jenna took the paper and unfolded it, spreading it out in front of her. She glanced over it, and sadness filled her eyes.

"Read it, now."

"To the payee, Tom Franklin, in the amount of five thousand dollars. Signed, Christa Hart."

"What is the name of the company at the top?"

"Elegant Grace Designs."

Adam nodded his head and then looked at Tim. "Do you know who Tom Franklin is?"

Tim shook his head and then softly replied, "No. I don't know him."

"He's the owner of an auto repair shop in Atlanta. Now, Jenna dear, read the date."

With dread, she replied, "October 21, 2009."

Adam reached into his other pocket and retrieved another sheet of folded paper and tossed it to Tim. "Your turn. Open it up and read it aloud, Tim."

Tim grabbed the paper and opened it, and the color drained from his face. "I had no idea! I promise!"

Adam took two steps toward Jenna and stuck a gun under her chin forcefully. Jenna cried out in pain. "I said read it. Don't give your stupid comments. We're presenting the facts tonight, something that was never done three years ago."

Tim swallowed. Slowly he read, "I examined the brakes to a 2001 Honda Accord belonging to Kimberly Lewis Kolar. The brakes were not working sufficiently. They were long overdue for repair. It is in my opinion that the crash very likely could have happened due to brake failure. Signed, Tom Franklin, owner of Franklin Body and Repair Shop." Tim set the paper in his lap and bowed his head.

"You're missing a key fact, Tim. Read the date."

Tim closed his eyes and took a deep breath. Finally he answered, "October 22, 2009."

Adam removed his gun from Jenna's chin and stood between them once more. He stated for the sake of the recorder, "So, to summarize the facts, Tom Franklin received five grand one day prior to his report. Something doesn't sound legit, now does it?" Adam turned his face toward the dark hallway where Lilee sat. Their eyes met, and Lilee felt a chill run down her back as he asked, "What do you think, counselor?"

***

A black sedan pulled along the street two houses down from Marla Kay Abbott's home. Behind Trevor, who was driving the sedan, were four marked police cars. Forest picked up his radio and said, "Roberts and Jones, take the back right corner. Jansen and Carter, I want you at the back left corner. Mitchell and Clark, you're on crowd control. Don't let anyone come near the Abbott home. Brown and Jenkins, you're with us on front. Stay down and vigilant. Move out."

Two doors quickly opened and closed on the black sedan as Trevor and Forest stepped out and ran a few feet down the street and onto the Abbott property. Like a well-oiled machine, the team worked efficiently together as they closed in with weapons in hand.

Forest tried the front doorknob, found it unlocked, and nodded to the three men behind him. They split and moved lower around the windows and peered inside for a visual.

"Jones here," said a voice quietly over their radios. "I got visual on one male gunman and two who appear unarmed. Kitchen, second window on right."

"Affirmative. Watts and Styles moving in from the front. Silence on radios," announced Forest and then turned to Brown and motioned for him to move toward the garage and Jenkins to watch the front door. Slowly Forest turned the doorknob and quietly entered the dark foyer with Trevor right on his heels.

As Lilee was announced, she noticed how Jenna jumped and turned to her left, startled that they hadn't been alone. Adam spoke loudly for the recorder. "Atlanta's best city prosecutor is present. Please state your name loudly for the recorder."

She took a deep breath and answered, "Lilee Parker."

Forest heard her voice and silently gave thanks as he glanced to Trevor, who nodded back to let him know he had heard her as well.

"Yes. We have Lilee Parker, the city prosecutor, present here tonight to help us clear up some facts that she grossly misrepresented to her boss, District Attorney Daniel Maggs, three years ago."

Lilee silently cringed. It was so long ago. So many cases had since come and gone, but she vaguely remembered looking over the case of Kimberly Kolar and advising Maggs that they didn't have a case. Listening to the deranged Adam Kolar tonight, she wasn't so sure of the decision she had made so long ago.

Adam kept his gun pointed at Tim. He wasn't too concerned about Jenna. She didn't look strong enough, mentally or physically, to stop him. Tim, on the other hand, did, so he kept him in his sights at all times. He glanced at Parker briefly and continued. "Now, Ms. Parker, please answer this question. What do you think of the fact that a five thousand dollar check was written by Tim Hart's mother at the same time a report was submitted laying fault to the other driver, Kimberly Lewis Kolar?"

With a shaky voice, she replied, "It looks suspicious."

"Suspicious. You don't say?" he said sarcastically. "What about the fact the check was written from her place of business instead of a personal check from the Hart's personal bank account?"

"Even more suspicious."

"Yes, it does, Ms. Parker. But tell me, why didn't you take this case seriously enough when I requested? A simple check into Tom Franklin's bank account would have been sufficient to launch a full-scale investigation, would it not have been?"

Lilee didn't answer. There was no answer she could give to satisfy this madman, so she remained silent.

"Answer the question. Why didn't you do your job as I requested?"

She noticed that his hand shook slightly as he held the gun. He was so angry, and he looked as if he was about to explode. She tried to think of what she could say that would help, help them all out of this mess. All of their lives were in danger, and she didn't know what to say to save them. For the first time in her life, Lilee Parker was speechless.

Suddenly she saw movement behind Adam. Someone was in the house with them. She focused hard on what she should say, anything that would hold Adam's attention so he wouldn't turn around. *Think, damn it!* she told herself. *Out of all your big moments in court, you've never frozen. Damn it! Don't do it now!* She willed herself to fight.

Lilee Parker straightened her back and opened her mouth. "As the city prosecutor who was first presented with this case, I move that all charges of negligence be dropped against Kimberly Lewis Kolar spanning from the accident that took her life on the night of October 12. Also, I ask the court that a thorough investigation be brought against Christa Hart and her son, Tim Hart. Last, I ask the court to call Tom Franklin to the stand to testify of the financial exchange that took place between Christa Hart and Franklin Body Shop and Repair.

"Please reconsider my earlier lack of judgment that was brought to my attention by the late Kimberly Lewis Kolar's husband, Adam Kolar. I was not aware of the evidence presented today. I'm truly sorry for my lack of judgment."

Adam laughed out loud. "Well, how noble of you, Ms. Parker. Unfortunately one of those requests is impossible."

Lilee got a good look at the man around the corner. *Forest!* She tried to remain calm and asked Adam to expand to keep him focused on her. "Which request? Which request is impossible?"

"Tom Franklin is dead."

"Oh? I didn't know. How did he die?"

Adam gave a twisted smile, and Lilee's stomach churned at the thought.

Suddenly Tim saw something out of the corner of his eye and jerked his head to his right. Adam, who was engrossed with Lilee's question, didn't react fast enough. Soon a hand came down hard upon his shoulder, and Adam fired his gun as he was knocked to the ground. Lilee screamed as Jenna slumped forward and her head hit the table. Blood soon soaked her gray T-shirt and then dripped to the floor. Tim cried out, "No! Jenna, no!" He ran toward her and gently lowered her to the ground.

A brief wrestle took place, but Adam had no chance. Trevor Watts' large frame covered him, and the gun was safely taken away. Once Adam was secure, Forest met Lilee's eyes. But it was brief, too brief. Soon everyone's attention was on Jenna, who was bleeding badly. Forest spoke on his radio. "Secure. Ambulance needed ASAP. Enter through the front and sweep the house."

Tim looked up at Forest. "Find Rosemary. She's three. Um…our daughter."

Forest looked over at Lilee and she responded, "I'm fine. Go."

Jenna heard Tim and cracked opened her eyes. She tried to smile at his words. She was fading. The pain was so great, and darkness tugged at her brain. Tim was pressing hard on her chest wound and screaming, "Hang on, Jenna! Help is on the way. No. No. Jenna, don't go!"

Everything happened so fast. Lilee watched as more officers entered the room, took Adam away, and bagged the gun. Trevor kneeled beside Jenna as Tim frantically searched for a pulse.

An officer Lilee didn't know walked her way, quickly freed her, and helped her to her feet. "I'm alright. Really. Help find the girl."

"You're bleeding."

Lilee reached up and felt her head. She had an injury. "It must have been when he attacked me."

Suddenly his radio came to life. It was Forest's voice. "Little girl found in back bedroom. Unresponsive but breathing."

Lilee reached out and grabbed the officer. "Take me to him."

He asked a series of questions to check her vision and hearing. Finally he said, "OK, but you will need to be checked out." He touched her elbow and helped her walk around Jenna and the others on the kitchen floor and into a narrow hallway.

Soon they found the bedroom and Forest hovering over the little girl. The small toddler known as Rosemary had her feet and arms taped and lay on her little toddler bed. Lilee grabbed a stuffed animal, ran to the other side of the bed, and placed it by the beautiful dark-headed girl.

She was so small. The officer who had freed her took out a knife and immediately cut the tape that bound her small frame.

"Her pulse is steady," announced Forest.

Lilee asked, "Was she drugged?"

"I don't know; maybe."

Forest reached out and briefly touched Lilee's face. "I thought I had lost you. I went to your home and found Andy Kane. I...I thought you were..."

She quickly touched him back and shook her head. She placed his hand over her heart. "I'm here, and very much alive."

Forest smiled briefly, but then his attention went back to the little girl and he removed his hand. Neither said another word until the ambulance arrived. Hearing the sirens, Lilee finally thought to ask, "Is...is Andy Kane dead?"

Forest looked into her green eyes. "I don't know. He was barely hanging on when I found him. I'm sorry."

She nodded.

A paramedic entered the room and both of them stepped aside. Quickly he checked the little girl's vitals. "Blood pressure low. Let's get her loaded up."

Neither Forest nor Lilee moved as they watched the small girl being placed on the large stretcher and pushed out the door. Forest turned to Lilee and hugged her tight, kissing the side of her head. He whispered, "I never thought I would hold you again. I...I was so worried." Suddenly he jerked away as his hand felt her head. "Oh my God. You're bleeding."

"Yes, but I think I'm fine."

"Do you remember what happened?"

"I think he hit me on top of the head with something."

"Let's get you checked out."

Slowly Forest pulled away when Trevor entered the room. His shirt was smeared with blood as he announced, "They took Jenna away. It doesn't look good." He stepped closer and added, "Officer Brown told me you were injured in the head?"

"Yes, but I think I'm fine."

Forest replied, "We're taking you to the hospital. You need to get checked out."

"OK, but I need to call Charli."

Forest looked at Trevor and asked, "Has someone notified Marla Kay Abbott?"

"Yes. General is the closest, so she will see both of them there." Trevor held up a tape recorder. "We found this."

Lilee stepped away from Forest and explained. "Adam Kolar, the gunman, he was trying to create a trial, and I was...I don't know...someone who would listen and help."

Forest squeezed her shoulder. "Let's get going. You can tell us more and call Charli from the car."

Lilee nodded, and Forest gently guided her down the small hallway and out the front door.

Four hours later, Lilee sat in a hospital bed with five fresh stitches in her head. A MRI and CAT scan had been performed, and the doctor had decided to keep her overnight for observation. When the door opened to her small room, she looked up to see Forest holding flowers. She smiled as he walked in and closed the door behind him.

"They are beautiful. Thank you."

"You are welcome. Doctor says you have a slight concussion."

"Yes, so I get my own personal room for the night."

He walked closer and touched her cheek and then grabbed her hand.

"I heard Andy Kane still might make it," she said. "Is that true?"

"I was told if he made it through the night, his chances would improve."

"What about Jenna Abbott? Any word?"

He shook his head. "She didn't make it."

A tear rolled down her face and she closed her eyes. Forest carefully eased down in the bed beside her and held her tight. He stayed with her through the night.

Two Months Later...

A lit Christmas tree stood in a small corner of the Jordan house. Ronny Jr. sat on the floor playing as Johnny Rae and Marilynn stood in the kitchen cooking dinner together. The last several weeks had been hard on them all, but especially Carly. She had only taken two days off for her son's funeral. Finances were hard once more, and Johnny Rae had stepped up and taken more hours at work to help. Everyone was grieving in their own way, but life went on and bills had to be paid.

Marilynn heard a noise at the front door and turned just in time to see Carly enter carrying a small brown sack and the mail. Ronny Jr. saw her and began clapping with delight. Immediately she set her purse and bag down, picked up the baby, and held him tight.

"I'm teaching Johnny Rae how to make my grandma's lasagna recipe," Marilynn said. "It's legend in our family."

Carly had a serious look on her face as she walked over toward the two in the kitchen.

"Oh, how kind of you, dear. Thank you."

Johnny Rae saw her expression and set down his spoon and walked over. "What's wrong, Momma?"

"Nothing's wrong." She pushed an envelope toward him. "It's the results from your GED test."

Marilynn held her breath and anxiously waited for Johnny Rae to take the white envelope and open it. When he didn't move, she let out a deep breath and encouraged, "Come on, Johnny Rae. Open it up!"

"You do it. I can't."

She looked at him, hesitated, and then took the envelope and opened it with shaking hands.

He laughed nervously. "You just as scared."

She stopped and looked him in the eyes. "I'm not scared, Johnny Rae. Not anymore. You already took the hardest step by showing up for the exam. If this isn't the results we want, we'll study more together and you'll try again until you succeed."

He narrowed his eyes at her. He couldn't believe a girl like Marilynn had fallen for him, and she believed in him so much. Just a few weeks ago he had made a tough decision. His friends had tried to convince him to join their gang. A couple of night excursions had left him feeling excited but at the same time a coward for sneaking around behind Marilynn's back. Her unwavering faith and trust in him made him want to be better, so he chose her and ditched some friends and the idea of becoming a gang member. Looking at her now, he knew he had made the right choice.

Carly stretched out her free hand and squeezed Johnny Rae's hand as Marilynn removed the white paper, opened it, and began to read.

***

A red curtain rose on stage at the downtown theater, and the room erupted with applause. As several young ladies filled the stage in their costumes and ballet shoes, Derrick hurried down the narrow aisle, found his wife, and maneuvered past three others and into the empty seat.

Andrea stopped clapping as she turned and faced her husband with a shocked look on her face. Yes, she'd saved him a seat like always, but he had always failed to show for these yearly productions. Her voice broke as she spoke. "You…you made it."

Derrick got comfortable in his chair and looked ahead and found Kimmy and Mekenzie on stage. Each had her long hair wrapped up high upon her head in a neat little bun. Kimmy wore red, and Mekenzie wore the matching outfit in green. They were beautiful as they began to dance and twirl around. Derrick smiled and then leaned in closer to Andrea and whispered, "There's nowhere else I would rather be."

***

The Hart estate had very few Christmas decorations this year. Normally Christa decked the halls with holly, and Christmas cheer filled each room. Not this year. A wreath hung on the front glass doors, and only one Christmas tree stood in the house, in the corner of the living room. The usual twelve-foot pre-lit tree still sat in its box in the attic. To Christa's surprise, Todd had brought home a six-foot live tree just the night before. No one had decorated it yet.

Christa sat in the quiet living room, staring at the tree. Her sons had finished with their semester at Auburn the week before and come back home. Life was trying to get back to normal, but it was hard. Christa had physical therapy four times a week in her home, and she'd placed her business on hold till the New Year. Every time she walked, she felt soreness, a constant reminder of the harm Adam Kolar had done that horrible evening in October.

The case had finally been put to rest. Christa Hart was advised by her family lawyers to allow them to do all the talking. With Tom Franklin dead, and obviously unable to testify, the lawyers provided documents proving that the Hart family had paid the mechanic thousands of dollars to fix Jenna's car, not to pay off Mr. Franklin for giving false testimony about the worn-out brakes on the car driven by Kimberly Kolar.

Since Tim's admission of driving was coerced that night on tape, and Jenna was now dead, the district attorney had no choice but to drop the investigation and focus all their attention on building their case against Adam Kolar. Mr. Kolar would stand trial early the next year for the deaths of William Hart, Nina Famas, Officer John Norman, Nick Woods, Tom Franklin, and Jenna Abbott. Also, he would face attempted murder charges for Lilee Parker, Andy Kane, and Daniel Maggs as well as charges for kidnapping a minor. The three-year-old daughter of Adam and Kimberly Kolar had been taken into child protective services until a proper family member could be found and arrangements made to care for the child.

Christa tried to block out the last few months as she looked around. The house felt empty and cold without William and Nina, their housekeeper of eighteen years. Yesterday, Andrea and Derrick popped in for a short visit breaking the silence. A wonderful surprise. For once, Christa never thought of the ugly one night stand between her best friend and her late husband. When Christa renewed her wedding vows with William last summer, life became more pleasant with forgiveness instead of a heart filled with hurt and anger. She made a choice then to never let Andrea know that she knew since William had admitting his weakness and begged for forgiveness.

Christa spotted the gold wrapped gift under the bare tree, given by Andrea. A smile formed on her lips. They shared a special bond. A friendship that began almost twenty years ago and one that would continue to grow. Hearing a noise, she turned her attention back toward Tim who was in the kitchen making something. Todd had left again, claiming he had to run another errand. *God, I hope it's not another tree for the foyer,* she thought.

Suddenly she heard the front door open just as Tim came out of the kitchen holding two cups of hot chocolate. Both looked toward the foyer waiting for Todd to enter. Just as Tim set the cups on the coffee table, they heard the voice of a little girl. Instantly a smile formed on Christa's face and she placed a hand to her mouth just as Rosemary walked in wearing a frilly little red dress carrying a large present.

Tim watched as Rosemary made her way over yelling, "Nana Hart!" and soon his eyes met Marla Kay's as she walked in, followed by Todd. Marla Kay held two large shopping bags, and Todd carried five large boxes of gold and red shinny balls for the tree.

"Mom, Tim, I thought it would be nice for the Abbotts to join us this evening."

Christa nodded and smiled at Todd as she wrapped Rosemary into her arms, forgetting for a fleeting moment the pain in her arms and chest. Todd looked away and found Tim still standing in the same spot. He searched his brother's face for some reaction and finally let out a deep breath when he heard Tim speak.

"Marla Kay, I'm glad you're here," he said and knelt down beside Rosemary and asked, "So, Rosemary, are you going to help decorate the tree?"

She pulled away from Christa and gave him a hug. "Yes, Daddy. I picked out an angel. I hope you like it."

Tim smiled. "I love it."

***

The annual Christmas party for City Hall was in full swing at a banquet hall in downtown Atlanta at one of the nicest hotels. At seven thirty, Forest Styles and Lilee Parker walked in holding hands and smiling. At first Lilee was worried about their relationship and how it would impact the ongoing case against Adam Kolar. But soon her worries were put to rest when Maggs pulled the case from her and gave it to Wes Shultz. She couldn't blame him. The day after she was released from the hospital, Maggs had visited and reassigned the case. Surprisingly she wasn't mad. For the first time in her life, she wanted to put a relationship ahead of her work.

Mark and Charli Pepper saw them and waved them over. Hugs, kisses, and compliments were all shared, and soon they found their table. Forest pulled out a chair for Lilee and asked, "What can I get you to drink?"

"Red wine, please."

Forest kissed her cheek and left for the bar and Mark followed, leaving them alone. Lilee noticed her water and asked, "Not drinking tonight?"

Charli turned and gave a coy smile. "Not a good idea in my condition."

"What? You're pregnant?"

Charli leaned in and placed a hand on her lips. "Shhh! Can't announce it yet. Besides, I plan to turn in my notice at the first of the year."

Lilee was taken aback. "What? Why? Is something wrong with the baby?"

"No, silly. I've decided I want to stay at home and be a full-time mom."

"I see. Wow."

Charli squeezed her hand. "I know. It will be tough when I walk out that door come March, but this is more important to me now, and with Mark's new salary, we'll be just fine for a few years."

Lilee forced a smile. "I will miss you like crazy. Work will never be the same."

"No, of course it won't. But I'll still be around."

Lilee genuinely laughed now. "Yes. You will still be around."

"So, you and Forest? The way you look at him. You never looked at Landon like that."

Lilee turned her head and searched for Forest. He was grabbing her glass of wine and holding a beer. He turned, saw her, and winked as he headed in their direction. She smiled back and then leaned into Charli and replied, "No, I didn't." She whispered, "I'm in love."

Forest and Mark saw the two girls huddled together smiling. Forest set down her wine glass, took his seat, and asked, "What are you two conspiring?"

Lilee moved away from Charli, leaned in and kissed Forest tenderly on the lips, and responded, "Nothing."

Forest watched as she pulled back with a smile. He smiled back and then asked, "Dance with me?"

"Yes, I would love too."

Forest stood once more, held his hand out for her, and grabbed his beer and they headed toward the dance floor hand in hand.

Here is a sneak preview…

Glass Shadow

Coming Soon

Early 2013

Chapter 1

Pain. So much pain. *What the hell is taking so long?* Angela looked around for help but saw no one. She stumbled down the aisle of the subway train hoping to see another passenger up ahead in the next car. *Move. You've got to move!* She willed herself to take another step. Another pain ripped around her body from her lower back, paralyzing her. She closed her eyes and tried to breathe, but it was so hard. She felt her lungs collapsing, and the car filled with empty seats began to spin. Slowly she let go of the steel pole as she slid to the floor unnoticed.

"Ma'am? Do you know your name?"

Angela felt her body moving. Someone was carrying her. No, she was riding on a raft. She slightly opened her eyes and found people, lots of people, who seemed to be flying by as she was pushed away by a man in white. The man's face was etched with worry, and his big brown eyes looked moist. Then he was gone. Angela closed her eyes once more, and the pain pulled her under for a deep sleep.

***

A sudden noise jarred Evelynn Holt in her sleep. Her husband, Donald Holt, grabbed the phone off the nightstand and answered in a groggy voice, "Hello?"

Evelynn rolled over, looked at the time, and groaned. *Who would call at two fifteen in the morning?* She pushed up onto her elbows just as Don turned on a small lamp. She rubbed her eyes and tried to interpret the one-sided conversation.

"Of course. No, don't call anyone else. We're on our way!"

Don placed the phone back into the cradle and faced his wife of five years. "Evelynn, they have a baby for us. We got to move, now!"

"Wh…what? A baby already? I…I don't understand. How can that…"

Don pulled on a pair of jeans that lay draped over a loveseat by the window. "Doesn't matter, baby. We're getting it now, at least if we can make it there in the next thirty minutes."

Evelynn yanked the covers back on their king-size bed, ran to her large master bath, and entered her equally large walk-in suite. She pulled down the first cotton dress she came across and pulled it over her long blond hair. Turning around, she found Don grabbing a red knit polo. The hanger fell to the floor as he ran back out and over to the toilet. She only had time to grab her brush and shoes before Don pulled her away and down the hall toward their enclosed garage.

"Wait. My purse!"

Don paused and saw his wallet lying beside her purse on the small end table. "Get my wallet too."

Evelynn stumped her big toe on a high-back chair but continued running after her husband, who had already pushed the garage door button and gotten into their black Mercedes. She opened the passenger door and paused. "Where's the car seat?"

Don cussed, got back out, and ran to the other side of the garage and picked up a box with a brand new car seat inside. Quickly he opened the door to the backseat and threw it in. He looked at his watch: only twenty-five minutes left. He ran back around, jumped in, and reversed out of the garage, hitting the garage button on his visor.

Once out of their gated estate, Evelynn asked, "Where's the baby at?"

"Downtown, at the intersection of Fifth and Walnut Street."

Evelynn pulled her seatbelt on, closed her eyes, and prayed, *Please God, please let this work.* Feeling Don's hand on hers, she opened her eyes, turned toward him, and met his blue eyes. He smiled and then turned his attention back to the road. His dark brown hair stuck up around his head, and she reached out and patted it down. "Don, did they say if it was a boy or a girl?"

"No."

She pulled her hand back, placed it on her pale yellow dress, and closed her eyes once more to steady her breathing. She was nervous. She was about to become a mom, something she had almost given up on. In a soft voice, she asked, "What about Drake? Will he be there?"

Drake Williams, the family lawyer, had set the ball rolling for an adoption three months earlier. Lots of meetings had since taken place between Drake and Don, and she was told repeatedly that it could happen sooner than later. She never believed them, though. Adoptions took a long time, with many never receiving their bundle of joy. Don had told her not to worry. Money and power could buy a lot of things in life—even a baby.

"Yes, and he will have papers ready for us to sign. And Evelynn, we have to be ready with a name."

She finally smiled. That wouldn't be a problem. Names had been picked out years ago.

On the north side of town, another couple had been alerted by a different lawyer. Carmen and Wayne Knight were more prepared. They had been waiting over four years for their adoption paperwork to be approved by all the government agencies involved. Now, at ages thirty-five and thirty-eight, it was finally going to happen. New, washed clothing hung in the painted nursery's closet for a boy or a girl. Each week, the baby sheets were washed and the room vacuumed. The car seat, already assembled, was fastened correctly into the back seat. Now, all they had to do was arrive and receive their baby. They were first alerted a week ago that an unwed fifteen-year-old wanted to give her baby up for adoption, and, if all went well, they were next on the list.

Wayne, a commander in the Air Force, had alerted his staff and requested time off when the big day arrived. The ladies in the office had planned a quick baby shower and brought in a cake. Carmen, his wife of eight years, was a chef at one of New York's finest restaurants and had given her notice on Monday. Her boss wasn't so happy. Together they drove hand in hand along the quiet, dark interstate.

"Honey, how exactly does this work?"

"We show up, sign some papers, and choose a hospital suitable for the examination."

Carmen was confused. "We aren't meeting the agency at the hospital?"

"Well, yes, we are, but we still get to choose a different location if we want."

"Why would we?"

Wayne took his eyes off the road and faced his wife. "Cause it's downtown in not such a good area."

"Oh. I see."

Wayne concentrated on driving but continued to hold her hand. "Relax. Everything will be fine. She should be arriving at the hospital any minute, and if we do choose a different location, they will move the baby by ambulance once it's safe to."

"OK. Oh, Wayne, I'm so excited!"

He squeezed her hand. "I know, dear. Me too."

***

Don turned left onto Walnut Street and saw the parked ambulance in an empty mall parking lot. His lawyer's shiny new black Porsche was parked at an angle right beside the ambulance. After scanning the area, Don decided to leave the car running. "Stay here. Don't move until I tell you."

Evelynn nodded and Don got out. Immediately the back door to the ambulance opened and Drake climbed out with a paper in his hand. "You made it just in time. The mother needs to get to the hospital. Another family has already been alerted."

"What? What do you mean?"

"Relax. There' two. I chose the one weighing over six pounds. The other one is under six."

Before Don was able to reply, an EMT placed a newborn wrapped in a blanket in his arms. Don could only watch as the door quickly closed and the ambulance sped away. Drake looked around. "We need to get out of here. Follow me. We need to find somewhere safer."

"But, I don't…"

Drake opened the passenger door and saw Evelynn. "Give the baby to her, we got to move, now!"

Evelynn was confused but had enough sense to listen to Drake, who seemed rattled. "Give me the baby, Don. Let's go."

Don walked over and carefully handed the baby to Evelynn and then shut the door just as another car pulled into the lot.

"Move, now!" Drake yelled and ran to his Porsche.

Don ran around, jumped in, and floored it behind Drake. Looking in his rearview mirror, he was relieved the other car hadn't followed them. Over the next ten minutes, Evelynn asked questions, but Don had no answers. Finally she stopped talking and began to closely examine the baby. "Don, it's a girl!"

For the first time since getting back in the car, he smiled. They drove the next five minutes with Evelynn describing their beautiful little girl. Soon Drake left the interstate and pulled into a twenty-four-hour truck stop. Don remained seated and let Drake come to him. Looking around, Drake finally climbed into the backseat with the papers. "I need a name."

Evelynn answered, "Elizabeth Ann Holt."

"OK. Now I need you two to sign here."

He passed a paper and pen to the front seat, and Don signed. Some juggling took place, and Evelynn finally signed her name below his. "Now what?" asked Don.

"Take the baby home. I've called a midwife. She should be there in the next twenty minutes."

Evelynn opened her mouth to speak but stopped when Don said, "Thank you, Drake. Come by tomorrow, and we'll talk more then."

"I'll be there at eight."

Evelynn watched as Drake eased out of the backseat, got back in his car, and drove away. Don placed a loving hand on Evelynn's cheek. "Let's get Elizabeth home."

Slowly she pushed the million questions out of her mind and nodded. "Yes. Let's get Elizabeth home."